THE CRIME

THADDEUS MURFEE

JOHN ELLSWORTH

His Wranglers down at his ankles and his cowboy boots still on, Russ Lowenstein sat on the couch in his office at the sale barn with a naked coed bouncing on his lap, her breasts jiggling with each penetration. The problem was she was trying to control the pace, and it was getting Russ nowhere closer to where he wanted to be. So he dug his fingers into the soft pink flesh at her waist and started pumping her up and down. At first she resisted, and their bodies clashed with the different rhythms, but one hard yank on her long hair down her back, and she succumbed to his will.

She was nineteen—a young nineteen—and an art student at NAU in Flagstaff. A bit flighty with her head in the clouds, but a great body, the kind only a young woman can have with a flat stomach, perky tits, and round ass. She had even shaved her pubic hair for him when he'd asked.

Her name was Cindi with an *i*, as if that made her special, and her father had been abusive while she was growing up, smacked her around, so she was looking for a compassionate father figure and found Russ. Russ was thirty-seven. He loved young girls and was glad to take care of her. And, oh, had he taken care of her, mostly in his office after hours—on the desk, on the couch, even on the floor. Agile young things like Cindi didn't worry about comfort like the older ones with their fluffed pillows and satin sheets. Like animals, they'd rut anywhere.

Sometimes, he'd splurge for a motel room, but it was rare. As much money as he made through livestock sales, he spent it as quickly. So much money was out of his pockets these days. And today was just another day for Russ, but for Cindi with an *i*, this was their last screw, the day he broke it off with her.

There had been drunken lovemaking the first time after they met at Collins Irish Pub, but then he had told her he had feelings for her and she was hooked. He planned on it lasting maybe a month, then casting her aside. He'd done it many times before with NAU students.

But she'd fallen in love. God, he hated when that happened.

While Russ was enjoying no-strings sex, or so he'd thought, Cindi was wondering whether their eighteen-year age difference was fatal to their relationship. She decided it was not, and she would adjust to the mature mindset of someone Russ's age. After this decision, she had purposely begun remaking herself as a thirty-year-old. She began wearing women's suits. She landed a job at the NAU library and told Russ she was an administrative assistant, when in truth she was the best-dressed bookshelver in American upper education. She was confident the sell was working, and he was seeing her as her older self. She prayed every day it would work.

With a grunt and a long groan, Russ finally made it across the finish line. When Cindi still kept going, trying to reach her own climax, he yanked her off and across his lap and thumbed her hard until she came, her long blond hair fanned out over the couch armrest.

"Of course, I love you," he'd said when prompted by her, "but I can't ever leave my wife. It's a long story, but my first wife owns half of my assets. Now my second wife owns part of the remaining half I got after the divorce. So that doesn't leave me much, ya know? Plus, there are my kids from my first marriage, Cindi. My kids are almost as old as you. How does that work, this huge age difference?"

"How does it work that you're married, Russ? Isn't that the real question between us? You're not even available when you lied to me and told me you were single. How's that work?"

From his sitting position, Russ leaned forward and backhanded the girl across the mouth. "Enough!" he cried. "Neither one of us got into this with any expectations. If you decided you were in love, that's on you."

No more nice-guy Russ, no more "caring" Russ. He was about to show her what happened when a girl didn't listen. He pushed her into the couch pillows and sat across her mid-section, pinning her down. She kicked her legs, bucking against him. Using all his power—Russ had wrestled at 178 in the 174-pound weight class in college—he forced her legs apart. Then he buried his face between her thighs.

"Ow!" she cried. "You bit me, you creep!"

Russ pulled away. He smiled at the girl. Then he shook his head and raised one cautioning finger as if to say, "Don't make me."

"Don't touch me! Bite me again, and I'll kill you!" Cindi screamed, tears already forming in her eyes.

No one screamed at Russ. No one. Hammered with rage, he leaned forward and slapped her again, this time with his other hand on the other side of her face. "Grow up!" he yelled. "And stop with the tears!"

She pushed away at his bare midsection. Then, without warning, she balled her fist and drove it straight into his testicles. Russ doubled over, howling, and fell sideways off the couch. Rolling around as he pounded the carpet, he cried out her name and swore he'd kill her. Which wasn't lost on Cindi, who was terrified at what she'd done and even more terrified by his threat. She gathered her clothes and slipped her feet into her sandals, lifted her bookbag to her shoulder, and fled his office.

In the bathroom down the hall, she locked the door behind her and finished getting dressed, first her panties and bra, then her jeans and T-shirt. After she pulled her hair back into a ponytail, she looked into the small mirror over the single sink in the bathroom and fingered the bruises that had come up on her face. Her cheeks throbbed where he had hit her on both sides of the head, and her eyes were puffy from crying. The fucking prick!

Cindi sobbed as she braced her arms on the side of the sink. Russ was just like her father, smacking her around like she was nothing. Their dog had gotten better treatment than Cindi had when she was growing up.

It had been a bad dream, the time she spent with Russ Lowenstein. She had wanted something to come of it, but she'd only been lying to herself. Now here she was staring into the face of a death threat. And that bite between the legs! What was with that? That was psycho stuff, that was. Like he wasn't all there in the head.

When Cindi heard Russ's receptionist come in and holler her good morning at Russ, she wiped her snotty nose on her sleeve and then took a deep breath. The motherly type receptionist knew about her lovemaking with Russ in his office but didn't seem to care. Cindi often saw Dot on her way out in the mornings. Once, Dot even offered her coffee. She'd be safe to slip out now that the woman was here for work.

She could barely see through her one eye where it had swollen from his slap. She started shaking again from the fear of what Russ might do to her. And then, at another glimpse in the mirror, that fear turned to rage. Look at her face! What would she tell her mom? What would she tell her friends? She couldn't go to classes looking like this. She'd be the gossip of NAU.

She gritted her teeth. He couldn't do anything to her if she killed him first. But she wasn't a killer, was she? If she was, she would have shot a hole in her dad's head years ago for all the bruises he'd left on her body. But she was younger then. She was older now, not her dad's "baby girl" anymore.

She'd get the prick before he got her.

2

Sheila Lowenstein walked into Thaddeus's office wearing a T-shirt, cargo shorts, hiking boots, and a blue bandanna around her head. Her longish blond hair was pulled back in a ponytail and she wore reflective sunglasses. This was Flagstaff, where half the town was out hiking, rock-climbing, and hang-gliding while dressed very much like Sheila. But Sheila had gone the extra step and wore a nine millimeter Glock in a belt holster on her left hip. Arizona was an open-carry state where the wearing of guns out in the open was legal and common. She might have been going for a hike in the woods or a run on the back roads and, because of the remoteness of the mountain areas and Forest Service roads, it sometimes made sense to carry protection in the wild and woolly west. All these things considered, Thaddeus didn't give much thought to her armament.

Until she sat down and told him, "Mark it, Mr. Murfee, May Second is the day I will kill my husband." Then she watched his every move as Thaddeus calmly got up from his desk and closed the door that she'd left open. When he was seated, she wasted no time whipping out a hundred-dollar bill and laying it on the desk. "You're hired. Now tell me what to say to the police after I shoot him."

Thaddeus didn't answer immediately. It wasn't the first time someone had threatened to kill another in his office. People, in general, were on edge these days. Thaddeus had never taken the time to hypothesize why violence was happening more and more in contemporary society, but it reminded him of the Wild West when you knifed someone for cheating at cards or challenged someone to a gun duel if a guy looked at your gal the wrong way. Everyone seemed poised between slaphappy and downright crazy.

It was time to do legal triage, talk her down, and get her some help. He picked up his phone and told Carleen to cancel the rest of his afternoon visitors. He looked up, spread his elbows on his desk, leaned forward while maintaining eye contact and said, "There are better solutions, Ms. Lowenstein. I don't know what's going on, but there are always better solutions than murder."

She worked her sunglasses up on top of her head so that they lay over the blue bandanna. The way she wore them reminded Thaddeus of that old rock star, Axl Rose, from Guns N' Roses. She said with a bite, "You have a better solution than murder? Uh-huh. Says you."

Her pupils were dilated and, combined with her agitated state, Thaddeus worried Ms. Lowenstein wasn't in her right mind. In his calmest voice, Thaddeus said, "Let's start over. Why don't you tell me just why you think you need to kill the man?"

"Man? I'm married to a dog, Mr. Murfee."

"What, exactly, has he done to achieve dog status in your eyes?"

"Russ has been sleeping with my daughter."

Now that got Thaddeus's full attention. "Is she Russ's daughter, too?"

"No, my daughter with Jim Sam Walston, my first husband. But my daughter likes Russ, or used to at least. And then he goes and rapes her. Damn nation! Aren't the other women enough for him that he has to take my daughter, too?"

When she burst into tears and sobbed into her hands, Thaddeus slid the Kleenex box across the desk. She clutched several and began wiping and dabbing. After removing the bandanna in her hair along with the sunglasses she'd just placed there, she loosened a three-inch device that was a cross between a barrette and a bobby pin. "Know what this is?"

Thaddeus shook his head once. "I don't."

Her words were jumbled as she spoke through her emotion. "It's a spy cam. I'm going to record his execution. Then I'm going to post it on YouTube as a warning to all stepdaddies. Hands off!"

Thaddeus knew the first order of business was to keep the stepdad alive—at least until he was murdered in prison by an inmate that got him for child sexual abuse.

"I suggest not telling your ex-husband yet. If you tell him and he goes out and murders Russ, then your daughter is going to feel responsible in some way. She doesn't need that kind of burden just now."

"I didn't think of that. Let Jim Sam get his hands on the shit." She tucked the barrette back into her hair. "PJ will get over it."

Get over her real daddy being in jail? Thaddeus didn't think so. He tried a different approach. "How old is she?"

"PJ is fourteen."

"That's statutory rape, Sheila. Let the court lock him up and throw away the key."

"I thought it was statutory rape."

"So I'd like to see you go across the street to the DA's office and sign a complaint against Russ. The cops will serve the complaint and arrest him."

"Does he go to prison then?"

"After a trial. But even that depends on evidence."

"Such as?"

Thaddeus nodded thoughtfully before beginning. "Well, I would hope that a physical exam by a gynecologist would be done. As well as tests for STDs. I'd like to see the DA do a full sex crime workup. Additionally, if she keeps a diary and made a contemporaneous diary entry about the rape, that would be huge. Plus, she'd have to testify. That's the difficult part."

"PJ will have to testify?"

"She'll have to testify at the trial. What does 'PJ' stand for, by the way?"

"Patricia Jean. And you can forget about her testifying at trial and all that. I'm not putting PJ through hell. Russ can swallow a bullet. That's the least he deserves. Humiliation and torture would be better first, but I ain't got the time."

Thaddeus reached for his hour-old coffee. "Can I have Carleen pour you a cup?"

"No, I need whiskey."

"I can't offer you whiskey."

"You don't keep whiskey?"

"No."

"Teetotaler?"

"I don't drink. You don't need to either just now. We need your best thinking."

Sheila Lowenstein leaned forward, placing her elbows on the desk like his. "So tell me. What's the best way to kill this man and stay out of jail?"

"I can't advise you on that. It would make me an accomplice."

Her sobs had turned into anger, her sadness to determination. It was in the flush and set of her features. "It's going to happen, Thaddeus. Russ Lowenstein will never leave PJ alone now. He is a violent, nasty man. A pervert. I didn't know he had an eye for the young stuff. He's always been a cheater, but never children. Nineteen is too young, but fourteen? And my daughter? Uh-unh. Now he's as good as six feet under."

"Russ *Lowenstein*? Isn't he the auctioneer at Western Cattle and Powder?"

"That's him. He's a full partner. Russ makes great money auctioneering cows off to slaughter."

A memory came to Thaddeus. "I've been to the sale barn where he works. He beats the desk with a piece of rubber hose whenever a sale is final. 'Sold!' he cries, and *whap!* He slaps that hose down and everyone knows. *Trust Russ with your stuff*—isn't that what his business card says?"

"Exactly. That's my husband, Mr. Murfee."

"Please call me Thaddeus."

"Okay, Thaddeus, I'm gonna send his sick ass off with the cows. Dead before they hit the ground."

"Look, Sheila, why don't we give this whole thing a timeout and let me talk to Chief Meisner at the PD? Let me see if we can work around this without having PJ testify."

"You do that. But I'm not saying I won't drill his stink in the meantime. We're all better off with one less Russ in the world."

"Let me speak with the police first. Can you commit to that so I can try?"

She eyed Thaddeus in the manner of a blackbird in a pine tree eyeing a mouse below. It was only a matter of time.

"No," she at last said.

"Well, can we at least talk to a counselor about this? I'll go with you this afternoon to Coconino Social Services, and we'll find someone there. Someone with a license to help people in crisis."

She shot upright and laughed. "Hah! The only one in crisis is Russ! He just doesn't know it yet."

"Is that a hard no?"

"That's a no. Write it down for later, Thaddeus. They'll know you tried to steer me right."

"My notes are confidential, Sheila. No one will ever know anything about what we've discussed."

"You're certain about that?"

"I am."

"Then what about this... I ambush him in the driveway when he pulls in tonight. I'm thinking a twelve-gauge shotgun. Or would I be better off with this nine millimeter?" Again, she clapped her hand against her holstered gun.

Thaddeus held up one hand in supplication. "Please. I think we'd best break this off and let me go talk to the cops. See if we can get Russ charged with statutory rape. That way we can protect PJ."

"But no names?"

"I can't disclose your name. It's against the law for me to tell anyone. I wouldn't anyway because I'm here to help, Sheila."

She abruptly stood and whipped her gun out of its holster. His heart flip-flopped. In one fluid move she worked the slide on the Glock. Then she re-holstered it. He raised his hands. "Maybe next time we meet you can leave the gun at home."

"Next time we meet, I'll be wearing handcuffs."

"Not good," he said. He felt he was running out of ideas.

"You better believe it, Mr. Murfee. Russ is about to make the front page."

"Please, Sheila."

But she was turning away, and in two steps had her hand on the doorknob.

"Tra-la, Thaddeus. You've talked me down. Send me your bill."

"There's no bill. Just promise me—"

With a laugh and a nod of her head, she was gone.

He immediately got on the phone. The Chief of Police was on direct dial. "Chief Meisner? Thaddeus here. We need to talk."

"I've got a tee time at nine o'clock, Thaddeus. Can it wait?"

"Cancel your tee time. Unless you want to watch one of your constituents get his head blown off."

"Canceling, Thaddeus. I'm on my way."

Thaddeus hung up the phone and went into the outer office. Carleen, his receptionist of seven years, was speaking into her phone and watching people on the sidewalk beyond her panel of windows.

"Carleen, put that on hold, please."

After telling the caller she'd be right back, she deftly pressed her finger on the hold button. "Yes, Thaddeus?"

"I need you to call Rim Country Security."

"And tell them what?"

"Tell them I want this morning's video erased."

"Your office video?"

"My office video."

"Are you sure?"

"Carleen, just make the call, please. You really don't want to know any more than that."

"Sorry I asked." She looked contrite, but Carleen was tough as nails. She knew when to proceed without question if Thaddeus directed.

"Don't be sorry, Carl. And take Sheila's name off the computer calendar."

"Mrs. Lowenstein?"

"Sheila Lowenstein. Remove all evidence she was here."

"Wow. Is she planning on shooting someone?"

Thaddeus's breath caught in his throat, and it took a moment for him to be able to get the words out. "No, nothing like that. No more questions, Carl."

"Okay..."

He turned and retreated back into his private office where he shut the door behind him.

What the hell? Was it that obvious? Planning on shooting someone?

He ripped his meeting notes from the canary legal pad. Then he turned in his chair and fed the single yellow sheet into his shredder.

He turned back around and faced the chair where Sheila Lowenstein had made her case for help. She had said he'd talked her down. Meaning, in plain English, that he'd talked her out of murder. Lawyer ethics would require him to divulge to the authorities a crime about to be committed. But she had walked out saying he'd talked her down, so there would be no crime. And so there was nothing to divulge to anyone. Well... maybe, maybe not. Fifty-fifty.

"I'm going to have to dance around this thing," he said to the empty chair where the Flagstaff Chief of Police would be sitting in five minutes.

Just then, his intercom buzzed, and he picked up.

"Thaddeus, I called Rim Country Security. They put a tech on the line, and he says there's no way they can erase a video."

"Can't or won't?"

"Won't. They said it would be breaking the law."

"What did you say?"

"I told them I'd talk to you and then call them back."

"Okay, don't call them back, Carleen. Just drop it."

"We're not telling anyone we've got an active shooter situation here?"

"Where are you getting that?"

"The Rim Country Security tech checked your morning video. Sheila Lowenstein told you she was going to shoot Russ. He's my cousin. You're going to warn Russ, right, Thaddeus?"

Shit. He honestly had not known that his receptionist was related to the man that his client, Sheila Lowenstein, had just threatened to kill. "Carleen, I want you to sit at your desk until the chief of police comes. Then show him in here. Then sit at your desk and don't call anyone or go anyplace until you and I have talked."

"What if Russ gets shot, and I'm just sitting here?"

"Carleen, what we do here is confidential. You can't say anything to anyone about what you've learned here."

"But, sir, I can when it's family."

Thaddeus's heart jumped in his chest. "Come in here, please."

She appeared in his office moments later.

"Get your steno pad and get ready to make some notes when the chief of police and I talk."

"Okay. Be right back."

Thaddeus sat back and groaned. He might be able to hold the lid on this thing for the next thirty minutes if he kept Carleen in view.

She wouldn't be able to call anyone as long as she was with him. By that time, the police would be alerted and on the job.

Seated at his desk, Thaddeus became aware that line one was in use when the light on the phone line turned solid.

"Carleen!" he shouted. He jumped up and ran for the reception area.

There, lying on its side, was the telephone handset.

But there was no Carleen.

He walked around the desk and picked up the handset. A thought occurred to him. "Hello?" he said into the mouthpiece. "This is Thaddeus Murfee."

"What in the hell is going on over there?"

"Who is this?"

"Russ Lowenstein. Carleen says my wife was just there."

"What do you mean?"

"I mean Carleen told me that Sheila was talking about shooting me. And you told her not to call me and warn me? What the hell is that all about, Mr. Murfee?"

"Russ, have you called the cops?"

"No! I'm still talking to you! I'm sitting here in my office with the door locked."

"If I were you, I'd stay right there. Don't open that door unless you're certain it's the police on the other side."

"Oh, my God," Russ moaned.

"What?" There was no answer, only silence on the other end of the phone, so Thaddeus shouted, "Russ? Russ, what's going on?"

"No, don't do it!" Russ shouted.

Which was the moment a single gunshot tore through the telephone earpiece. Thaddeus snapped the phone away from his ear, but still he heard. He heard seven more shots ring out as the intruder peppered the corpse of Russ Lowenstein. Shortly after, the phone call disconnected.

Thaddeus dialed 911 to report the shooting. He was sure the police had charged off with their sirens screaming and lights pounding, but they were too late. Thaddeus had heard the gunshots. It had happened so suddenly that he had no time to prevent the shooting.

Besides, hadn't Sheila told him she was no longer a threat? Does a lawyer have a duty to turn in a client where there is no threat? Just where, he wondered, is that line drawn, the line between a lawyer's public duty and the duty of silence he owes his client? She had said *You've talked me down.* Wasn't that the deciding factor that required him, as a lawyer sworn to silence, to stay uninvolved? He shuddered to think of it. He could almost feel the family suing him already. Worse, he felt terrible for Russ. Should he have tried to restrain his client and call the police? Seriously? What lawyer does that? Even more, what rule or law requires that? Absolutely none, he decided. But wow—it was a close call. So close.

Thaddeus stood up and stretched. There was no longer any hurry. The chief of police must have diverted to the crime scene as he still hadn't shown up fifteen minutes later.

A half hour later, his last thought as he walked out his front door and headed for the office of the District Attorney was that this case was going to write itself. And in the end, he just might lose his law license. And Sheila Lowenstein just might find herself on death row.

Or maybe he'd choose the right jury and walk her out a free woman. That was always a possibility.

But no matter which way it broke, Russ Lowenstein wasn't going to care. His jury had already returned. Thaddeus smiled at the irony as he headed upstairs at the courthouse.

Russ had gotten eight votes, a unanimous finding of guilt by his full metal jury.

3

The District Attorney's office was on the second floor of the courthouse, down the hall and to the right. Thaddeus went inside where he was greeted by Inyoue Greenpath, the receptionist. She looked up from her screen and saw it was Thaddeus. She slowly shook her head.

He asked, "You've already heard over here?"

"Just. She said you're her lawyer."

"She's my client. Please let the police know I don't want her talking to any cops or detectives without me present."

She ignored his request. "Leon is expecting you so go on in."

Leon Leewitten was a tall drink of a cowboy, maybe six-four in boots, a slow-talker with just a hint of drawl he picked up in Texas when he was stationed there for Air Force jet pilot training. He shook his head when Thaddeus appeared in his doorway. Then he curled a finger. "Come to papa, poor ol' Thaddeus."

"Son of a bitch, Leo, I tried." Thaddeus pulled out a chair across from Leo's desk and sat heavily with a grunt.

"I'm sure you gave it your all."

"Off the record, her daughter was raped by Russ Lowenstein. So let's start thinking about cutting her some slack, shall we?"

DA Leewitten pushed away from his desk. "Whose daughter?"

"You know. Sheila's daughter, PJ."

"PJ was raped by Russ?"

"Yes. So her act of shooting him was no greater an offense than manslaughter."

The DA clapped a huge hand on each kneecap. "All right, we got that out of the way. By the way, Thaddeus, who the hell are we talking about, for the record?"

"Sheila Lowenstein," Thaddeus replied.

"Before you say anything more, Russ Lowenstein was shot and killed. We're questioning the mother, Sheila Lowenstein, at the scene as we speak. So far, the mother has confessed basically to premeditated murder. She's told Detective Snow she went to Russ's office to execute him for raping PJ."

Thaddeus remained silent. It was time to clam up.

"Are you sure you want to defend this woman?"

"I'm at least willing to talk about possible guilty pleas if she's already confessed."

"What do you have in mind, Thaddeus?"

"Heat of the moment, temporary insanity. We should talk about an involuntary manslaughter plea. Something to wrap it up with a year in jail and five years of probation. Something like that."

The prosecutor extended his arms and cracked his knuckles. "Funny, that. I'm thinking first-degree murder, prison with no possibility of parole."

"He was sexually assaulting her daughter, for crap's sake, Leo. There's no possibility of a jury finding first degree. Maybe second, but that's even stretching it. I think we're talking manslaughter."

"Voluntary manslaughter, three years in prison, ten years of probation."

"You're coming to your senses, Leo. Look, let me talk to her and get a feel for what happened. Then I'll get back to you, and we can maybe wrap this up."

"Don't talk to me. I'm turning the case over to Jon Logan."

"Really? I thought Jon was in line for the next judicial vacancy."

"He is, but that won't happen for at least a few years."

"Tell Jon I'm looking to deal it out pretty quickly. I want to send PJ to Jim Sam's home—

Leo interrupted, "Wait a tick. Who is Jim Sam?"

"PJs biological father." And without missing a beat, Thaddeus continued, "I want to keep her out of this as much as possible. I don't want her to have to testify."

"Understood. Can't argue with that, Thaddeus."

Thaddeus stood, preparing to turn and leave.

"Thaddeus, one more thing."

"Yeah?"

"Chief Meisner was bending my ear the other day. Turquoise is working for her mom now?"

"Yep."

"Chief Meisner wants to offer her a detective job with the PD. And I'd like to offer her a job myself. As a special investigator out of the DA's office."

"I'll pass it along, but I think she's pretty happy where she is."

"I'm only passing it along for the PD, too, you understand."

"No, Leo, you're trying to edge out the PD and grab her for yourself. Bastard," said Thaddeus, but he had a smile on his lips.

Leo tossed back his head and laughed. "Got me. Good for me, Thaddeus. Good peeps are hard to come by."

"Thanks. As her dad, I couldn't agree more."

"Okay, then." Leo slapped his hand on his desk in finality.

Thaddeus pinched his lips together and nodded. "Okay."

They shook hands, and Thaddeus departed the DA's office. He walked around to the front of the adjoining building and entered the jailhouse.

It was time to hear what Sheila had to say for herself.

4

The police had just returned from the scene of the crime so Sheila Lowenstein was still up front at the jail, awaiting processing after her interrogation at the scene had concluded. When Thaddeus arrived, she was moved into Attorney's Conference Room 3. Her honey-blond hair was still in a ponytail, but the bandanna was missing. He imagined cases where distraught inmates had garroted themselves with bandannas. She was still wearing the T-shirt and cargo shorts ensemble she'd worn to Thaddeus's office a short while ago. But this time there was no pistol strapped to her waist. That had gone the way of all weapons homicidal. Her gun was in police custody, headed for the crime lab already.

Thaddeus took a seat at the metal table. They faced each other without speaking at first. She was an attractive woman in her late thirties, maybe early forties, no gray showing in her hair, but wrinkles at her eyes. There were no defining features on her face, no dimples or moles, no outlandish lips or big doe eyes. It occurred to him just then that she appeared like so many other wives and moms out there. Generic to a T. He pulled out a legal pad and sighed. "Okay."

"Go ahead, Mr. Murfee, ream me out. I know I've got it coming." She was red-faced and weeping, clutching a handful of paper towels the jail had given her. It appeared from her jerky movements and racing words that she was "on something" as well. She'd been agitated earlier, but nothing like this. She must have popped a pill for courage before the big blowout.

"First, please call me Thaddeus. Everyone does, and I'm your lawyer now. Officially. I'm not here to ream anyone out, Sheila. You had your reasons. I get that."

She looked up, red-eyed and wet-faced. "What's the DA saying?"

"How did you know I've talked to the DA?"

"Detective Snow said you were at his office."

"Did you confess to the cops?"

"I told them I shot Russ fair and square. My gun, my bullets, my trigger finger. Good riddance."

"I know you think that, and I'm not here to argue the justification angle, not yet at least. What I'd like to hear about is your state of mind when you pulled the trigger. Were you blinded by rage? Had you lost control? Were you on drugs? Help me here, Sheila."

"I was cool as a cucumber, Thaddeus. I was there to execute the bastard. I've saved the county a million dollars in legal fees and court costs. They should be giving me a bounty."

"Yes, well, let's not let the media latch onto that angle of 'bounty hunter seeks reward.' That's not our best angle. No, I want you to come across in all situations as the mom who lost it, who went nuts for a couple of minutes and took out the man who raped her minor child. That's your angle."

"I did take out the man who molested my daughter. The same man who seduced me, you might say, with his words and smiles five years ago. He was smooth, that one."

"What about drugs? Were you on anything?"

"OxyContin. I'm being treated for that addiction."

"How does the Oxy make you feel?"

"It puts me in a good place. Like all is well."

"Well, why would you shoot someone in that state of mind?"

"I felt like I was taking out the trash. That's how I felt when I shot Russ." Her tears had paused for a minute, but now they broke through again. "D-do-do you think they'll let me have my OxyContin in jail?"

"Is it prescription?"

"Yes."

"What's it for?"

"Back pain."

"You have back pain or you're being medicated for back pain? Remember, huge difference here, Sheila."

"At one time I had back pain. Anymore, not so much. But I'm hooked on oxycodone. I don't know what to say."

"I'll speak to the jail doctor. It complicates things. Also, if they take your history while deciding which drug you receive in jail, stay away from talking about the shooting. Do you follow me?"

"Because anything I say, even to the doctor, can be used against me?"

"Technically, no, but as a practical matter, yes. Prosecutors can usually find a way to get even privileged statements you make to your jail doctor put into evidence for the jury to hear. It's a dirty game, so don't talk about the shooting or events leading up to it."

"All right." She took the wadded tissue and threw it in the wastebasket and then pulled a fresh one from the box on the table.

"Sheila. Let me get some background for my file. First, what work do you do?"

"Jobwise? I'm a youth counselor at First Christian Church."

"You can't mean that." He was blinking hard, trying hard to believe what he'd just heard.

She narrowed her eyes at him. "Of course, I mean that. I have my Master's in Pastoral Counseling with an emphasis on youth. Why, should that make me immune to having real feelings about rape?"

"No, I—I— It just came across as odd to me. A pastor murdering someone."

"We're human, Thaddeus."

"But it seems..."

She crossed her arms and raised an eyebrow. "Hypocritical? Perhaps, since I preach to turn the other cheek. But I'm sure God is on my side with this one. Think of me as an avenging angel. I would have done the same for any of my flock."

It was hard to argue when they pulled that card. "Okay, I'll stay away from that for right now."

"Good idea."

"Any other kids?"

"PJ is an only child. Russ and I tried to have a kid together, but I'm too old. Ran out of eggs."

"What about your own siblings? Brothers or sisters?"

"My sister died two years ago from breast cancer. I have one brother who's a golf pro in Jupiter, Florida. We love each other, but he's busy year-around because golf is year-around in Florida."

"I'm sure it is. Parents alive?"

"Mom passed..." She looked to the ceiling as if thinking. "Three years ago, June it was. My dad's in a home in Scottsdale. Peter, my brother, and I share the expense of Dad's care."

"Tell me about your marriage to Russ."

"Basically he caught me on the rebound after Jim Sam and I got divorced. I met him at Happy Hour Shit Show Karaoke at The Green Room. We shared some laughs and drinks at the bar, and I was hooked just like that. Like I said, he's a snake charmer."

"Why did you and Jim Sam divorce?"

"Just grew apart. That and his gambling addiction. He wouldn't get help. It wasn't a big deal, maybe a couple hundred a month, but it was always going out, never coming in. So we fought a lot about money. Youth Counselors don't make much, ya know. Which is ironic, now that I think of it, because I'm addicted to pain meds. Now I know how hard it is to quit an addiction. Anyway, PJ never forgave me for the divorce. She still tells me she hates my guts. She loves her daddy, Jim Sam. I was the one who asked for the divorce."

"Do you think PJ might have been paying you back by letting Russ use her?"

"I don't know. No...maybe... It wouldn't surprise me. Jim Sam always said that PJ and I are so much alike, and that's why we clash sometimes." She cradled her forehead in her hand, the elbow bent and resting on the table. "My life's been a wreck, Thaddeus."

"It does sound complicated. Now, let me ask, do you and Russ own property in the state?"

"We own our house. But no equity. Why, do you need money right away?"

"At some point, I will. We won't know how much until I meet with the DA again and see how they're going to handle this. But I'm thinking money for bail. I want you out of jail during the pendency of the case so you can help me and so you can take care of PJ. So I will look for equity that can be used for bail. And I'll look at your community contacts."

"What's that mean?"

"It means I have to show the judge you have significant contacts with the community, that you'll likely not flee. Home ownership, employment, family, assets—all are indicia of stability. You'll also have to surrender your passport."

She was crying again, seated at the steel table, rocking up and back, handcuffed, shuffling her feet without letup, and several times saying nonsense phrases that alarmed Thaddeus. Clearly, she wasn't all there.

A knock sounded on the steel door. It was pulled open, and two deputies stood waiting. "Mr. Murfee, we need to process Sheila Lowenstein."

"Sure. Just make a note that I don't want her giving any statements to anyone, please."

"Her file's already flagged for attorney restrictions. No one will try to take her statement."

"And see to it she's single-celled, too. She has an opioid addiction and can't be in the general population as a known drug abuser."

"Yessir. The doctor will single-cell her."

Which made Thaddeus feel just a bit better. When a client was single-celled, it reduced the chance of a cellmate coming into court and claiming the client confessed to them. He always preferred no cellmates for that reason.

"Could you close the door one second, Ester?" Sheila said to the largest deputy. "I have one more thing to tell my lawyer."

Ester, the bigger of the two female deputies, nodded and shut the door.

"Remember I asked you to help me figure out how to shoot Russ and stay out of jail?"

"I do remember," said Thaddeus.

"Well, I figured it out. These charges aren't gonna stick, Thaddeus."

"Why's that?'

She touched the side of her head and smiled.

Thaddeus's brow furrowed in concern. "What's that mean?"

"You'll see. Just don't worry so much."

"I need to know what you have up your sleeve, Sheila."

"You will, just not yet."

It was clear they were finished now. Thaddeus thumped the steel door, and Ester came right back inside to collect Sheila.

He retraced his steps to the front of the jail and walked outside. It was a beautiful, sunshiny, northern Arizona day with fluffy cumulus clouds ringing the San Francisco Peaks.

Not the kind of day where someone would want to kill anyone. But it had happened.

He headed across Birch Street toward his office. It was time to get ready for tomorrow's initial appearance and figure out how to get Sheila's bail set low enough she might remain out of jail during the pendency of the trial.

Parked along Birch, just south of Agassiz Street, was a white van with dark windows. Just adjacent to the van on the sidewalk was a young petite blond woman with a mountain bike. The bike looked beefy comparative to her own slight frame but had grooved tires for street use instead of the normal knobby tread. A helmet dangled from one of the handlebars. It was an expensive aluminum frame bike with all the bells and whistles, handlebar extensions, double water bottle holders, saddle bag, even fork suspension. She smiled at Thaddeus before he passed by the van. He nodded at her and kept going.

When he had crossed Agassiz and was walking with his back to her, she locked up her bike and headed for the jail. It was time to take Mom's medicine to her.

5

The following morning, Thaddeus was at the courthouse early. He first visited the Clerk of the Court's office to make sure his client was on the calendar for initial appearance that day. He was told she was. He then obtained a copy of the criminal complaint and began reading. Ordinarily, he would be seeking a preliminary hearing this morning as part and parcel of the initial appearance, but he knew the DA would only protest, telling the court that an indictment was imminent and thus a preliminary hearing unnecessary.

When Sheila arrived 20 minutes later, she came into the courtroom accompanied by two female deputies and was taken to the empty jury box and seated there with the other prisoners already waiting for their time before the judge. She was wearing an orange jumpsuit and no makeup and her hair was braided back from her face so that her cheekbones seemed more pronounced today. From the circles under her eyes, she appeared to have gotten little sleep the night before. Thaddeus walked over to her, shook her hand, and gave her a smile. "I'll do the talking," he said. "Nothing is going to happen today that I haven't handled hundreds of times before."

"I thought about it," she said, "and I don't mind spending time in jail at all. After all, I murdered my husband, and there will be ramifications for that."

"Really? That's quite a cavalier attitude, don't you think, Sheila? Most clients are horrified at having to spend time in jail. You surprise me yet again." After yesterday's discussion at the jail, Thaddeus had thought that he had arrived at a kind of *détente* with Sheila. But as it turned out, he hadn't. He had completely misread her. And now her unconcerned attitude was becoming an irritation, to say the least. She changed faces every time he saw her. One day she was sobbing, begging him to get her out of jail on bond, the next day all but clam-happy to spend time in the joint.

"No, just a simple change of heart, Thaddeus. With much prayer last night, I'm ready to take on my fate. God will walk with me."

"Fair enough, Sheila, but your change of heart every other day makes it difficult to prepare your defense."

"I'm sorry about that, really I am, but it will all work out. Have faith."

He wanted to say more, something poignant that would get through her haze of withdrawal, because that was what must have caused her flippancy, but instead, Thaddeus turned away and returned to his seat behind counsel table. In fifteen years around court rooms, he'd never been told by a criminal defendant that they didn't mind spending time in jail, that they were guilty and were willing to face the consequences. On the contrary, criminal defendants were notorious for denying all responsibility and for complaining without letup that they were being railroaded and being held illegally in jail.

Judge Able M. Watertown assumed his perch above the participants then nodded, instructing everyone to be seated.

The clerk then called the first name on the list of cases to be heard
that day, and they were off and running. Twenty-five minutes later,
Sheila Lowenstein's case still hadn't been called, so Thaddeus
made his way to the clerk's table and requested that Sheila's case
be called next. The clerk was amenable to reshuffling the deck and
told Thaddeus he would be up next.

Shortly after, the clerk called the case of *State of Arizona versus
Sheila Lowenstein, Defendant*, and Thaddeus made his way to the
lectern. He turned to wait for his client to be brought to the lectern
in the company of the two deputies. Once she was beside him, he
stated his name for the record and that he was appearing for the
defendant who was present with him.

Judge Watertown dispensed with the preliminaries and asked the
district attorney whether the death penalty was being sought in
the first-degree murder case. The prosecutor, Jon Logan, stood up
to advise the court that, yes, indeed, the state would be seeking the
death penalty.

Thaddeus heard his client suck in a quick breath. At least her
hearing was all right, he thought. That revelation seemed to have
gotten through.

That revelation also changed the complexity of the case, of course,
and had a huge bearing on whether bail would be set so that the
defendant might be released from jail pending trial. Capital
murder cases were all but impossible to obtain bail, but Thaddeus
had prepared and filed a motion to set conditions of release, a
motion in which he set out many unsworn facts about Sheila
along with her request that she be released pre-trial on bail.

Judge Watertown asked Thaddeus whether he wanted to be heard on his motion. Thaddeus replied that he did. He had filed just that morning the defendant's motion for conditions of release in which, he explained, he was seeking bail in a reasonable amount due to the defendant's inordinately strong case of contacts with the community.

He then said to the judge, "Your Honor, this is one of those cases where the defendant has significant ties to the community. She is a lifetime resident of Flagstaff, she is a graduate of Northern Arizona University, she owns a home in Flagstaff, her child is in school here, and she has a Christian counseling business here."

"Counsel," said Judge Watertown to the prosecutor, "what is the state's position?"

Attorney Logan was immediately on his feet, saying, "Judge, it should go without saying the defendant is not entitled to make bail in a capital case where the evidence is clear and the presumption is great. In this case, the defendant admitted to Detective Snow that she had, in fact, gunned down her husband and she had planned the whole thing out, providing a solid foundation for a finding of premeditation, making it but a short step, then, to a finding of first-degree murder."

Judge Watertown nodded as the district attorney spoke, indicating his agreement with the prosecution's position that bail should be denied. He then turned to Thaddeus and asked whether he had anything further to add. Thaddeus had much more that he wanted to add but, in order to protect his client's case, much of what he knew couldn't be gone into at that stage of the proceedings.

"Your Honor," Thaddeus replied, "there's much more on this issue that I am unable to reveal at this point and would ask leave of court to return to this matter at a later date if bail is denied here today."

Judge Watertown wasted no time saying, "Bail is hereby denied, defendant's motion for conditions of release is denied, and the defendant is remanded to the custody of the Coconino County Sheriff."

Thaddeus then told the deputies that he would like five minutes alone with his client in the attorneys' conference room off to the side of the main courtroom. They took Sheila into the room, stationed themselves just outside the door, and Thaddeus went inside and closed the door behind him.

"What's troubling to me," Thaddeus said to his client, "is the ease with which you're willing to remain in jail. I need you to tell me what's going on with you so that I'm sure I'm doing everything I can to help. Do you actually *want* to be in jail, Sheila?"

Sheila was adamant that she belonged in jail because, after all, she was guilty. She had committed a heinous sin and was ready to do her penance. There were no tears at the judge's denial of bail, and now she looked more determined than defeated. Her lips were pressed tight and her hands clasped in front of her on the table with the manacles still secured.

Thaddeus plowed ahead. He talked for several more minutes about what might happen next, if the motion for bail were to be revisited. But Sheila again indicated she wasn't all that concerned if bail was not allowed.

Thaddeus came away from their brief meeting with the feeling his client was anxious to be found guilty of the murder of her husband. She was trying too hard, laying it on too thick. It was a moment unlike any he'd ever known before in the defense of murder clients, and it left him feeling confused but determined to find out everything he could about Sheila's case.

Walking back down Birch Street to his office, he was lost in thought. Why would she want—almost hope—to be found guilty?

She had a daughter. A daughter who was sexually assaulted by Russ Lowenstein. So how did that fit in?

Unless.

Unless the daughter should have been the one behind bars. And the mother was protecting her child.

It was time someone told him the truth so he could help.

6

The day of the initial appearance, Turquoise Murfee walked down and picked up the police report from Flagstaff PD. Thaddeus and Katy had adopted Turquoise when she was a teenager. She was a full-blooded Navajo miss, now almost twenty-seven, who had spent five years in the LAPD before returning to Flagstaff to take up an investigator's position with her stepmother's law practice. But she was currently on loan to her dad. Turquoise didn't mind. She would do anything for either of them, whoever needed her help. She enjoyed working with both of them equally.

While she was picking up the police report, she was spied by Chief Meisner, who said he'd like some time with her that week about "a business proposition." She'd smiled and said sure, to call her. Then she paid for the police report and left the FPD. She spread the report out on her dad's desk and began reviewing what the PD had done and learned.

"Russ's office is on Gander Lane?" commented Turquoise. "I thought he was north on San Francisco Street."

"Evidently not. It's not a new building, if memory serves, but it's part of the livestock sale barn up there. It wasn't a sale day, the sales were over the weekend, and the few offices around him were deserted. Except for Dot Marchant, the secretary who answers the phones."

"We can assume Dot knew Sheila and let her come through the front door and just walk right past to Russ's office."

"Sure, she would've known her. Let's see what Dot has to say..." Thaddeus scanned the paper. "Here we go. She evidently told the police she was keyboarding, facing the double doors, when Sheila walked in. Sheila wasn't hurrying and didn't seem upset at all. Oh, this is interesting. Evidently their daughter, PJ, was already in visiting her dad. She'd had a 4-H steer that went through the sale and he was cutting her a check."

Turquoise was reading the documents next to Thaddeus. "Says PJ was going to buy a new mountain bike and wanted her money."

Thaddeus nodded. "That makes sense. PJ is what, fourteen? Are kids that age still in 4-H?"

"I was. I was all through high school, Dad. I think the age limits are eight through eighteen. Younger than eight is Cloverbuds."

"I'd forgotten you were in 4-H all the way through high school. My bad."

"You were gone a lot, Dad. You've always been gone a lot." Turquoise wasn't whining. It was more stating a fact. And yet a fact he hadn't really dwelled on until now. All the children that Christine and Thaddeus had were always so thankful and rarely complained. But some of them had come from dire situations, so there was that. Never had one of them mentioned they felt neglected of his or Christine's attention. But then...children were often just happy with what time you did give them.

But it was true; he was always gone, away from home and his family. He said, "I'm sorry I've been away so much. It doesn't mean I love you and the others any less. It's just law... Well, practicing law is a huge commitment, twenty-four hours a day, seven days a week."

"I know that, Dad. You don't have to defend what you love to do."

Did he love practicing law? He wasn't sure anymore. And was his love for justice more important than his love for his children? Every time he turned around, they seemed to have grown older, grown taller, right in front of his eyes.

Turquoise lay her hand over his. "Hey, I wasn't trying to guilt trip you or anything, Dad."

He wrapped his free hand and arm around her shoulders and gave her a sideways hug. "I know you weren't. You're not like that." But a thread of guilt had attached to his heart, and he worried that perhaps it would wrap itself around so tightly that he'd never get it unknotted.

Turquoise interrupted his melancholy. "Hey, Dad, it's cool. Don't worry. I know I can speak for the others when I say we all love you and Mama Chris very much. And everything you guys do is for us. We know that." She lifted from her seat and grabbed his coffee on the other side of the table. She set it next to Thaddeus. "So let's get back to it. I have a full day, and I know you do, too."

And just like that Turquoise was able to brighten his mood. She was a gem, she was, and wise beyond her years.

"Right, back on track." Thaddeus turned back to the task at hand. "PJ was at Russ's office before Sheila. We don't know how much earlier—it could've been five minutes, or it could've been an hour. Skip down the page, Turq. Whose gun was it?"

"Let's see..." Turquoise was running her finger down the page, skimming. "The gun was—the police didn't find a gun. That's odd." She reread what she'd just gone over. "I thought Sheila had walked into the office with a gun in a gun holster."

Thaddeus was thoughtful. "She had a gun and gun holster when she was at *my* office, but Dot doesn't mention seeing one. She might have had it, though, or Russ could have had one in his office that PJ could have found. I'm still open to the shooter being someone other than Sheila, Turquoise. What if PJ did the shooting, and Sheila is confessing to the crime in order to protect her daughter?"

"Crossed my mind, too. Either one has plenty of motive, but I'm thinking the mom would carry the bulk of the anger over the whole mess."

"Sounds about right. Still, we need PJ's statement. I don't see one attached to this report and I don't know why. You should run on out and talk to her just on the off-chance the cops haven't yet. Get her nailed down."

"Totally. I'm on it. You shouldn't go with me, old Fire Horse."

"Yes. She'd probably be much more open to talking to you than to me, Turq. Let's make that happen today yet."

"Where's she staying?"

"With her dad, Jim Sam."

"Sheila's ex-husband? Got it."

"He's also a suspect in my book."

"No indication he was there. Dot doesn't mention Jim Sam."

"I know. I just like to cross off all the possibilities, though, no matter how remote."

"I hear that. I'll slip my recorder under his nose, too, and see what comes out."

"Excellent."

"Anyone else, Dad?" Turquoise was nothing but thorough, and Thaddeus loved that about her. She was perfect as an investigator. Not only clever, but courageous. For one who had been through so much of her own abuse on the reservation, as an adult she was quite grounded. And it was perhaps that childhood abuse that drove Turquoise to find the truth, to help others.

"Not at the moment. Put a pin in it, though." He winked at her.

"Pinned." Turquoise rose from her chair and walked away. At the door, she turned and smiled at him. "And try not to worry too much, Dad." With that and a wave, her lithe figure disappeared down the hall.

7

"Mr. Murfee, as long as we're on the record here, just let me say your client gave us the fastest confession I've ever heard. And I've been a detective for fourteen years. She was almost anxious to confess to killing her husband."

Detective Jason Landis was speaking. Thaddeus held up one finger and turned on his recorder. "I'm going to want to take one statement at a time. Detective Snow, since Detective Landis has already begun, would you mind leaving the room?"

"No problem. Just holler when you're ready for me." Snow got up and exited the conference room at the Flagstaff Police Department. It was just before lunch, and Thaddeus was chipping away diligently at his to-do list.

Jason Landis was a much older man than Detective Snow and the senior detective of their partnership. Perhaps a twenty-year gap or more separated the two, but Landis's smoking made it hard to determine his actual age. Smoker's creases lined his mouth, and a yellow stain was most likely permanently imbedded on the inside of his index and middle fingers of his right hand. A full ashtray was on the table before him. He spun it around and around. Even from across the table, Landis reeked of cigarettes. He wore his hair in a kind of messy brush-back that had separated and was drooping.

As if Turquoise had caught him staring, she elbowed him gently to begin. She would also take notes, and they would compare impressions after the interviews.

"Detective Landis, my name is Thaddeus Murfee. With me is Turquoise Murfee."

At the mention of his daughter, Detective Landis surveyed Turquoise with a look of appreciation in his eyes. As a man, Thaddeus could understand it; Turquoise was a beautiful woman with an athletic figure, long dark hair that she wore today pulled back with a turquoise headband that matched the blue in her eyes. She was striking. But as a father, he would always flinch at a man's interest in his daughter. As tough as she was, he was still her protector.

He cleared his throat for the detective's attention and continued, "We're going to take your statement about the Russ Lowenstein shooting, and we're going to be recording the statement. Do we have your full knowledge and consent to record you?"

"Yes."

"Now, you just made a statement off-the-record when we came in. About the speed of my client's confession. Would you repeat that?"

"I said your client gave us the fastest confession I've ever heard. I've never heard anyone go off like that, not in fourteen years on the job."

"All right, thank you. She was eager to confess, is that what you're telling us?"

"Correct."

Thaddeus, sitting across the conference room table, was making meticulous notes about his client and her confession. Here it was again, her being anxious to confess. The more he heard this, the greater the suspicion in his mind that something was out of whack.

Landis said, "I was the first detective to enter the shooting scene. One of the uniforms had Mrs. Lowenstein off to the side and had brought her a Styrofoam cup of water. She was crying—sobbing, actually—and you could tell the whole thing had really shaken her up. Which is what kind of got to me."

"How's that?"

"Well, if it was going to bother her so damn much, why'd she shoot the guy in the first place? It didn't make sense. Still doesn't. She was hysterical when we first got there, yet she confessed to me, she confessed to Detective Snow, hell, she'd confess to the butcher if he'd listen to her. Then her daughter showed up and Mama confessed to her, too. I was right there waiting for the forensic photographer to arrive, so I heard all this."

Thaddeus said, "Let me interrupt you there for a second. You said, 'her daughter showed up.' Does that mean she wasn't at the scene when you got there?"

"Not that I saw. The scene was pretty full of techs and uniforms, and she could have been in a different room, but she had her bike helmet under her arm like she'd just arrived. Then Snow took them into the library off the dead guy's office. We wanted them out of the scene so stuff didn't get moved around and all that. But I could hear her crying even from the next room over. Damndest thing I've seen in a long time. If you love someone, don't shoot them. Duh."

Turquoise spoke up. "Detective Landis, I served as a detective in the LAPD, and we had a policy there of taking everyone's statement at a shooting scene. I'm sure you do, too. So, did you get a statement from Mrs. Lowenstein's daughter? I believe her name is PJ?"

"I did. Took it myself this morning. Mr. Murfee has been given a copy just now."

Thaddeus slid his copy of PJ's statement to Turquoise seated at his right. She scanned down through it and then looked up. "Seventh sentence from the top. 'I knew my parents were having trouble before the shooting.' Did you see that?" she directed at Detective Landis.

"Yep." But he didn't elaborate, only pulled a soft pack of cigarettes from his breast pocket, shook it once so that a cigarette popped up, and pulled it free with his mouth.

"Did you ask her what kind of trouble they were having?"

"No, but I think I know," he said around the Marlboro in his mouth. Without asking if it was okay to smoke in front of Thaddeus or Turquoise, he dipped his finger into the same pocket, retrieved a small Bic lighter, and lit the cigarette.

"You know, how?" Thaddeus asked.

"I know because I know Russ." He blew out a long exhale. "Old Russ was a rounder, a ladies man. It wouldn't surprise me to learn he'd been cheating on Sheila Lowenstein."

"Do wives usually shoot errant men?" asked Thaddeus.

When Turquoise waved a hand in front of her face to fend off the drifting smoke, Detective Landis leaned back on the feet of his chair and cracked a window. There were gray, heavy clouds forming, and the wind through the window ruffled the papers on the table. "You mean cheaters? Not usually. They either get payback by cheating or by divorcing the guy. Most of them aren't shooters."

"So wouldn't it make sense there was something besides infidelity going on between the defendant and her husband?"

"Like what?" asked the detective. "What else might've been going on?"

Thaddeus decided to reveal what Sheila had told him about PJs molestation. "Like maybe Russ was making advances on Sheila's daughter? On PJ? I mean, what if he was sleeping with her? Perhaps even sexually assaulting her without consent?"

"There could definitely be a shooting over that."

Thaddeus pushed it one more step. "Well, did you ask Mrs. Lowenstein or PJ whether Russ was having sex with the daughter? Did you even try?"

"I didn't ask, no."

"Why not?"

"The daughter wasn't there when I first arrived. She came later."

"Wasn't there? Like I asked before, isn't it possible she was there and you just didn't see her?"

"Anything's possible, Mr. Murfee."

"So it's possible, even, that the daughter pulled the trigger. Isn't that possible? And the mother's covering up for her? And maybe that's why the mother is so anxious to confess? Most mothers would do that to protect their kids, wouldn't they?"

"I can't speak for most mothers, Mr. Murfee. But, yes, as a general proposition, mothers are extremely protective of their kids. That could be our case."

"Really? Would you tell that to the judge, that maybe you've arrested the wrong person?"

"It's pure conjecture, that one. I wouldn't swear to it, no."

Thaddeus sat back, nodding. Then he sighed and plunged ahead. "Please describe the shooting scene."

"When we arrived, Russ was slumped in his executive chair behind his desk. His body was angled to his left, but his right arm was hanging outside the chair."

"No gun?"

"No. When I asked where the gun was, Sheila started crying. The daughter was frozen and wasn't talking. Shock, I figured."

"Did you ask the daughter about the gun?"

"Well—I sort of thought—I mean, I asked Sheila Lowenstein if anything had been moved. She said no, Russ was just like she found him."

Interesting that Sheila had expressed that she "found him." That didn't seem like the right words if you had just killed someone.

"Was she in the room when the shot was fired—a funny question since you've arrested her, but what I'm asking is whether it's possible he shot himself?"

"Eight times? Not possible. Not according to her. She says she shot him. Then she said she dropped the gun on his desk. But it wasn't there."

"Do you have a preliminary report on the blast distance?"

"Preliminary expert report from Detective Sivert says the gun was about six feet away when the shot was fired that killed him."

"So we can rule out suicide?" He was purposely ignoring the other shots fired, trying to see what the detective had to say, his version of the murder.

"If Detective Sivert is correct, yes. He's a gunshot expert, and he's performed preliminary testing with the same caliber gun and its blast pattern before. He says six feet."

"Which means someone else pulled the trigger of the fatal shot?"

"Evidently. I can only go with what he says."

"How many bullet wounds?"

"One, just above his left eyebrow, one in his shoulder, and six in his abdomen."

"What did the mother say? We're talking about Sheila Lowenstein."

"As soon as we approached her, she raised her hands. 'You caught me,' she says. 'I shot Russ.'"

"Did she convince you she was the shooter?"

"What's that mean?"

"Did you believe her?"

"Sure, what's not to believe?"

"Did she sound convincing?"

"She sure did. I told her to turn around, and I cuffed her."

"You did a gunshot residue test on the mother's hands at the scene?"

"Detective Snow did one."

"Test result?"

"Inconclusive."

"Did you see Detective Snow swab Mrs. Lowenstein's hands?"

"I did."

"And apply the reagent?"

"I did. And the test was inconclusive."

"What about the gunshot residue test you did on the daughter's hands. Results?"

"We—we didn't test the daughter's hands."

"You didn't test her hands? Why not?"

"Because the mother was confessing."

Thaddeus left off questioning right there. The next question, the obvious one, would be saved and asked at trial. He wouldn't give Landis a chance to prepare an answer for the jury by asking him the question prematurely here today. He also knew the detective was a bright guy; he already knew the next question, anyway.

"What else about this case have I not asked you about, Detective Landis?"

"About Eleanor Garcia. We found out about her from Russ's cell phone."

"What about Eleanor Garcia?"

He finally stubbed out his cigarette. "Her number consistently came up on Russ's call history. Looks like he's been calling her for six months. So Snow and I drove out to Williams and talked to her. Turns out she's been having an affair with Russ. So maybe that's what got him shot, right, Mr. Murfee? I mean, that was the conclusion reached by Detective Snow and me. We decided the real troublemaker was Ms. Garcia."

"Did you ever test Eleanor Garcia's hands for GSR?"

"Gunshot residue on her hands? Naw, too much time had gone by. GSR wears off in hours sometimes. We didn't talk to her until two days after the shooting. If she'd just washed her hands with soap and water, there wouldn't be any gunshot residue."

"Did you ask her when the last time was she saw Russ?"

"The day before the shooting. They had breakfast at her condo in Williams after he spent the night Saturday. Then he came to work in Flagstaff for the livestock sales that day."

"How old is Eleanor Garcia?"

"Thirty-three."

"You asked whether she was perhaps pregnant?"

"Yes, I mean no. No, she wasn't pregnant."

"At the scene, did you ask the daughter, PJ, whether she was having sex with Russ, her stepfather?"

"No."

"Why not?"

"It just never came up."

"Well, it never came up, Mr. Landis, because you never brought it up. Am I right?"

He shrugged. "I suppose—yes, that's right. We didn't think to ask that."

"So you didn't test the daughter for gunshot residue even though she was at the scene the morning of the shooting. And you didn't ask the daughter whether Russ was sleeping with her even though we know he had a reputation for sleeping around. How am I doing so far?"

"No, no, I don't argue with any of that. But our investigation isn't over, Mr. Murfee. We asked her this morning."

"Who's we?"

"Myself and Detective Snow."

"What about this morning? Did you ask whether she was having sex with Russ?"

"Yes. She denies it."

"What about Ms. Garcia? Did she have an alibi the morning of the shooting?"

"She says she was home alone, having coffee and reading the paper."

"Does she have a witness to corroborate that claim?"

"No."

"Do you plan to talk to her again?"

"Probably. We haven't made that decision just yet."

"Detective, will you supplement your police report and see that I get copied as you continue your investigation?"

"Certainly."

"Turquoise, any more questions for the officer?"

She drummed her fingers on the table, looking directly at Detective Landis, but when he started to squirm in his seat, she finally said, "No." Thaddeus was a proud Papa. Turquoise was not only a beautiful person, but had turned into a tough cop. And now a smart investigator.

"All right, Mr. Landis, I'm turning off the recorder unless you have something else to add."

"No, nothing. At least not yet," Landis said.

"Fine. Thank you for your time. I want to take PJ's statement before Detective Snow's interview. Please tell Detective Snow I'll call him a bit later."

"Roger that."

Walking out to his truck, Turquoise said to Thaddeus, her teeth gritted, "I would've been fired in L.A. for that investigation. They would've had my badge. This is ridiculous."

"He didn't ask the daughter the key questions at the scene because it didn't come up? Have you spoken to her yet?"

"She's been evasive, but I have an appointment."

"When and where is your appointment with her?"

Turquoise checked her watch. "Eleven minutes. We're meeting at Kathy's Koffee. She wants anonymous, and she wants away from Jim Sam's home."

"Makes sense. Have you spoken with Jim Sam, by the way?"

"I haven't, but his interview is this afternoon."

"Good. You're making your dad proud."

"Just doing my job, Dad."

"I know. But it's still great to have you back with us and helping out. Christine's loving it."

"Chris is easy to work for. She's so smart. And tough. She would've made a great cop."

"She was a platoon leader in Iraq. Not much gets past her."

"Drop me at Kathy's Koffee, okay? I'll walk back to the office."

"Done."

8

Turquoise doctored her coffee with cream and sugar while she waited for PJ to arrive. When she looked up, a girl wearing a bike helmet rode past the window to the bike stand. She removed the yellow helmet and hung the strap on the handlebars. Then she took a U-lock from her backpack and secured the mountain bike.

Turquoise caught her eye as she walked through the door and gave a small wave to identify herself to PJ. She watched as PJ ordered at the counter, waited for her coffee to be made, then took her time at the milk and sugar counter. Even though she knew Turquoise was waiting, the girl didn't seem to be in any hurry to accommodate Turquoise.

When PJ finally slid into the bench opposite, Turquoise asked, "How are you today, Patricia Jean? Or would you rather I call you PJ?"

"Yes, PJ is what everyone calls me."

Their booth was next to the dormant wood stove. Turquoise looked down through her notes, deciding how she would go with the interview. "Do you mind if I record this?"

"You're buying. Record away."

Turquoise switched on the recorder on her iPhone. "The record will reflect that I'm sitting in Kathy's Koffee with Patricia Jean Walston on Wednesday, May fourth at twelve-oh-seven p.m. She has given me permission to refer to her as PJ and to record our conversation. Is that true, PJ?"

"Yes, you have my permission."

"How old are you?"

"Fourteen. I'll be fifteen next month."

"Thanks for agreeing to see me, PJ. I know how tough it is for you right now."

"Not really so hard. I mean, yeah, the thing with Mom is horrible. The Russ part of it's a joke. He got what he had coming to him."

Well, at least PJ wasn't holding back. It was worse when you had to pry information, and therefore motivation, from an interviewee. "You sound very angry at Russ."

"I hated Russ. I guess you already know why. My mom told you, right?"

"Your mom said something about sexual abuse. But she also told my father, Thaddeus Murfee, that you liked Russ as a step-dad."

"Mom's delusional. I never liked him. He was raping me. How sick is that? I'm glad she shot him."

"Did she?"

"Did she what?"

"PJ, did you see your mom shoot Russ?"

"Did I see it? Yes, I saw it."

"So you were in the room with her?"

She gave Turquoise a typical teenager sneer. "How else would I have seen it?"

Turquoise considered the information that Detective Landis had just given them. PJ hadn't been in the office when he and Detective Snow arrived, but had come in just after. So where had she gone after her mom shot Russ and before the police arrived?

Turquoise decided to try another track. "Why were you there that morning?"

"It was a 4-H thing. He was paying me for selling my cow."

"He was writing you a check?"

"Yes. I netted over twelve-hundred-dollars on her."

"You must be proud!"

"I am." She took a sip of her coffee in a to-go cup. "Except Russ caught me in the barn a lot. That's where he molested me. Now that my cow is sold, I never want to go in a barn again."

"How did that make you feel?"

PJ gasped and spread her hands wide. "Why do you keep saying that? My step-dad was screwing me, and I'm only fourteen. It was happening since my thirteenth birthday! How did that make me feel?" She nodded, her lip curled in disgust. "Yeah, which time?"

"I'm sorry. You're angry and I don't blame you one bit."

"Angry? If Mom hadn't killed Russ, I would have myself sooner or later."

"Tell me what you saw your mom do that morning in the office."

"She came in with her left hand on her hip. It was funny because she was carrying her keychain in her right hand. She never carries it in her right hand because she's left-handed. She always carries the keyring around two fingers."

"What did that tell you?"

"That she was hiding something on her hip."

That seemed like a stretch. Turquoise could understand a left-handed person always predominantly using their left hand, but because her hand was on her hip didn't mean she was necessarily hiding something. At her dad's office, Sheila had been angry and could have ended up in that stance naturally. Although Dot had said she didn't seem agitated when she passed through reception. Things weren't adding up. "And was she hiding something on her hip?"

"Only a gun."

"Your mom brought the gun to Russ's office?"

"Yes."

"What were you wearing that day, PJ?"

"Jeans, T-shirt, Patagonia shell."

"Did the coat have pockets?"

"Pockets for your hands? Of course."

"You're sure the gun didn't come to the office inside your coat and not your mom's?"

PJ leaped to her feet, placed her hands on her hips, and bent forward. "What's the matter with you? Mom said you were here to help us, not get me in the middle of her fight."

Turquoise nodded her head. "Sorry, PJ. Please sit down. It's just my job to ask everything I can think of. I'm going to write down that you had nothing to do with the gun. By the way, was it Russ's gun?"

"I think so."

"Where did he keep it?"

"In his nightstand, top drawer. There's always one in the chamber, too."

"One in the chamber? Are you a shooter, PJ?"

"Russ taught me to shoot. He did stuff with me like that. Sometimes I didn't hate him, not before it started happening."

"So you knew where the gun was kept, you were angry at Russ, and you were going to his office that morning to get money for the cow he made you sell. Is that about right?"

"I didn't take the gun, period. Mom had it in her holster. Then she pulled it out, leaned across his desk, and shot him right between the eyes. He went flying back. It was pretty sick."

"Pretty sick as in cool, or pretty sick as in disgusting?"

"Cool sick."

Turquoise worked hard to keep her expression passive. "You didn't mind seeing him shot?"

"Not one bit. It was my mom, and she was protecting me."

"When did your mom find out Russ was sexually assaulting you?"

"That morning. I broke down crying. She finally got it out of me."

"What was her reaction when you told her?"

"She got very quiet, and her mouth was hard. When Mom goes quiet, you want to look out. And when her teeth are clenched like that, you've had it."

"Did she confront Russ that night?"

"No, it was a sale day, and he was sleeping on his couch at the sale barn."

"Why did he do that?"

"He never leaves until every rancher has his sale money from that day's sales. Most sale barns don't give a damn. Russ always did."

"He didn't come home, so you went out there for a check. If everyone got paid the same day as the sale, why were you not getting paid until the next day?"

"Because my check was coming from the sale barn itself. That's who bought my cow. One of the accountants, Bernice I think is her name, has to sign the checks and wouldn't be there until Monday morning. So I went in before school on Monday to get my check. Mom went to see your dad Thaddeus, then she came in and shot Russ, and that was the end of that."

"Did you ever get your check?"

"I did. Bernice mailed it to me. It came yesterday."

"Was Bernice there Monday morning?"

"I didn't see her."

"But your dad was still writing you a check?"

She shrugged. "I guess so." She grew agitated, shifting around in her seat. "I don't know who had to sign the damn check. That's just what Russ told me. Come back for my check the next day."

"I get it." Turquoise decided to change tactics. "Has your mom told you what she discussed with my dad as her lawyer?"

"She told me she told your dad she was going to kill Russ."

"She did? What did my dad do?"

"He said she should try counseling. Totally lame." She looked at Turquoise over her raised cup. "Sorry. I know he's your dad and all."

"Did he try to stop your mom?"

"She said that was the funny thing. She told him she was going to kill Russ, and your dad didn't try to warn him. I wonder why?"

"That's the question, all right. So what happened after your mom shot Russ?"

"The bangs were real loud. But no one came in. My mom dropped the gun on the desk and stepped back."

"Did she say anything?"

"She said, 'It's all I know to do to protect you, PJ.' Something like that."

"Like she did it to protect you?"

"Yes. Who can blame her for protecting her kid?"

Turquoise nodded vigorously. "Exactly, and I think that's your mom's defense. It's called defense of another, and it's an affirmative defense."

"Wow. Are you a lawyer, too? Or just a police officer?"

Turquoise smiled. "Neither. I'm an investigator for my mom, who's also a lawyer. But right now I'm on loan to my dad. It's a long story." Turquoise riffled through her pages on the table. She took a sip of her own cappuccino that had chilled to lukewarm. "Let me back up. I want to go over one part a second time. Is that okay?"

"Sure, you're buying."

"I want to make double-sure it wasn't you who shot Russ."

"I don't like this. They've already arrested my mom for it."

"Please answer my question."

She huffed and crossed her arms over her chest like a child having a tantrum would. "I didn't kill Russ. I couldn't do something like that. I'm just a kid, and I don't even think that way."

Turquoise reviewed her notes. Before, PJ had said to her, *Angry? If Mom hadn't killed Russ, I would have myself sooner or later.* Turquoise realized at that moment she couldn't really trust anything that PJ said. What was a lie and what was the truth? "Might you think that way if he was sexually molesting you?"

"I don't know." She flailed her hands in the air. "Maybe, I don't know."

"Were you mad at Russ the day he was shot?"

"Mad about what?"

"Mad about anything," Turquoise said. "Had you just had words?"

"We weren't fighting, no."

"Why were you at his office?"

PJ's face scrunched up in anger. "I told you! He owed me money for my 4-H cow. I was just standing there waiting outside his office until he wrote my check. Russ was on the phone. Then my mom came in."

"Please tell me what happened once your mother arrived."

"She came in, but like I said, Russ was on the phone."

"Did you take a gun to Russ's office the morning he was shot?"

"No, why would I?

"I just have to ask, I'm sorry."

"Are you Thaddeus Murfee's daughter?"

"I am."

"You're Navajo, am I right?"

Turquoise nodded. "I am. Obviously adopted."

"Where's your mom?"

"My mom, Katy, died. She adopted me with Thaddeus."

"I'm sorry. I won't ask anymore."

"Fair enough. Did you take a gun there?"

"I did not."

"One last question, PJ. Did you want Russ dead?"

"Yes and no. I was confused beyond anything. One minute I hated him, the next minute I didn't care. I didn't like myself anymore."

"Did you ever think about killing him?"

"No. I don't think like that ever."

Which was contradictory to what PJ had just told her earlier. If her mom didn't do it, she would've done it. So she had considered it at some point. "You wouldn't take matters into your own hands?"

"No, I wouldn't."

Again, a direct contradiction. But there were no "tells" of her lying, no looking up to the left or fidgeting with her hands or coffee cup. And she'd retained Turquoise's eye contact their entire conversation. But that said, Turquoise remembered being a teenager, and how often they lied. "Do you believe your mother would kill Russ if she found out he was having sex with you?"

"She did find out. And she did kill him."

"All right. Anything else I should ask you?"

It was a standard question in an interview but PJ looked confused. She finally answered, "No."

"And your statement has been freely given with the full knowledge that I'm recording everything we've talked about?"

"I'm cool with it."

"All right, I'm turning it off now." Turquoise ended the iPhone recording and slipped the phone back into her purse. She picked up her coffee cup, but before she took a sip, she said, "Oh, one more thing."

PJ had risen to leave, but at Turquoise's words plopped back down on the seat with a heavy sigh.

"What time did you get to the office that morning? You said you were on your way to school."

She twisted her mouth back and forth, her eyes raised to the ceiling as she thought about it. "Probably was around eight-fifteen or so? School starts at eight-thirty."

Turquoise nodded. "And was there anyone else in the office when you got there that morning? Other than Dot?"

PJ shrugged. "I didn't see anyone. But then I was waiting in the reception area. I didn't go back to the other offices or the bathroom, so there could've been. But usually it's pretty quiet after a sale. I guess Russ's partners always take the Monday off after working the weekend. At least that's what Mom told me."

Turquoise sat quietly to see if PJ would fill in the silence with any other information, but finally PJ excused herself, saying she had to get back to school. Turquoise offered to drive her even though she'd watched PJ arrive on her bike, but PJ declined, which was a good thing since she'd left her Mustang at her dad's office. PJ had her bike, she said, and got up and left.

Turquoise made some notes after she was alone. She then loaded her small iPad into her purse and paid for the coffees at the register.

She went outside and turned her head to the sky. The sun was behind a dark cumulus cloud, but some beams shined through the cracks. The sky teased rain a lot, but then it never fell when the desert needed it. Turquoise drew in a deep breath of fresh air and started her walk back to her dad's office. She decided that tonight she'd exchange the gun at her side for one of her paintbrushes. There was nothing so soothing as painting a sunset landscape of the Navajo reservation where she grew up. She often painted to reconnect to her roots and found peace in blending her watercolors, the bright iron reds bleeding into a subtler orange and then a soft pink.

After a day like today, she well needed it.

9

Detective Linus Snow was a young black man, long and lanky with a quick smile and eyes that could freeze a fly in flight. Thaddeus immediately got the impression that he would be fair as long as you were being fair, but if you were dishonest or withholding, he would double-down on you in a hot second.

Detective Snow had dropped by Thaddeus's office once he had finished up with a preliminary hearing in court. He was wearing khaki pants with a blue button-down, his collar unbuttoned and his necktie flapping free. On his feet were Roper boots and on his head was a Stetson Cattleman hat. Other men were wearing straw already, but not Detective Snow. A preference, probably, but the hat would be terribly hot by July.

They were in Thaddeus's private office. Two bottles of Lipton's tea were open on the desk, resting on small cork coasters. The detective took a seat and thanked Thaddeus for the drink, tipped the bottle at him, and then took a swallow. "Good, that. Now, how can I help, Thaddeus?"

"I want to ask you about Sheila Lowenstein, Detective. Can I snap on this recorder?"

"Dealer's choice. Snap away."

Thaddeus pressed RECORD and placed the recorder between them on the desk.

"First off, my name is Thaddeus Murfee, and I'm recording a conversation today, May Fourth, with Detective Linus Snow in my office. Detective Snow has been kind enough to come here voluntarily and freely. No law or rule requires him to be here at all. Detective Snow, is this recording with your consent?"

"It is."

"You happened to respond to a shooting scene involving Russ Lowenstein?"

"I did. My partner Jason Landis and I responded to a call from Flagstaff PD Dispatch."

"When was that?"

"Second of May."

"Describe what you saw and did and heard."

"We arrived at the scene and found the front office abandoned. Dot Marchant, the receptionist, was out front, standing at the far end of the building, smoking a cigarette. She had a female officer with her, and they were talking. I could hear Dot talking through her tears, crying and weeping.

"We went inside the sale barn where two uniformed officers who met us at the door showed us to the back offices. In one office, we found Sheila Lowenstein and her daughter, PJ Walston."

"What happened next?"

"Officer McIntyre had Mrs. Lowenstein off to the side. He was encouraging her to take some water. She was highly emotional and agitated, saying over and over, 'I did it! He had it coming!'"

"What did you do?"

"We wanted a pristine scene, so I took Mrs. Lowenstein and her daughter into the next office. I sat them down and gave the Mrs. a box of tissues I found on a desk. She blew her nose and wiped her tears, but both of them were still crying. No, I'm wrong. The daughter wasn't crying, just the mother. The daughter was grim, and her face was blank. I thought she was in shock."

"What made you think she was in shock?"

"A lot of times when people go through something traumatic, they might appear calm and quiet afterwards. But I've learned over the years it can be a sign of shock. So that's what I decided about the daughter. My God, her stepdad was just gunned down by her mother. That's pretty horrifying to most people."

"What occurred in the room with the two women?"

"They talked back and forth. The mother asked the daughter if she was all right. The daughter reached over and rubbed the mother's back. It was all pretty low key as long as the mother wasn't crying, but then she'd break down and start up again. There wasn't much I could do. But I did ask them both what happened. The mother said, 'I shot Russ.'"

"What about the daughter? Did she answer your question?"

"No. She just looked at the tabletop and then looked at her mom. She wouldn't make eye contact with me, but that's normal with a kid that age. They're pretty shy around the police."

Or they didn't make eye contact when they had done something wrong and didn't want to get into trouble. He'd seen it with his own kids. That's why he and Christine insisted when their kids talked to them, they used respectful eye contact. So much could be viewed, could be understood, through the expressive eyes.

Detective Snow took a quick sip of his tea and then continued, "Later, Detective Landis came in, and we did a swab test on the mother."

"A gunshot test?"

"Right. But the test was inconclusive. Which wouldn't be unusual. She might have washed or rubbed off the gunshot residue."

"Let's talk about that. When you first arrived, the mother was in Russ's office?"

"Correct."

"Then you took her into the next office?"

"Correct."

"And you swabbed her hands and tested for gunshot residue?"

"Correct."

"And it was inconclusive?"

"Don't forget, Officer McIntyre had given her a cup of water. It might've sloshed and washed away any residue from her gun hand. It can happen that easily."

"What about her shirt? Did you test her shirt?"

"She wasn't wearing a shirt. She was wearing a halter top."

Which was interesting because when Sheila visited him that morning in his office, she was wearing a T-shirt with sleeves. And afterward, in the jail, she was wearing the same T-shirt. But it could have easily hidden a snug halter top.

"What about the halter top? Did you test that?"

"Yes. It came back negative."

"So her gun hand was inconclusive. How about the other hand?"

"I swabbed both hands. Both inconclusive."

"Knowing this, did you then swab the daughter's hands?"

"No."

Thaddeus held back the sigh of frustration building in his chest, so ready to be released. "Why not?"

"Mainly because the mother admitted to shooting Russ. If I could go back and change things, I would've swabbed the daughter. I made a mistake, and I own it."

"Thank you for that." As honorable as it was for the detective to admit fault, as often the police did, it never helped Thaddeus when it came to defending cases.

"Hey, truth is truth, sir."

"Who else have you talked to in your investigation into the shooting?"

"Dot Marchant, the receptionist. I put those notes in your court-house mailbox."

"Thanks for that. Did Dot say anything useful in identifying the shooter?"

"She said Sheila walked by her that morning and she was wearing a gun. Dot didn't think much of it because Sheila looked like she was going hiking. Guns are common in the woods around here."

"What else did she say?"

"Just that Sheila swept right in and right on by, smiling hello as she went past."

"What about PJ? Was she already there?"

"Yes, PJ was there to get a check for her 4-H cow."

"And the shooting didn't occur until after Sheila arrived?"

"Correct."

"Did you find a gun on the premises?"

"No."

"Did you find a gun on Sheila? In her holster?"

"No." As if in thought, Detective Snow slowly spun the Lipton bottle on the table. "By the time we arrived, there was no gun."

"Did a second gun ever figure in? Ever located?"

"No. You should have all the police reports. No officer on the scene mentions a second gun. Or a first gun, for that matter. We couldn't locate a gun after searching all through the office, out back in the dumpsters, everyplace on the premises. We also searched both female subjects and their packs and purses. No gun."

"Do you have a recorded statement from my client?"

"No, they said you were her lawyer by the time we got back to the jail so we didn't record her."

"But she did confess to you that she shot Russ?"

"Yes."

"Did you ask the daughter whether she shot Russ?"

"No, the mother was already confessing."

"Did the mother give you anything in writing?"

"No."

"What about the daughter? Anything in writing?"

"No."

Thaddeus studied his notes. Then he asked, "Did the mother ever tell you why she shot Russ?"

"Yes. She said he raped her daughter."

"Did you ask PJ about that?"

"Yes. She said she'd rather not talk about Russ."

"Did you push it?"

"Lord, no. I didn't want her anymore upset."

"But you mentioned she wasn't physically upset, and she wasn't showing any grief in tears or otherwise."

"That doesn't mean she wasn't upset. A lot of people hold in their emotion. And as a minor, we didn't feel it was necessary to provoke her."

"Got it, fair enough." Thaddeus tapped his pen against his notepad. "Who else have you spoken with?"

"Spoken with? No one. We have crime lab reports, police reports, medical examiner report, and so forth. But we haven't talked to anyone else." Thaddeus remembered that Landis had said they had spoken to Eleanor Garcia, who Detective Snow had failed to mention just now.

"What about video? Any closed circuit TV?"

"Yes. In the outer office, it shows the daughter arriving, then the mother arriving minutes later."

"She's wearing a gun?"

"The video doesn't show her waist."

"What about the daughter? Any gun? Backpacks?"

"Backpack, yes. It was a school day."

"Did anyone search the backpack?"

"Yes, as I mentioned earlier, we looked through her backpack, but there wasn't anything relevant there. Only school stuff, ya know, like books, folders, a packed lunch, a set of keys." Detective Snow finished his tea and then screwed the cap back on. "The mother's butt pack was searched for weapons and evidence, but there was only a cell phone, keys, a small wallet, Chapstick, and... that's about it, I think. It's all in my report."

"Any other CCTV?"

"Yes, we have a short clip of Sheila, from the back, walking into Russ's office and firing the gun at Russ Lowenstein."

"You mean, there is an image of a shooter, so whether it's Sheila is still yet to be determined."

"If you say so."

Thaddeus did. It seemed one too many times the police latched onto a suspect without really giving a crime the thorough investigation it deserved. Thaddeus could tell by Snow's choice of words that they already had Sheila locked down as guilty and were doing very little to research other avenues.

"Did you search the daughter's motor vehicle? I think she arrived first?"

"She had no motor vehicle. Just her bike."

"Did you search her bike?"

"I didn't. I was busy with the mother and the shooting scene. I assume the uniforms or crime lab had a look at her bike."

"Why didn't you search it?"

He sighed, a long exhalation of exasperation. "Because the mother was confessing. I'm thinking you don't believe your own client, Mr. Murfee?"

Thaddeus smiled. "Just doing my job. If I ask you these things now, I might be able to skip them in court. Win-win for everyone." He took a long sip of his iced tea before he asked, "Did the girl's bike have a bag on it?"

"Honestly? I don't know. I never saw the bike."

"So you didn't search the bike at the high school? Your partner said her bike was searched when the police finally followed up later about her bike."

"I didn't, I know that much. It was probably a couple of uniforms. It would all be in the reports."

Thaddeus riffled through his notes one last time. "I think that's all for now. I'll follow up if I need anything else later. I would like a copy of the CCTV."

Detective Snow gave the table a friendly smack like a judge would a gavel. "Done. I'll put it in your box."

Thaddeus rose and offered the detective his hand. "Thank you. And thanks for coming."

"You're welcome." He gave Thaddeus's hand a good solid shake and then strolled out the door. The way his arms moved while he walked, along with his long limbs, reminded Thaddeus of a praying mantis.

10

Thaddeus and Turquoise made an appointment to meet with Dot Marchant late in the afternoon of Russ's funeral, which was the Thursday of the same week of the shooting. They met at the sale barn in the reception area she presided over during working hours. Dot was still wearing her little black dress with a fine strand of pearls and sunglasses. She had been crying. Her red, rheumy eyes told Thaddeus all he needed to know: here was a loyal employee greatly saddened by the loss of her boss. She would be likely to tell the truth.

After he introduced Turquoise, the three of them gathered around Dot's desk. "I don't have coffee to offer," she said. "Just don't have the wherewithal to whip it up."

"Not to worry. This won't take long," Thaddeus told her.

"Do you mind if I record our conversation?" asked Turquoise at the ready with her iPhone.

"I don't mind," said the receptionist. "I don't know how much help I can be, though."

"Dot, let me ask a couple of preliminary questions," Thaddeus said with a smile. "Your full name is Dorothy Marchant and you're a first cousin to Russ Lowenstein?"

"Yes, your receptionist Carleen is also his cousin through marriage. Russ is actually Carleen's husband's cousin. That's Mitch. Which sort of makes us all family." She smiled. "Very loosely speaking. But I was much closer to Russ than any of them."

"Sure, sure," Thaddeus replied. "How long have you worked for Russ Lowenstein?"

"All of ten years. He was my second boss out of high school. A good man, too."

"How much did you know about Russ's private life?"

"Are you talking about his girls?"

Thaddeus looked up from his notes. "Excuse me?"

"You know, are you talking about Russ's girlfriends? It's no secret he kept plenty of them around. He even brought them here to the office."

Thaddeus exchanged a subtle look with Turquoise who raised her brow. When others had told him that it was no secret that Russ got around, Thaddeus hadn't realized it had been so obvious that those closest to him had turned the other cheek. "Were you here in the office when they were?"

"A couple of times they were leaving as I was coming in that morning, but it's not my place to say anything, ya know?" She blew her nose and deposited the tissue in the waste basket next to her legs. "I mean, he's my cousin, and I love him like a brother." She sobbed into a new tissue she'd collected from her empty box on the desk. "And now he's gone."

Thaddeus was about to forge ahead with his questioning when he felt Turquoise's knee knock with his own. When he glanced up, she shook her head, just a quick, almost imperceptible, movement. She was right. Thaddeus had to give Dot a moment to collect herself. She was in the middle of grieving and had just come from the funeral. Probably not the best time for an inquisition, but a lawyer had to act fast.

Dot took a deep breath and blew it out slowly. She looked Thaddeus in the eye, as if to tell him she was ready. He nodded and continued, "During the time you worked here, did Russ ever receive any angry calls that you were aware of? I'm speaking specifically of non-business types of calls now."

Dot toyed with her gel polish. "Yes and no. I've had to intercept a couple of husbands who just showed up ready to kill him. One of them had gotten a private eye to follow Russ and his wife. He came into the office waving pictures around, saying he was going to shoot the son of a bitch."

"How long ago was that?"

"Mr. Manning? Hmmm...a good five years, I think. Maybe six. He eventually got divorced and moved back to Denver."

"Did he ever return after that first time with the pictures?"

"No, but his lawyer took Russ's deposition. Mr. Manning was getting divorced from Cecilia. It was pretty nasty. They settled out of court, as I recall."

"Any other upset callers?"

"A few phone-ins, yes."

"Can you help us with any names?"

Dot looked up from the examination of her nail gel. "I'm gonna have to think about that. There were times when I had to balance a few women on the phone—Russ's wife, Sheila, and Russ's girlfriends. It got touchy once or twice."

"Let me direct your attention to last Friday, the day of the shooting. Please describe what happened that day before the shooting itself."

"Sure. I was here early because we had another cattle sale the next weekend, and it takes a lot of work to organize the big auctions. It was my job to call all the cattlemen who would be delivering livestock to make sure they remembered. I also checked to make sure I had their payment accounts accurate and ready to go. So I was doing all that. It was just after eight when PJ arrived."

"Would it be unusual for PJ to come here?"

"You could probably say 'unusual' and be pretty accurate. Remember, she wasn't his daughter by birth, and there wasn't that familiarity and love for your offspring like normal. Anyway, she showed up, came in carrying her backpack, earbuds in her ears, and didn't really say much to me. Just a wave of her hand and a smile and she went on back to her stepdad's office."

"I have to ask this—was she armed, wearing a gun, carrying a gun, holster, anything?"

"No, it wasn't like that. Just a hello and goodbye. I wasn't paying that much attention anyway."

"So she goes back to see her stepdad. Then what happened?"

"Just minutes later, here comes Sheila, and she *was* wearing a gun. She just blew past me and went into Russ's office. It wasn't two minutes later than I heard the gunshots."

"What did you do?"

"Honestly? It scared me so much I ran out the front door and ran down to the end of the building. I was hiding around the corner when the cops arrived."

"Who called the cops?" There would be a record if anyone called 911 or the police from here, but Thaddeus wanted to hear who Dot thought it might be. That said a lot—remorse, for one thing.

"I don't know. Maybe PJ or Sheila? I don't know why they would, but it never occurred to me before. Who did call the cops?"

Thaddeus ignored her question and focused on the information he needed. "All right. What happened next?"

"The police arrived five minutes later. They came in with their red lights flashing and went into my office with their guns drawn. They were doing that thing where one runs ahead and then poses with his gun, then the next one runs ahead and poses with their gun, then the other one runs ahead. That thing. I called to some of the police who stayed outside, and one of the uniformed officers came to talk to me. He had his hand on his gun as he approached me."

"What was said?"

"He asked me who I was, asked if I was okay, asked who was inside, asked what the heck had happened."

"Anyone else talk to you that morning, Dot?"

"One of the detectives asked me some questions. I forget who it was, though."

"Did you ever speak with Sheila or PJ again that morning?"

"Me? No."

"Ever hear them say anything that morning?"

"Not really. I went back inside after the officer said it was safe, but they already had the yellow crime scene tape up across Russ's office door. They were all in there, and I couldn't hear a thing. I was in shock, but they let me sit at my desk to call Russ's partners to notify them of the tragedy."

"You did that?"

"I called them, yes."

"Have you spoken with anyone else who claims to know what happened inside Russ's office that morning?"

"No. I mean, only PJ and Sheila know what happened, am I right?"

"I assume so," Thaddeus said. "So let's talk about video cameras. The office has video security?"

"Oh, yes. Lots of money passes through here. We have cameras everywhere."

"Cameras in this area?"

"Yes. Several."

"Cameras in Russ's office?"

She thought a minute. "I don't know. I assume so, but I don't know for sure."

"Have you ever reviewed any of the video recordings from that morning?"

She reared back, a crumbled tissue stretched between both hands. "No. I wouldn't even know how to."

Turquoise asked, "Who is the security company that handles your surveillance?"

That was a good question by his girl. If Dot did the finances, she'd have to know who she paid at least.

"Allsafe Security out of Phoenix. I have their contact details if you would like them. I gave it to the detectives, too."

"That would be great," said Turquoise with a smile. She stretched one of her new PI business cards across the desk. "My email is on here if you could send it to me today yet. That would be much appreciated."

Thaddeus had to admit his daughter was better at this than he was. Her detective work in L.A. had really honed her people and interrogation skills. There was definitely a craft to interrogation— a quick grasp of each individual, reading between the lines, understanding what wasn't said was just as important as what was said. And Turquoise's greatest skill, showing sympathy to the witness and relating to their current emotional state.

Thaddeus glanced briefly at his phone for the time. It was downright rude to an interviewee to show their effort wasn't as important as anyone else's. "Dot, was there anything about either PJ or Sheila that morning that you thought was unusual?"

"I'd never seen the Mrs. come into the office wearing a gun before. That definitely threw me."

"Anything else?"

"I mean, she was dressed for the woods, like she was going hiking or something. But that wouldn't be that surprising. She was a real outdoorsy type of person. She was always taking her church youth groups on hiking and camping excursions. Those often were the times when I'd find a girl here the next morning, if you know what I mean."

"I do now, yes."

"But there wasn't really anything else that might have tipped me off that someone was going to get shot."

"What about Russ that morning? Was he acting any differently?"

"Russ was Russ. He was always happy and joking and giving you a big smile. That morning he was just the same, even though he'd slept on the couch. Didn't ever seem to bother him. He was always friendly, never in a bad mood. Everyone loved Russ."

"Someone didn't," Turquoise said calmly. "Someone that morning shot him."

Dot looked at her. "What do you mean 'someone'? Don't we know it was Sheila who killed him?"

"We're working from that assumption, certainly," Turquoise said, "but nothing's written in stone."

"Meaning someone beside Sheila might have shot my boss?"

In the same neutral tone, Turquoise replied, "Not exactly. I didn't mean to suggest it was anyone else. We're just keeping an open mind at this point."

"You're not thinking I shot him, are you?"

Thaddeus's head jerked up from his notes. "Good grief, no. We have no such idea like that, I can promise you."

Dot began crying. "I know. I'm just very emotional. I loved Russ. Everyone did. I miss him already. I don't know about my job, either, Mr. Murfee. I don't know if I still work here or not. No one's said anything to me about it. Russ was family, you see? And he was the one who hired me, but that doesn't mean the other partners will want to keep me on."

"That has to be hard," said Turquoise.

"Yes." She sniffed. "It is."

Thaddeus pulled another tissue from the box on her desk and handed it to her. "Okay, is there anything else you want to tell us, Dot? Anything else we should know?"

Dot fisted the tissue in her hand, her demeanor turning from sad to angry in a second. She leaned forward in her chair. "Yes, how can you defend Sheila? She did it. Everyone knows it. You can't be planning to get her off, are you?"

"No one knows yet what the whole story is," Thaddeus said. "Let me get back to you on that."

"She did it. There was no one else here. He didn't shoot himself."

"No, no one believes he shot himself. All right, Dot, thanks for your time today."

"We recorded this with your full knowledge and consent?" Turquoise asked as she rose from her chair.

"Yes," said Dot. "I'm going to lock up now. Please don't leave until you see me leave. I've got the whips and jangles."

"No problem. We'll be out front in the Dodge Ram. We'll make sure you leave without bother."

"Thank you then."

Thaddeus and Turquoise gathered their things and left the office.

"We need to get ahold of the security company and find out about security inside there and what video coverage they have, including what Detective Snow told me about," Thaddeus said to Turquoise once they were back inside his truck with the engine running.

"I'm on it. First thing in the morning."

They watched Dot come outside, climb into her Corolla, and leave with a wave over her shoulder.

Then the sale barn parking lot was empty.

11

———

Magdalene Geneseo, a thirtyish correctional officer at the Coconino County Jail, nudged her coworker, Cindy Ralston. Both Magdalene and Cindy wore the jail uniform and a full utility belt. Both wore their hair pulled back tightly in a low bun. They were observing Sheila through the small window in the door of her cell.

"She hasn't eaten since she got here," said Magdalene. "Sheriff Joe says he's sending Dr. Butterieg back in."

"She just lays there on her bunk and stares at the ceiling. Spooky, Mags, if you ask me."

"I know." Magdalene shook her head, made a clucking sound with her tongue. "Doesn't look good. I'm gonna grab some snacks out of the break room and see if those interest her."

"I'll go ahead with our rounds. Catch you up front," said Cindy as she moved down the hallway, the bright halogen lights glaring over her head. She hated them. They made her sweat.

"All right, then." Magdalene walked back the other way, silencing her radio at her waist when it squawked.

Inside the cell, when she was sure the jailers were gone, Sheila sat up on her bed. She began humming Deep Purple's "Smoke On the Water." "Bom-bom-bom, bom-bom-be-bom."

Her bedding consisted of a bare mattress and a new paper bedspread, the type that would tear if any weight were put on it, designed to come apart if a prisoner attempted to hang themselves with their bedclothes. The idea was to prevent a type of suicide that had long prevailed in jail due to the availability of bed covers that could be torn into strips and used for hanging oneself.

Sheila removed her orange jail-issue blouse and pulled and yanked and bit at it until it came apart. She then tied the parts together in a long, single ropy configuration. She looped the thin end around the spigot on her sink and tied it there. She then tied the other end around her neck and backed up to the sink, taking up slack as she neared the appurtenance. Then it was down on both knees and a fall forward, causing the noose around her neck to tighten as she hung there, suspended in a 45-degree angle to the floor. She waited in this manner for her oxygen flow to be cut off.

She had waited for the officers to make their rounds on the women's side of the jail compound. Now it was time to die, time to put PJ out of the reach of the cops by convincing them the mother, in a fit of despair at having murdered her husband, ended her life. It was to be her final gift to PJ, a life without being forced to testify at a trial about Russ and his seduction of her, a chance for PJ to avoid the horror of talking about those things for the entire city—and the girl's friends—to hear about.

THADDEUS GOT THE CALL FROM THE JAIL JUST AFTER SEVEN THAT night. His client had been taken to Flagstaff Memorial Hospital and was on suicide watch.

He arrived, parked his Dodge truck, and ran for the elevators. Up to her floor where he flashed his identification for the deputy on duty outside the room. He stood with his hands clasped in front of him, his legs apart, right in front of the door.

After a quick look at Thaddeus's bar ID card, the deputy stepped aside to let him pass. "She's restrained in the bed. Just her right wrist, so she can't leave us."

"Got it," Thaddeus said before hurrying into the room.

She appeared asleep, but then her eyes opened. "Thaddeus," she whispered, "sorry about this."

"What the hell?" Thaddeus whispered back. "I thought we were way beyond this, Sheila. I'm there for you, and I'm going to cut a deal you can live with. This was totally unnecessary."

"I got to thinking about PJ having to testify. I can't have her go through that."

"She won't have to, Sheila. Let me work with the district attorney's office and let's see what I can make happen. But this"—he pointed at the ligature marks on her throat—"can't happen again. It's unnecessary. Please, Sheila, promise me you won't try this again."

Tears washed across her eyes. "I can't promise that, Thaddeus. I just keep thinking about my poor little girl. I brought that monster into our house, and it was my job to take him out. Just like taking out the trash—I think I told you that the other day. That was just how it felt. But also, they've refused to allow me my Oxycontin. The shrink has me on something to reduce the withdrawal. But it's been hell. I don't think I can survive that monster, too."

"You've got a lot on your plate. Just know we're all here pulling for you, Sheila. Has PJ been to see you?'

"They wouldn't let her in. They say regular visiting hours still apply even though I'm in the hospital. You're allowed in because you're my lawyer."

"I'll do what I can to get her in for a visit. Count on that happening before they return you to the jail."

"That would be wonderful if I could see my daughter. I'd be grateful."

"Would you be grateful enough to tell me this won't happen again?"

"Yes, I would. If you'll get her in to see me, I won't try again."

"Deal. Let me go talk to the DA's office in the morning. We'll make it happen, Sheila."

"Please, Thaddeus, you need to understand how close I am to my daughter. I'd do anything for her."

"I think I understand that you would, Sheila. You're a classy mother."

She began crying then. Thaddeus went to her bed, sat on the bedside, and held her in his arms. "Easy now. I promise I'll get you out of this. There, there."

She plucked a handful of tissues from the bedside box and dabbed her eyes. Then she managed a laugh. "You should've seen the look on Russ's face just before I shot him. I know it's not funny and I know I'm in serious trouble, but it was almost worth it to see his life finally catch up with his penis. Reality show, Russ. Bang bang!"

Thaddeus released his hold of her, and Sheila moved back to sit up against her pillows.

"Do the cops all believe I did it?"

"That's a funny question. I mean, you confessed, Sheila. Why would they have any other suspect besides you?"

"I'm just making sure. I don't want anybody thinking it might've been PJ, and I'm just covering for her. My suicide attempt should squelch that thinking."

Thaddeus stood and took a step back. "Is there something you're not telling me, Sheila? I'm getting uncomfortable right now when you're talking like this. Did PJ have anything to do with Russ's death?"

"How could she? I'm the one who shot him. I'm just trying to make sure she's not under any kind of suspicion. Do the cops think she might've been involved? At least tell me that."

"None of the cops seem to think PJ shot her stepdad, no."

"Do you?"

Thaddeus smiled and placed his hands on his hips. "It doesn't matter what I think or don't think. My job is to walk you out of the courtroom a free woman."

"Thaddeus, you're going to do just that. I can promise you."

His eyes narrowed. "See, when you talk like that, I get suspicious. What are you trying to say?"

She touched the side of her head. "I've got it covered. You just do your job, Thaddeus. That's all I'm asking. By the way, my brother sent your retainer, correct?"

"He did. I'm putting it in a trust I'm setting up for PJ's college expenses. Turquoise said she'll probably need financial assistance, especially with the cost of universities these days."

"My God, that's nice of you. I've never heard of a lawyer doing that."

"These are dire circumstances, Sheila. Your family is in need. I'm just doing what I'm able to do. Don't give it another thought."

"Well, I don't know what to say."

"Just say you won't try to kill yourself again, and we're even."

"I won't try to kill myself again. I promise."

"Then we're even. That's what I came here to get, your promise." He turned to leave. "By the way, say nothing to the doctors about the shooting, right?"

"I won't. I haven't."

"Good enough. Good night, Sheila."

"Good night, Thaddeus."

Thaddeus exited the room and thanked the deputy for calling him. The man nodded and shook Thaddeus's hand.

Then Thaddeus was off, back to the office this time. He'd gotten a text from Turquoise to say the CCTV video had arrived at the office via Fed Ex, and he wanted to pick it up for a quick look before bed.

12

The security video system operating in Russ's office was old and tired and produced a very grainy black and white picture. This is what Thaddeus and Turquoise learned once they had acquired twenty-four hours of video, twelve hours before and twelve hours after the time of the shooting.

The video started at 12:01 a.m. The father and daughter team was able to place the time of the shooting at 8:32 a.m., May 2nd. It was on a Monday.

The camera must have been positioned just over the door since the view was of only about a half of the room. Straight ahead was Russ's desk, facing the door, with two office chairs set up across from it. Slightly to the left of the large corporate desk was the back door that led down a flight of stairs and directly into the sale yard. It remained closed. Russ's desk was littered with stacks of papers. There was a large computer screen front and center on the desk and what appeared to be a phone on the right side. But the image was so grainy it was hard to determine what anything was. He and

Turquoise went back and forth at guesses of the items they could see.

Thaddeus knew from police reports that there was a three-seater couch along the left wall with a small end table in the corner of the room. These were both out of range of the camera, and he assumed that if Russ brought his "girlfriends" back to the office, that was on purpose. If what Sheila and PJ said was true, Russ should be sleeping on that couch as the minutes passed.

At just after seven a.m., what appeared to be a set of boots was captured in the frame, midway down the screen. Thaddeus mused out loud to Turquoise that it was as if Russ had slept in his boots and just sat up on the couch. Turquoise tilted her head back and forth, trying to get a better understanding of what they were looking at. But the boots didn't move, as they both expected them to, followed by a groggy Russ getting up from sleep. The most peculiar bit was that either Russ was wearing long jeans so that the material bunched at his ankles or they were, in fact, not looking at a pair of cowboy boots at all.

At 7:14 a.m., the boots disappeared, and at 7:22 a.m., a small blur appeared in the bottom left corner of the screen. Too bad there wasn't color.

Thaddeus clicked the pause button. "What do you reckon that is?"

Turquoise tapped her mouth with her index finger. "I have no idea. Can you zoom in?"

Thaddeus laughed. "I'm not that computer savvy. You give it a go."

Turquoise fiddled with the screen a bit until she could magnify the corner. Then Thaddeus rewound and ran that segment a half dozen times before he and Turquoise, with a pretty good certainty, could ascertain it was hair on the top of the head.

Was this Sheila or PJ? Had Dot gotten the times wrong? It was a distinct possibility. If she wasn't watching the clock and was busy right away with office work, she could have been very wrong on the times. Or was this one of Russ's dalliances? So then had Dot lied to protect Russ, the cousin that was like a brother?

When they kept the video running, Russ could be seen moving across the screen to his desk where he sat and buttoned up a plaid shirt, the kind with the colors that cowboys often wore.

Then he powered up his computer, and that kept him busy until just after eight a.m. when Dot Marchant entered his office carrying two large containers of Buffalo Cafe coffee. She set both on Russ's desk and left out of the range of the video camera. This opened up a new question to Thaddeus: was it possible the second coffee was for Sheila because Russ knew she was coming to the office? Or was the coffee for the person that was already there? The question remained unanswered by the video itself.

8:14 displayed on the screen just as a young blond woman appeared with her backpack dangling from her hand and sunglasses perched on her head. She wore a T-shirt and jeans. They spoke—no sound—and then the girl turned around toward the camera. From her features, it appeared to be PJ, but her and her mother looked quite similar, just their statures were different. She left through the door. From the police report, Thaddeus had learned PJ had told the police she was headed for the ladies' room. But from Turquoise's notes, PJ had said she'd never entered the room and stayed in reception because Russ was on the phone.

At exactly 8:31 a.m. a blond woman wearing shorts and a T-shirt entered the frame, seen from behind. She strolled up to Russ's desk and raised a pistol. Without pausing, she then leaned across Russ's desk and shot him squarely in the face, just between the eyes. He flew backward in his chair, whereupon she came around the desk and fired the gun repeatedly, seven more times. With great aplomb, as if she was proud of her work accomplished, she stood upright, turned left, and then crossed the room to the back wall. She pulled open the door, walked through, and closed it behind her.

"Dad, I never did see her face."

"Neither did I. Let's run that part again."

Again, frame-by-frame, they stepped through the video. Still no face revealed.

"Amazing," said Turquoise. "Isn't there a video shooting toward her? A video from the far wall area?"

"No, this is it."

"Well, we know what happened, but we don't know who she is, actually, not from the video," Turquoise said.

"And where's PJ? I thought she was supposedly there when the shooting occurred?"

"Not in the frame."

Thaddeus added, "Unless the shooter is PJ."

"Maybe the daughter brought a gun and shot her dad. And we're sitting here, like the cops, believing the shooter was the mom. It's far-fetched, but I don't ever believe what my eyes tell me first time around."

"I like how you think, daughter. That's the kind of open mind that solves homicides."

"Speculation, Dad."

"Isn't it all at this point? You know what? Judging from the backside, the shooter could even be a man. I'm going to have our video analysis folks measure the backside of the shooter and compare that to the measurements of the mother and daughter. This could be much deeper than it is even made to look. Because we also have this third head briefly in the video."

"Wow, talk about speculation."

"Well," said Thaddeus, "part of me wants to believe what the client tells me, but another part of me never believes the client. Not without corroboration, anyway."

"So, there we are, Dad, thinking like the cops. We've got video proof of Sheila murdering her husband."

"Or else we've got video of a plot to make us think Sheila is the killer. We know both mother and daughter had motive."

"The rapes, yes."

"And probably both had the mental state—the anger—to propel them to gun him down," Thaddeus said.

"Yes, any jury is going to feel the same way. The abuse began when PJ was thirteen. That's going to make some jurors want to turn the mother loose and say the father had it coming."

"This is incredible," said Thaddeus. "We have video of the actual murder, and we still don't know who pulled the trigger."

"So what's next, Dad?"

"Well, we have our video people do their workup. Then we'll go from there."

Turquoise said, "It's going to be difficult. Mother and daughter are not that different in build. Although I think PJ is a bit shorter than her mother. I've never seen Sheila, so I could be wrong about that."

"And I've never seen PJ, so I don't know how they compare, either."

Turquoise said, "They could be the same size, for all we know at this point."

"And what about the mystery head? Do you think it's Sheila or PJ?"

Turquoise sat back in her chair, crossed her legs, and tented her fingers in front of her on her stomach. She was the kind of person who thought before they spoke. "It could be either, really. Or someone completely different. But it does add in another element to our investigation."

"Agreed." Thaddeus shut down his computer. "Okay, that about wraps it up for today. Let's mark the video as one of our trial exhibits and enter it into the case log."

"Will do."

"Will you go ahead and get physical measurements of both women? We're going to need that."

"No problem."

Thaddeus sat back in his office chair. "Wait, one more thing. Are you ready for the two of us to talk to Carleen?"

"I am if you are. What are we after?"

"Well, the day of the shooting she was on the phone trying to warn Russ. And who knows what else."

Turquoise looked at her watch. "It's a bit late, almost nine-thirty. I'll catch her first thing in the morning tomorrow to set up a time for a chat."

"Please do. She's not a friendly witness. Approach her like you would a sidewinder."

13

The following morning, Thaddeus phoned the sheriff and discussed Sheila's incarceration and visitor schedule. It was agreed that PJ could visit her mom without restriction. The sheriff was bending over backwards to help, and Thaddeus thanked him for being so understanding.

They then discussed Sheila's oxycodone addiction. Something had to be done, as going cold-turkey off the medication was very dangerous. Thaddeus pushed for a visit from an addiction doctor, at Sheila's expense, and the sheriff agreed that should be done without delay. After hanging up, Thaddeus called around and hired an addiction doctor to visit Sheila at the hospital. Preparations and observations would begin immediately.

When he felt like he had done all he could to provide for her current needs, he called her at the hospital to report back. She was grateful, and he was gracious. They were transporting her back to the jail after the morning rounds. The doctor still needed to sign her release forms.

But her life should improve considerably, even considering the ongoing incarceration.

Thaddeus hung up the phone and sat back, somewhat satisfied with his work. Then he made coffee and went back to the video again. Certain moments warranted repeated study before he was satisfied.

He cued the video, took a large swallow of his coffee, and sat back to watch.

Two hours later, Carleen appeared in Thaddeus's office. He'd been in there with Turquoise, discussing the Sheila Lowenstein case and planning out Turquoise's next tasks. Thaddeus looked up when Carleen walked in without knocking. He wasted no time.

"What is your family tie to Russ Lowenstein?" Thaddeus asked Carleen. He knew the answer from Dot but wanted to hear it from her.

The older woman hesitated, taking her time to sit and adjust in the chair across from him. Perhaps she had a lawyer who had advised her not to talk about the lawsuit. She was obviously operating from the premise that she was under scrutiny because she'd called Russ to warn him Sheila was on the way and was armed. "I'm his cousin," she finally said, "and as far as calling him to warn him, you would've done the same thing in my shoes, Thaddeus. In fact, you should have done the same thing. You should have called him and warned him. He might be alive today if you had picked up your phone and told him to go straight to the police for protection."

"I can appreciate your thinking, Carleen. Unfortunately, you're ignoring the legal ethics that I'm bound to operate by. In this case, I was restrained from telling anyone about my client's state of mind. Plus, she had assured me there would be no confrontation and no violence and that counseling sounded good to her. Given these things, I couldn't tell anybody anything. Moreover, you violated my ethics by acting on privileged information you gained from my talk with Sheila. When you called Russ to warn him, you essentially resigned from your job here."

She sat upright, crossing her ankles under the chair. "Meaning?"

"Meaning this can't ever happen again, not in my office. So I'm going to have to let you go, Carleen." And he was sorry. She'd been a solid worker. Showed up on time, rarely called in sick, was thorough in her organization, and could jostle a schedule better than an appointments coordinator at a medical center.

She narrowed her eyes at Thaddeus, cocked her head. "You better not let me go. Not unless you want a big fat lawsuit on your desk."

"Sue away," said Thaddeus, shrugging. "That's what we have lawyers for."

Carleen abruptly stood, her body rigid with anger. "Then I'm finished talking, Thaddeus. You're firing me so I have nothing more to say."

"Tell me one thing, please," he said to her as she rose from her chair. "Are you going to keep the secrets you've learned here over the past seven years? Or do I need to get a restraining order to shut you up?"

Her face turned beet-red, her hands fisted at her sides. "How dare you speak to me that way! You better get a restraining order, Thaddeus. I'm telling everyone I know that you cost Russell Lowenstein his life. And I know lots of people, sir." She stalked toward the door.

"I'm sorry you feel that way. I would've hoped we could keep this out of the courts." And Thaddeus did mean that. He had enough court time as it was, let alone adding in his own personal defense.

She turned on her heel and took two steps back toward him. "And you know what else? I filed a bar complaint against you, Thaddeus Murfee. The State Bar of Arizona will be investigating you starting Monday. I wouldn't be surprised to see you lose your license to practice law." She leaned forward, pointing a painted nail at him. "Your goose is cooked, mister."

"Fair enough, Carleen. We'll just have to let one of the judges help us here."

"Help, hell. I'm hiring a lawyer and suing you, Thaddeus."

"Suing me? Why?"

"For wrongful death. You plotted with Sheila to murder my family member. Now, we're furious with you!"

"So you're suing me. Jeesh!" Of all the rotten outcomes from one of his own employees.

"We'll make it stick, too. That's what Mr. Novack says."

"John Novack is your lawyer?" Thaddeus leaned forward in his chair and clasped his hands together. "I'd better call him and warn him what a crap case you have against me."

"No need. He promised he'd have the lawsuit on file tomorrow morning as soon as the court opened. You can read all about it when you get served today, sir."

"My word, Carleen. You didn't waste any time, did you?"

"Good luck, Turquoise," she said to Thaddeus' daughter, who had remained silent throughout the exchange. "You're going to need all the luck you can get working for your dad. He's dishonest and a cheat."

Turquoise leaped to her feet. "You'll want to get out that door before I come around this desk after you, Carleen. Get the hell out and don't look back."

"Done! I wouldn't stay here another second. See you fools in court!"

The door slammed behind her. Thaddeus followed her out, back into the waiting room. She'd already boxed up her things and was struggling to get through the door with her hands full of a large cardboard box. Turquoise came up from behind and pulled open the door.

"Good riddance," Turquoise said to Carleen. "Don't let the door hit you in the ass."

"We can add you to the lawsuit, too, Turquoise, know that?"

"Add away. I haven't had the chance to kick ass in a couple of weeks now. So spell my name correctly and make me part of your nowhere case."

"Well, goodbye then, Turquoise. I would've expected more from you." She huffed and then squeezed herself out the door.

"'Bye, Carleen," Turquoise said in an overly cheery voice while waving. She then let go of the door so it swung closed behind their old receptionist. "Wow, she turned into a bit of a cow."

14

Thaddeus arrived at his office the next morning to find a local process server, William Maxton, sitting in his waiting room. He stopped to speak to the man.

"Uh-oh, Maxie. I'm in trouble?"

"I hate bringing this, Thaddeus. Looks like Russ Lowenstein's family is suing you and Sheila."

"Okay, Sheila I get, but why me?"

Maxton handed a sheaf of papers to Thaddeus. "You're officially served. I glanced through the complaint. They're saying you had a legal duty to warn Russ that Sheila was coming for him."

Thaddeus immediately knew Carleen was behind the filing. Evidently, she had gone to the family and given them enough dirt that they got angry and added Thaddeus to the lawsuit they were filing against Sheila.

Thaddeus sighed and shook Maxton's hand. "I'm served. But don't worry. I don't take it personally, and I'll still use your services for my lawsuits, Maxie. Have a good day now."

"Thank you, Thaddeus. I was afraid you'd be pissed."

"You're only doing your job. I get that. Can I buy you a cup of coffee?"

"Thanks, but no. I've got a whole front seat full of stuff to serve yet today. I'm on my way."

"Later, then."

Maxton hurried out of Thaddeus's office. There was a bounce in his step, Thaddeus observed. Probably damn glad to make it away unscathed. He sighed and took the lawsuit into his office along with a fresh cup of coffee. At his desk, he flipped through the clerk's documents to the meat of the paperwork, the lawsuit itself. There it was, black-and-white. *Heirs of Russ Lowenstein, Deceased, vs. Sheila Lowenstein, Defendant, and Thaddeus Murfee, Defendant.* He started reading while sipping his coffee. Soon, a smile was playing across his lips. Definitely Carleen's handiwork since the family was claiming Sheila had foretold Thaddeus that she was on her way to murder Russ, and Thaddeus had responded only by attempting to have his video erased. There was nothing mentioned about the call Thaddeus had taken from Russ Lowenstein, in which Thaddeus had told Russ to get out of the office. Of course, Carleen probably was unaware of what had been said in the call unless she was listening in, which he was almost positive she was not.

He had wrestled with these questions before, the questions of what duty a lawyer owed a stranger versus the duty he owed his client to keep a confidence once the client said *You've talked me down*, as Sheila had promised Thaddeus. Wasn't a lawyer entitled to believe his client? Or was he required to have the wisdom of Solomon and the psychology of a Dr. Phil to understand when he was being lied to? It was the same problem.

Thaddeus let out a long sigh. He knew what was coming next: the dreaded bar complaint the family would now make to the State Bar of Arizona, claiming Thaddeus should be banished from the practice of law because of his negligence. Yes, that would be coming in the mail in the next few days. He could taste the bitter pill of the bar complaint like some terrible medicine a lawyer has to ingest every year or so just to keep them humble. It was his turn in the barrel, and he hadn't even collected a dime in personal compensation for his troubles. Suddenly, he was tired and felt like saddling up Hearsay and disappearing a couple of mountains over. Which he decided he would just do.

He headed his Dodge Ram northwest on US 180 out of Flagstaff and gunned it up to the speed limit. It was a bright day, and his glasses darkened against the sunlight. In his drink holder was a venti Starbucks he had picked up on the way out of town. Life was good at such times. He had already called his horse wrangler, Wiley Sutter, and told him to have Hearsay ready to ride.

At the ranch, Thaddeus pulled the truck up to the stable. Wiley was waiting with a bucket and brush and a newly saddled Hearsay, Thaddeus's two-year-old quarter horse. Thaddeus swung open his door and stepped down. First, he removed his necktie and rolled up the sleeves of his office shirt. He was already wearing his Ropers, which would do just great in the stirrups. He reached back in and grabbed his coffee and two bottles of water and slipped those into a saddle horn bag. Then he swung a leg over Hearsay and loosened the reins. Off they went, down along the north-south road adjacent to their pasture and up the hill toward the Coconino National Forest his acreage abutted. In the distance, he could see Humphrey's Peak, the highest elevation in the park. The sun was almost directly overhead, so it wasn't long before Thaddeus reached for his first water bottle.

From there, they wandered aimlessly on the Forest Service roads that crisscrossed the precious land in every direction. There were patches that were still bare from logging after all these years, the land mottled with red barberry, claret cup cactus, Parry's agave, locoweed, and the rare sego lily. In other areas, the pines had been replanted, the forest floor bare of much other than pine needles.

As he and Hearsay set a slow wander through one of these regrowth forests, Thaddeus grew contemplative, even a bit melancholy. He couldn't remember the last time he and Christine had taken the kids out on the horses for the day. They each had a pony, even Jamie, although he didn't ride. And maybe that was why Thaddeus subconsciously didn't push for more family outings. Their family wasn't whole without Jamie.

But that didn't mean he couldn't arrange a vacation for all of them. Maybe a trip soon again down to Mexico, or Chicago perhaps where Jamie loved all the museums, especially the Museum of Science and Industry. Thaddeus personally preferred the History Museum, but nothing was comparable to Jamie's look of utter happiness when he visited the new science exhibits.

So...Thaddeus was a big fan of lists. At any one time, he had multiple lists on his yellow legal pads. He had yet to start making lists on his phone, which Christine had informed him numerous times was possible with an assortment of free apps. He tried it once, and it just wasn't the same. Never looked at the thing again. So instead, he was making a mental list for his family. And the first thing added was:

Vacation.

15

C hristine, reading through the Detective Landis investigation notes, came across the name of Eleanor Garcia, the woman Russ was seeing in Williams, Arizona. The town was about twenty-five miles west of the Murfee ranch, not that far, and Christine wanted to talk to her, so she loaded into her Mercedes and headed west from the ranch. Thirty minutes later, after a gasoline stop, she was pulling into the driveway of the Garcia woman's small, neat house on the east side of town. She parked and approached the front door of the bungalow.

There was a small sign next to the doorbell that instructed callers who were patrons of the beauty salon to come around to the garage entrance on the side. Christine rang the front door because it was still early in the morning and she doubted the Garcia woman's beauty salon would be open yet. She was right, and the door swung open in seconds. There stood a well-coiffed woman wearing gray sweatpants and a navy shirt that said *Runnin' Rebels*. She was holding a coffee mug that said, *Your Hair is My Lunch.*

Christine smiled inwardly and wondered what people thought of some of her own at-home getups.

Christine introduced herself. "I'm a lawyer and colleague of Thaddeus Murfee. Thaddeus is defending Sheila Lowenstein. One of the police officers on the case gave us your name, and I've come over to spend a few minutes with you about the case. May I come in?"

Eleanor Garcia pushed open the storm door and stood aside so Christine could enter. "Sure. I figured you all would be coming sooner or later. Let's get it over with."

Christine stepped inside and offered to take her shoes off but Ms. Garcia waved her off. She herself wore a pair of purple flip-flops, the cheap kind a person could get at a discount store for a couple of bucks.

She pointed with her mug. "Let's go into the kitchen. I'll get you some coffee."

"No need. Just had my coffee, Ms. Garcia."

"Eleanor."

"Eleanor, then. The living room is fine."

The woman backed up and motioned to the room with her free hand. "Be my guest."

It was a small room. Christine took a wingback chair with a large pheasant on the backrest. Ms. Garcia sat to her right on a short, low couch done in white with embossed swirls. She balanced her coffee cup on her knee and shrugged. "Ask away."

Christine took out a small notepad and readied her pen. "Do you mind?"

At the shake of Eleanor's head, Christine started, "You and Russ were seeing each other?"

"We were. Big mistake. I don't usually date married men."

"Why did you this time?"

"I met him in a bar in Flagstaff. Russ was hard to ignore. He was magnetic, handsome and fun. So we had a fling."

"How long did this continue?"

"Six months. It was off and on. He'd get bored and come over, and we'd usually hang out here with drinks and movies. It was all very low key. He was a terrible screw. I'm nothing to write home about myself, so we deserved each other, right?"

"Were you in love?"

"Honey, women like me don't fall in love. Love's too expensive."

"So it was just out of boredom, mainly? Loneliness?"

"Yes, loneliness. Williams is a very dead-end town socially. There's no one here for women like me. The good ones are all married. Then there's guys like Russ. You learn not to disrespect yourself after a while. It is what it is."

"Please tell me what Russ ever said about his wife, Sheila. Let me back up. Was Sheila aware Russ was seeing you?"

"Everyone was aware of everything Russ was doing. He was a guy who made no attempt to cover up anything. He made so damn much money at the sale barn that he just didn't care what people thought anymore. Did Sheila know? I assume so."

"Would anyone you can think of have wanted to harm Russ?"

"I know one man, Marshall Anders, who wanted him dead. Marshall caught Russ with his wife out at Mormon Lake Lodge. They were shacked up there. Marshall got wind of it and tracked him down. He beat the hell out of Lucy Dee and went out to his truck for his gun, but Russ got away. Word was Marshall threatened Russ with instant death if he ever contacted Lucy Dee again."

"And did he?"

Eleanor shrugged. "I don't know, but Russ's dead now, ain't he?"

"Do you know if Marshall knew Sheila Lowenstein, Russ's wife?"

Again, she shrugged. "If she drives a foreign car, there's a good chance he did. He's the only mechanic in Flagstaff that knows what he's doing."

Christine made a note to find out what kind of car Sheila drove. "How can I get ahold of Marshall Anders?"

She waved her hand in front of her face. "Oh, no, honey. No one gets ahold of Marshall. He's a hothead, and he's already done a stretch at Florence for killing a man in a barroom brawl that he started. You stay far away from the man."

"All right. Where does he live?"

"Flagstaff, out near Pine Canyon country club. He's a foreign car mechanic with a large shop that does very well. He works on my BMW now and then." She huffed a laugh. "That might make me sound posh, but my BMW is 1989. But no one knows cars like Marshall. You could trust he wouldn't rip you off, you know?"

Christine nodded. "Sure, I get that. It's hard to find a good mechanic. Where's his shop?"

"Eastern Avenue. Just below the small mountain on the east end of town."

"Do you know the name of the shop?"

"Classic Cars or something like that. Classic something. But you stay away from him. That man's not to be ruffled. Oh, I remember now, Canyon Classic Cars. All he does is foreign."

When Christine stuck her hand out, Eleanor shook it. They were going to remain friendly, their moment said. As far as Christine was concerned, Eleanor Garcia had nothing further to add to the conversation over Russ's death. Her role was minimal to none.

Christine drove off toward the Flagstaff freeway where she got up to speed and headed eastbound. She could take the Country Club turnover, go across the freeway bridge and double-back toward Eastern Avenue and Canyon Classic Cars.

It was time to talk to Marshall Anders. She had no fear of the man, just a notepad filled with questions she'd jotted down while speaking with Eleanor.

She pulled into Canyon Classic Cars. Christine parked her Mercedes between a classic Jag and a glossy MG of 1952 vintage. She opened her door, taking care not to allow it to touch the Jag on her left, and stepped down. With notepad in hand, she walked inside the shop through the overhead door.

A man in his early forties, clean-shaven but balding with his hair longer on the sides and in the back, came over to greet her just inside the open garage door, wiping his hands on a red shop towel as he came. "Yes?"

"Are you Marshall Anders?"

He squinted at her, then nodded. "I am. Who's asking?"

She held out her hand. "Hi, my name is Christine Murfee. My husband is Thaddeus Murfee. Thaddeus is defending Sheila

Lowenstein, who is indicted for murdering Russ Lowenstein. Russ Lowenstein, I have learned, was not one of your favorite people."

He ignored her offered handshake. "Cut the bullshit, lady. The cops have already been here. I had nothing to do with the death of Russ Dirtbag. Good riddance, I told them. I'll tell you the same thing. Damn good riddance."

Christine checked her notes. "Is it true Russ Lowenstein had an affair with your wife, Mr. Anders? I've heard that from another source."

"Who told you that? It's pure horseshit, and I'd like to know who's spreading lies about me."

"Sorry, but I can't divulge names. Everything I do is confidential, just like your information will be if you decide to cooperate with me."

He shoved the rag in his back pocket, like how Bruce Springsteen used to wear one on stage. But this man had no class. He oozed bad vibes. "Lady, I'm telling you what you're suggesting is all bullshit." He bared his teeth at her like an animal would. "And if you keep spreading lies about me"—he took a couple steps toward Christine and pointed at her chest—"I might be paying you a visit."

Christine stood her ground, didn't even flinch like she imagined most would. She imagined Marshall Anders got his rocks off on intimidation, enjoyed another's fear at his bullying. "Mr. Anders, know this. Know that I can take care of myself. Paying me a visit, as you put it, would be a huge mistake for your health and safety. A huge mistake. Now, you can either cooperate with me and help me with some answers that probably have nothing to do with you, or you can continue to threaten me. The one is the safe side of the street for you, the other is a dead-end if I catch you snooping around me, my husband, or my family. So which is it? Do you help me out or tell me to go to hell? In which event I'll leave and not bother you again."

He was practically hovering over her at this point. "Lady, that's twice you've threatened me right here in my own garage. That's a mistake. I'd suggest you leave before it gets much hotter in here."

Christine kept her cool, didn't allow any emotion to show through, just like she had back in Iraq. Even when soldiers twice her size tried to intimidate her, she never backed down. By the end of her last tour, she was famous for her nerve and backbone. "I'll leave. It's your right to refuse to talk with me. But know I've got my eye on you. If I think there's a connection between you and Russ Lowenstein's death, I'm going to work that connection and bring it to the jury's attention in Sheila Lowenstein's case."

"Sheila and I are friends. I've got no beef with Sheila. Just with that douchebag husband of hers. But he's gone adios, so end of story. You should leave now."

"I'll leave. Just remember, safety first, sir."

"Like now."

"I'm going," Christine said, turning on her heel and heading for her car. She stepped outside the garage into the bright mountain sunshine and felt a shiver travel up her back even though the day was quite warm. He was watching her—staring knives—she could feel it. She purposely slowed her gait and sauntered the last twenty steps to her Mercedes, just daring him to shout or catcall before she could pile into her vehicle and leave. But no snarky remark ever came. She hopped in, cranked the engine over, and lowered the window for a fresh-air drive. She started backing up. When she looked up from her rearview camera screen, she saw that he was still staring at her, arms crossed, a wicked smile on his face.

Christine raised her right hand and waved goodbye, a friendly gesture. He immediately became enraged so he must've thought she had given him the middle finger instead. He cursed at her and brushed his hand her direction, as if shooing her away. Then he shook his head and turned away, laughing angrily. "Bitch," he snorted.

16
_____

Back at the office, Thaddeus was reading the Lowenstein family wrongful death lawsuit once more, assembling the points of the complaint in his head and deciding one-by-one just how he would respond. On his second pass-through, Christine came into his office, her face glowing. He knew that face, one she wore when she was overexcited, adrenaline pumping through her veins.

She shut the door and walked around to his side of the desk. She swiveled his chair and sat down on his lap sideways. "I just talked to Marshall Anders. What a drip."

"Who?" He wrapped one arm around her back, the other he left draped across her legs. Hell, she had fantastic legs.

She took a sip of his coffee from the mug on his desk and made a face. "Yuck."

"It's cold."

She smirked at him. "I figured that out."

"So who is this Anders fella?"

"Let me back up. This morning I spoke with Eleanor Garcia, Russ Lowenstein's girlfriend. She was no help, and I believe she's innocent in all events surrounding how Russ died. Anyway, she gave me the name of Marshall Anders, a man whose wife had a thing with Russ. The man, said Eleanor, had threatened Russ's life, so I went down to Canyon Classic Cars to talk with him."

"The one on Eastern Avenue?"

"Yep," she said with a smile.

Thaddeus groaned. "I just wish you wouldn't take on guys like Anders without coming to me first. What's the point of going on your own, Christine? Are you just looking for a fight?" Half the time she was, but just because Chris wouldn't mind a good ass-kicking once in a while didn't mean Thaddeus thought it was a good idea. She was still his to protect.

"No." She kissed his cheek. "I was looking for information. I was polite and professional. He's the one who turned things ugly. It ended with him thinking I flipped him off. But it really was a wave. So I gave up and drove away. He got the message that I'm watching him."

"Holy shit, Chris! Why do you antagonize those kinds of men?"

She removed his glasses and kissed each eye. "Stop worrying. Those men are half-wits, more testosterone than brains."

Although Chris's touch usually had a calming effect on Thaddeus, it wasn't working today. He didn't know what he would do if anything happened to her. "That's what I worry about! Do I need to go talk to the guy myself?"

She gave him a quick peck on the forehead. "No, he isn't talking. And he might call the cops on us if we show up there again. But I do want to do this—I want to defend the lawsuit Russ's family filed against you. If you'll let me do that, then I can take Marshall Anders' deposition and get some answers I wanted from him."

"Such as?"

"My main question is whether he had anything to do with the lead-up to the shooting."

"Why would you think so?"

She crossed her leg and snuggled into his chest. "Well, the man has a history of violence. I'm thinking he might have supplied the gun used to kill Russ. Do you know what type of car Sheila drove?"

"Not off the top of my head...but let me check the police report." While Thaddeus looked back through the papers to get Christine her info, she peppered him with kisses along his chin. If she didn't stop soon, he'd be locking the office door and drawing the blinds. "Here it is. A 2017 Range Rover."

"So a foreign car." Christine chewed her bottom lip in thought.

Thaddeus nodded, but couldn't keep his eyes off her mouth. "Yep, it seems so."

"So far, the weapon hasn't been found. But I've got a hunch about him and Sheila. He said he knew her. I'll just bet dollars to donuts he was helping her somehow. Which would make him a co-conspirator." She unfolded herself from his lap and got up from the chair. She slipped on her shoes that had fallen off when she had sat on his lap.

Her absence always left the same feeling with Thaddeus. He missed her. Even when she was still right here. That's how much he loved the woman. "So how does that help my defense of Sheila? Adding him into the mix doesn't make Sheila any less guilty, does it?"

"If he supplied the gun, who's to say he didn't teach Sheila how to use it? My guess is his involvement is up close and personal. He wanted Russ dead, and he convinced Sheila to pull the trigger."

"I still don't get how that helps my case. She still pulled that trigger, at least according to her."

She had walked toward the door, but then came back and leaned both arms onto the far edge of his desk. "But what if she's fabricating? What if Marshall Anders planned the shooting for her? There goes premeditation if it wasn't Sheila who premeditated, but it was Marshall. Doesn't that weaken their case?"

"Hmm." Thaddeus tapped his pen against his lips. "That has a certain attraction to it. She was egged on by a man who taught her how to shoot and how and when to do it. Yes, I could use that to help show she wasn't acting entirely on her own, and the idea was planted and nurtured by him. Okay, let's keep looking at him. How can I help?"

"Let me defend the wrongful death case and let me depose Marshall. I can get him going at his deposition, and who knows what he might say? He might even threaten me, and we could use that in the criminal case."

"It's a stretch, but it's worth investigating. All right, you're now my lawyer on the civil case. But be safe, Chris. I worry about you. We shouldn't take his threats lightly. I know it doesn't bother you, but I can't bear the thought of a man making threats against my wife. Especially right in front of her."

She smiled and stood. "And I worry about you. That's our gig. Now, I'll get an answer to the complaint on file today. By the way, who's defending Sheila in the lawsuit?" She was already walking toward the door.

"Her homeowner's insurance has it right now. They might be defending under a reservation of rights."

"All right, I'll put in a call to them and see if I can turn up their attorney."

"Go get 'em, Chris." Thaddeus smiled. What a cracker Chris was! But he loved her passion, her pursuit of justice. One of the many things he loved about her. He was a lucky son of gun.

She waved, halfway out the door already. "Bye!"

17

Another complaint, this one by certified mail from the State Bar of Arizona. Thaddeus ripped it open with a heavy heart.

The bar complaint stated:

1. The Respondent, Thaddeus Murfee, came into knowledge that his client, Sheila Lowenstein, intended to kill her husband.

2. Even having said knowledge, Thaddeus Murfee failed to act: specifically, he knowingly and purposely failed to warn the decedent Russell J. Lowenstein that his wife, Sheila Lowenstein, intended to shoot and kill him and, further, Respondent Murfee failed to alert the authorities of his client's intention.

3. The Respondent, Thaddeus Murfee, acted with a clear disregard for the safety of others in failing to report his client's intention to commit a crime, which disregard resulted in the death of Russell J. Lowenstein.

4. Thaddeus Murfee should be suspended from the practice of law while this matter is investigated. A hearing on this request for suspension pending investigation will be held on Friday, May 13th.

THADDEUS CHECKED HIS CALENDAR. FRIDAY THE 13TH. HOW appropriate. Now, he wasn't a suspicious man, but he didn't reckon the date boded too well for him. The hearing on his license and his ability to practice law was only one week away. He'd need to get help and get help soon. He'd need an attorney outside his office to defend him.

So he made a call and then left his office and hiked up North Agassiz Street to the office of an old friend, a lawyer-rancher named Shep Aberdeen. He entered Shep's outer office and was told to go on in, that Shep was expecting him.

Shep was a muscular cowboy from Durango who'd gone to law school in his early twenties and, after knocking around in Denver in banking law, decided he was better suited for criminal law and migrated to Durango. He'd then come to Arizona and Flagstaff, his wife's hometown, where he raised whiteface cattle and defended people in serious trouble with the law. He was all of six feet with buzzed brown hair, a graying goatee, and rimless spectacles.

Thaddeus wordlessly plopped the bar complaint down on Shep's desk and turned it for the cowboy-lawyer to read.

Shep scanned the document and then re-read, slower the second time through. Then he looked up. "You do all this?"

Thaddeus shrugged and took a seat across from Shep. "Beats me. I was under the impression I'd talked her down. Then she went and shot the guy. I was as surprised as the next person."

"Were you really, or are you just thinking that now they're prying your license off the wall?"

He settled into his seat, crossed his legs, and then his arms. "Maybe a little of both. I should've called someone. I did call the cops, but I didn't report it as an emergency. I just told Chief Meisner we should talk. I did tell him a constituent was armed and dangerous."

"Did he ask if it was an emergency and he needed to dispatch someone immediately?"

"Not that I remember. He was getting ready to play golf, and I had to talk him out of that to come meet with me."

"So you did at least call the cops." It wasn't a question.

"I did. I also talked to Russ just seconds before he was shot. But he'd called my office, so I guess that doesn't count. I think he'd been talking to Carleen before she skedaddled."

"Not if he called your office, I'd say it doesn't. Did you tell him his special someone was on the way to blow his brains out?"

"He told me that Sheila was unlocking his office and coming in. He asked me if I'd called the cops, and I told him yes. I also told him to run."

"Did he try to run?"

"The way I understand it, there wasn't time. I heard the gunshots over the phone. It was clear she'd done what she went there to do."

"Lady kills man. Stupid damn lawyer fails to warn man. Damn, Thaddeus, I don't like the sound of all this. The State Bar is just looking for someone to blame."

"I'm not one of their favorites."

"No, because you defend every Tom, Dick, and Harry that comes along, even if they just iced the governor. You haven't gone out of your way to make friends in high places, Thaddeus."

Thaddeus slid to the end of his seat and pounded Shep's desk with his fist. "Screw high places and screw having those yahoos as friends. You know I don't do politics, Shep. You and I aren't so unlike in that respect."

"My thoughts exactly. Maybe that's why I hate you less than most people, ol' Thaddeus. I understand you, brother. You've got a bit of a crazy streak, just like old Shep."

Thaddeus couldn't help smiling. Shep was one of the few people who had him pretty well figured out. Christine was another one who did.

"So, will you defend me?"

"Sure. But what's our defense?"

"Shep, I'm paying you good money to tell me what our defense is. That's your job."

He chuckled. "Sure, but I'd just like to hear your take on it first."

"My defense is that I didn't do it. My defense is that I had no duty to warn, that I had a right to believe my client when she said I'd talked her down, meaning she wasn't going to do harm to her husband. That's my defense."

"Now, about that? Did you know her from before?"

"No."

"Was she referred by another one of your clients?"

"Not that I know of. She didn't mention anyone. And Carleen always tries to get that information out of them when they book their appointment."

"So how did she know to come to you of all lawyers?"

Thaddeus let out a loud sigh through his nose. "I have no idea. Maybe she'd heard I was good at defending violent crimes. I don't know."

Shep pinched his lips and opened his hands as if saying, *See? There's your answer.*

"C'mon, Shep. We can't go down that line of thinking."

Shep turned his chair sideways and looked out his office window, deep in thought. "Did you get the impression she could be trusted? Meaning, your first initial gut reaction to the woman when she came in."

"No. If anything, she was a bit twitchy, as if she was on something."

"That doesn't help. But there must've been something in her character or actions that made you think you'd talked her down."

Thaddeus made a face. "What do you mean?"

"Did she make you feel all warm and fuzzy inside when she said she wouldn't shoot the asshole after all?"

"Warm and fuzzy? Where does the law talk about warm and fuzzy?"

"That's what the hearing officers will be looking for at the State Bar. They want to know you had a reason to believe her, a history with her, if you will. But you didn't have any such history. She was just another nobody in off the street, looking for help. Why did she say she'd come to see you, by the way?"

"She said she came to see me to find out what she should tell the cops after she shot her husband."

Shep sat back and clasped his hands behind his head. He nodded repeatedly. "Thaddeus, my boy, we've got a bit of work to do."

18

The day of the bar complaint hearing rolled around on
Friday, May 13th. Thaddeus and Shep Aberdeen appeared
at the local offices of the Attorney General in the hearing room
designated for formal examinations. As they approached the
hearing room, Thaddeus spotted his old receptionist, Carleen
Hoven, sitting on the bench outside the room, speaking quietly
with bar counsel, who he recognized as Harriet Whiteman,
working out of the State Bar's office in Phoenix. Shep and Thaddeus passed by the two women with a nod and a smile then
ducked inside the hearing room.

"I didn't know it would be Harriet herself," said Thaddeus. "Were
you aware?" He was asking because Harriet Whiteman was the
Chief Bar Counsel, the attorney who had ultimate responsibility
for all state bar prosecutions. Her expertise and aggressiveness
were the stuff of legends among lawyers, and Thaddeus knew he'd
be in for a raging fight before it was all said and done that day.

"I knew it would be Harriet, yes. But let me tell you, she pulls on
her suit pants just like everyone else, one leg at a time, Thaddeus."

"Well, I know we're in for a fight. It might as well be the best the Bar has to offer."

"Given that it's you, Thaddeus, I would have expected no less out of the Bar. You're not their most popular guy."

They took their seats at counsel table. Shep opened his books and papers and arranged himself at the table while Thaddeus sat helplessly at his side. He'd known he was going to harbor feelings of vulnerability since he wasn't defending himself and wouldn't be acting as an attorney. Still, it was difficult just sitting aside and giving someone else the reins. He felt a cool bead of sweat break out along his spine, and he shivered though the room was warm that May day. Nerve-wracking, and he felt every inch of the complaint crawling on his skin.

Then the bar counsel, Harriet Whiteman, and the complainant, Carleen Hoven, entered the room and arranged themselves at the table to the right of Shep and Thaddeus.

At 8:59, a side door opened, and the three-judge panel in charge of hearing the case filed into the room. They took their seats at the front of the room on a raised dais. It wasn't a courtroom, but a hearing room, so their seating arrangement up front was a long wooden table and overstuffed executive chairs. Next, a court reporter came into the room carrying her machine and tripod and the official Supreme Court clerk entered as well, arranging herself at a table off to the side. Her job would be to mark evidentiary exhibits and control the flow of any paperwork in the case. At the exact stroke of 9 a.m., the hearing officer, flanked by the two other officers, began speaking.

"Good morning, counsel and parties. My name is William S. Sewell, and I am the presiding hearing officer on the case entitled *In the Matter of Thaddeus Murfee*. The case is brought by bar counsel of the State Bar of Arizona, counsel Harriet Whiteman appearing for the Bar. Appearing with the respondent, Thaddeus Murfee, is his counsel, Shep Aberdeen. Gentleman and lady, are we ready to proceed?"

"Ready," said Harriet Whiteman.

"We're ready," said Shep.

The hearing officer continued, "No agreement has been reached between the parties, so this contested hearing is held before this hearing panel, which includes the presiding disciplinary judge, a lawyer member, and a public member. At the conclusion of the hearing, the panel will issue a report containing findings of fact, conclusions of law, and an order regarding sanctions, if any are levied. The hearing panel may order dismissal of the charges, diversion, restitution, assessment of costs, admonition, probation, reprimand, suspension, or disbarment. The panel's order is final subject to the party's right to appeal. Appeal is to the Supreme Court of Arizona, of course. I am the presiding disciplinary judge. The lawyer member, seated to my right, is Mona Gonzales of Prescott, Arizona. The public member is Henry Davos, who sits on the local school board and is no stranger to public hearings. Henry, for the record, is seated to my left." Judge Sewell glanced at the small stack of papers in front of him. "All right. The burden of proof rests with the State Bar of Arizona so, counsel, you may call your first witness."

Harriet spoke up. "The State Bar of Arizona calls Carleen Hoven, the complainant. Ms. Hoven, please go forward and take a seat in the chair on the right."

Carleen did as instructed, carrying her purse with her and arranging it with a yellow notepad on the small table before her.

She was a slender woman, fiftyish, with a light brown bob haircut. Her mascara was tastefully done, not too heavy, but her lipstick was a garish peach color. Her blush was two small spots on each cheek instead of the shadowing Christine did along the bone. Carleen's nails were plain and short, not even painted from the first day he employed her, but on her left ring finger she wore a thin wedding band and a small diamond engagement ring. When she sat down, she met Thaddeus's gaze and didn't move her eyes away from his. He knew she was angry and determined, yet he harbored no ill will toward her. She was, he thought, doing what she thought to be right. And maybe it was right, he allowed. Maybe he had come up short in how he'd handled Sheila's threat that day.

"State your name for the record," said Harriet Whiteman.

"Carleen Hoven."

"Ms. Hoven, where do you live?"

"Winslow, Arizona."

"Are you married?"

"Twenty years to the same man, Jed Conway Hoven. We have three children."

"Do you know the respondent, Thaddeus Murfee?"

"I do."

"How did you come to know Mr. Murfee?"

"I heard through a friend that Thaddeus was looking for a receptionist, so I emailed him my resume. He hired me on the spot when I had my interview."

"Describe your relationship with Mr. Murfee while you worked for him."

"Very nice. Thaddeus is a kind and caring man, and he always treated me with respect and treated me fairly. I have no complaints about my job there."

"What is the nature of your complaint then, Ms. Hoven?"

"Thaddeus fell far short on May Second this year. That would be the day Russ Lowenstein was gunned down by his wife, Sheila."

Judge Sewell sat in a relaxed position, bent forward over the table, and resting his weight on crossed arms. "Take us through the day, please."

"Well, I left for work at my usual time, seven-thirty in the morning. I had stopped for a cup of good coffee on the way to the office and was sitting at my desk eating my Danish and sipping my coffee when Thaddeus arrived about five minutes later. He said hello, stopped and told me a joke, and went on into his office."

"A joke? What kind of joke?"

"An off-color joke. He loves off-color jokes."

"Can you tell us the joke?"

"Sure, he said, 'The lawyer said to the client, there's two sides to every story and you're a douche in both of them.' I laughed."

"You found that humorous?"

"He tells jokes well. Timing or something."

"What happened next? He went into his office at the far end of the hall. I heard him turn on ESPN on his computer and get the recap of the Diamondbacks' baseball game. He's a huge fan."

"Who did they play?"

"Giants. D-backs lost nine-to-six. He moaned, and I could hear him saying something back to the sports news, something about pitching."

"Then what happened?"

"His door closed, and I assumed he went to work on something. Just before eight in the morning, his first appointment showed up at the office. She'd just made the urgent appointment that morning. I'd barely sat down when the phone rang, but he always told me, 'Carleen, we are here to help.' It sounded urgent, so I booked her in."

"Who was that?"

"That would have been Sheila Lowenstein."

"Was Sheila Lowenstein the same woman arrested for the murder of Russell Lowenstein?"

"Yes, the same. She showed up wearing hiking clothes and a gun. I thought the gun was a little much but, hey, it's Arizona. Everyone's armed."

"What was said between you and Sheila?"

"Well, I offered her some coffee or juice, but she said no. She was nervous, flipping noisily through a *People* magazine and sighing long and loud. But we get lots of nervous and upset clients in, so I thought nothing of it. Then Thaddeus buzzed me, and I showed her down the hallway to his office. I knocked once and she went inside. After a moment, I heard him close the door behind them."

"What happened next, Carleen?"

"About twenty minutes later, she left our office. Didn't say anything to me as she passed, but that's not unusual. Only about half the clients who come and go ever speak to me. Then Thaddeus came out of his office and came up to my desk. 'Hey,' he said, 'I need you to erase all office video showing Sheila Lowenstein was ever here.' I just gave him a funny look. He told me to call Rim Country Security and have the video erased. Also, he told me to take her name off the day's calendar. He wanted no evidence she was there. So I got the number for Rim Country and called them. The tech was quite rude and told me there was no way they'd erase a video, that it came to them automatically and got stored on their servers and verified and dated and so forth. So I told that to Thaddeus."

"What did he say?"

Carleen flipped up the page on her yellow notepad. "I wrote it down here because I thought it was important. I can read it to you."

"Please do."

"I said, 'We're not telling anyone we've almost got an active shooter situation here?' He said 'Where are you getting that?' I told him the Rim Country Security tech checked your morning video. Sheila Lowenstein told you she was going to shoot Russ. He's my husband's cousin. So I asked him, 'You're going to warn Russ, right, Thaddeus?' and then Thaddeus said to me, 'Carleen, I want you to sit at your desk until the chief of police comes. Then show him in here. Then sit at your desk and don't call anyone or go anyplace until you and I've talked.'"

"So he didn't have you call the police?"

"No."

"Or call Russ Lowenstein to warn him?"

"No."

"Did he call either one of those?"

"No."

"How can you be sure of that?"

"Because his phone lines never lit up. He made no calls."

"What about a cell phone?"

"He might have called on his cell phone, but Thaddeus hates cell phones."

Ms. Whiteman addressed the hearing officers. "We have submitted evidence of Mr. Murfee's cell phone records, which show there were no calls out from eight in the morning until late that afternoon."

Mr. Sewell nodded. "Please continue."

"What happened next?" Ms. Whiteman redirected at Carleen.

"I called Russ myself, but I didn't get through to him."

"Did you warn whoever you were talking to?"

"Yes, Dot Marchant is the receptionist up there. She's also my cousin through marriage. Unfortunately she wasn't in reception at the moment, so I told the girl to get Russ on the phone and why. It was urgent. At that same time, Thaddeus told me to bring my steno pad into his office and wait for the Chief of Police to arrive. But I dropped the phone and took off for Russ's office."

Thaddeus caught one specific in all that. There was another girl at the office other than Dot who had answered the phone. Had it been PJ? And she'd transferred the phone call to her step-dad? Or was it the other figure that they'd seen in the video? Either way, it was another new element to the case that twisted an already bizarre situation into a tighter knot that Thaddeus was finding hard to unravel.

"Why did you take off like that?"

"My God, it was my cousin sitting up there, and a crazy woman with a gun was coming. I wanted to *warn* Russ."

"So you left Thaddeus's office to drive to Russ's office?"

"That's exactly right."

"What happened next?"

"Dot called me on my cell. She said there had been a shooting in Russ's office and she was hiding outside the building. She told me not to come."

"How did she know you were coming?"

"I told her as soon as I answered her call."

"Carleen, did you ever hear Mr. Murfee talk to the police or Russ or anyone to warn them Sheila was going to shoot Russ?"

"No, I didn't."

"Could it have happened, and you just didn't know?"

"No, I don't think so. I do know he called the Chief of Police, but that was because his door was open from when Sheila left, and I could just hear what he was saying."

"Which was?"

"He told the Chief of Police to come to his office, that he needed to talk to him."

"Was what you heard in the nature of an emergency call?"

"No, it was just a call like you might invite someone to lunch."

"Anything else you want us to know about that day?"

"Just that I don't hate Thaddeus or anything like that. I was just disappointed in him. I didn't understand his thinking. I still don't."

"Your Honors," said Whiteman, "the State Bar rests. We have no other witnesses."

Judge Sewell looked at Shep. "Did you want to cross-examine?"

When Shep declined politely, Judge Sewell said, "Please call your first witness, Mr. Aberdeen."

Shep put Thaddeus on the witness stand. Thaddeus identified himself, his place of business, his length of time as a lawyer, and the rest of the preliminaries.

"Directing your attention to May second. Can you tell us what happened that morning?"

"All right. I was in my office, reviewing the day's mail and planning my response to a plaintiff's discovery request. My phone beeped, and it was Carleen. A woman named Sheila Lowenstein had arrived for her appointment."

"Now, did you already know Sheila Lowenstein?"

"I did not."

"What happened next?"

"Carleen brought the woman to my office and knocked. I welcomed her at the door and asked her in. I closed the door after she entered. She was wearing a bandanna on her head—a blue

Harley-Davidson bandanna, a white T-shirt, khaki shorts, hiking boots, and a gun on her side."

"Tell us who said what once she was seated."

"Well, that would be confidential. She's not on trial here, and I don't think I have the right to breach her confidences. Which is what this whole bar complaint is about."

Judge Sewell then intervened. "Mr. Murfee, the court has anticipated the issue of confidentiality would surface in this hearing, so I've prepared an instruction to you based on the Rules of Professional Conduct for attorneys as adopted by our Supreme Court. Here is my order to you, sir:

"A lawyer may reveal such information relating to the representation of a client to the extent the lawyer reasonably believes necessary:

"One, to prevent the client from committing a crime or fraud that is reasonably certain to result in substantial injury to the financial interests or property of another and in furtherance of which the client has used or is using the lawyer's services;

"Two, to establish a claim or defense on behalf of the lawyer to establish a defense to a civil claim against the lawyer based upon conduct in which the client was involved, or to respond to allegations in any proceeding concerning the lawyer's representation of the client; or

"Three, to comply with other law or a final order of a court or tribunal of competent jurisdiction directing the lawyer to disclose such information."

Judge Sewell passed out a copy of his order, and Thaddeus and Shep read it through. Then Thaddeus looked up and said, "Judge Sewell, thank you for this. I was aware of the rule and know it well.

Based on the court's order, I'd like to add to my earlier answer that, when she first came into my office, Sheila Lowenstein's first words were that she wanted my advice on what to say to the police after she shot her husband. She then paid me one-hundred dollars to retain my services so I'd be speaking to her as her attorney. Needless to say, I was rather startled at her opening salvo."

Shep said, "What happened next?"

"Near as I can remember, I asked her a few questions about what had gone wrong in her marriage. It was then that she told me her husband had been molesting her daughter."

"A man not the girl's birth father was having sex with the girl?"

"Correct."

"And the girl was a minor."

"Yes, she is only fourteen years old."

"This might seem obvious, but please describe the mother's state of mind."

"She was furious. And, listening between the lines, I think she was frightened, too. I mean, it has to be one of the most horrific nightmares a parent can experience. Not being able to protect your child from pain and suffering like that. And right in her house, right under nose. She gave the impression she was totally committed to shooting Russ, but at the same time she was reeling like a boxer who's been beat down. She didn't really know what she was doing or what she should be doing. I had a lot of compassion for her just then."

"What was your reaction? What did you say to her?"

"Two things. First, I suggested a counseling session was in order. I was trying to come up with a way to defuse the situation. It was about to blow sky-high. Second, I wanted the police involved. I suggested she go talk to the police and swear out a criminal complaint against Russell Lowenstein. But she was too far gone for either of my suggestions. She left my office saying first that she was going to shoot him and then, just before she walked out, that I had talked her down."

"Meaning what by 'talked her down?'"

"That she wasn't going to shoot him."

"Did you contact anyone as a result of Sheila's visit?"

"I contacted the Chief of Police, Chief Meisner. He was getting ready to play golf but I told him to cancel and come to my office instead. He said he would. In the meantime, Russell was shot and killed."

"Did you ever contact Russell?"

"No. He called my office. He contacted me."

"What did he say?"

"Only that Sheila was there to shoot him. Then I heard the gunshots over the phone. Then the line went dead."

"Okay, Thaddeus. I'm going to leave it right here, but I will follow up again after you're examined by Ms. Whiteman."

The presiding judge said, "Your witness, Ms. Whiteman."

Harriet got on her feet and began pacing just behind her chair. "Mr. Murfee, tell the court about the call you made to 911."

"I didn't make a call to 911."

"Tell the court about what you did to warn Russell Lowenstein to flee. I'm sure you called him immediately after she'd left your office so it gave Russ enough time to get away or hide?"

"No, I didn't immediately call Russ. I called Chief Meisner."

"You didn't dial 911 and you didn't call your client's victim. Any reason why not?"

"Because she said I'd talked her down. I went with that."

"You went with that? Did you have any reason to believe she was telling you the truth and you had changed her mind?"

"No reason. It was a judgment call. Evidently I was wrong."

"Are you aware that *ER 1.6 Rule b* provides 'A lawyer shall reveal such information to the extent the lawyer reasonably believes necessary to prevent the client from committing a criminal act that the lawyer believes is likely to result in death or substantial bodily harm.' Did you violate this ethical rule?"

"I hope not. In retrospect, it doesn't look good for me. But hindsight is always twenty-twenty. I was operating prospectively. I didn't want my client taken into custody for something she'd just reassured me she was not going to do. I can't tell you how many times I've heard a client wish someone dead or broken or run over by the law. Lawyers hear this stuff almost every day in dealing with the public. We can't be expected to give away our clients' secrets every time something gets said."

"Isn't it different when a client brings in a gun and tells you she's on her way to kill her husband?"

"Lots of people wear guns. I see it around Coconino County just about every day."

"But coupled with a threat against someone's life? Doesn't that give you pause?"

"Objection," said Shep. "I don't think 'gives you pause' is the standard of care Mr. Murfee owed to the legal system. I think he is governed by the ethical rules, not a figure of speech."

"Sustained. Please rephrase."

"Withdrawn. So someone can wear a gun into your office, tell you she's on her way to murder her husband, pay you in cash for legal advice on what to tell the police after she murders her husband, but you still don't think you have a duty to dial 911 or call the prospective victim? Is that what you want the State Bar to allow you to do, Mr. Murfee, to remain silent in the face of these threats?"

"Yes. It was my judgment the threat had been defused. I was wrong, but I wasn't in violation of my ethical requirements."

"Well, we both agree on the first part then—you were definitely wrong. That is all, Your Honor."

Judge Sewell looked to Shep. "Anything further, Mr. Aberdeen?"

Shep flicked a front page of notes over and started again, "Thaddeus, do you regret your decision to not call 911 or Russell Lowenstein after Sheila Lowenstein left your office?"

"I do. But like I said, at the time I thought I was acting accordingly with the information that Sheila gave me."

"And what was that information again?"

"That I had talked her out of shooting her husband."

"And even though you didn't know Mrs. Lowenstein prior to her visit, you still believed her?"

"Yes."

Shep concluded, "That's all, Your Honor. I think we're beating a dead horse if we do another round of the same testimony. You're three bright individuals sitting in judgment today. You know what was said and you know what the rules are. I don't have anything else to add to that."

"Does either party have any other witnesses?" asked the presiding judge.

"No."

"No."

"Very well, the hearing stands in recess. The administrative officers will issue their ruling on the petition of the State Bar in due course. Thank you all for coming today."

With that, the hearing was suddenly over. Thaddeus and Shep gathered their books and papers to leave.

Harriet Whiteman turned to Shep. "I suppose you know they'll expedite. We should hear in the next seventy-two hours how they're ruling."

"Okay," said Shep. "And if it's adverse, we're off to the Supreme Court. Do those get expedited or is that a long wait?"

"Could be a long wait. Getting an expedited hearing out of the Supremes is very difficult, Shep."

"Well, then, we'll keep our fingers crossed."

"Goodbye, you two."

"Goodbye," said Thaddeus, and he turned to Carleen. He held out his hand. "No hard feelings, Carl. I know you're doing what you think is right."

She didn't shake it. "For God's sake, Thaddeus, Russ was family."

Thaddeus hadn't known that at the time, but there was no use in arguing the point. It shouldn't matter whether he was family or not. Ethical requirements were across the board. "All right. Well, have a good day, then."

With that, the hearing and its aftermath concluded.

19

Sheila's jury trial was slated for Monday, July 30th and the ruling on Thaddeus's license to practice law still hadn't been filed. Instead of an expedited ruling, the matter had dragged along for a full month after the hearing. Thaddeus and Shep had made repeated calls to the office of Chief Bar Counsel but those folks seemed to be as much in the dark about a possible ruling date as everyone else. Then, on Monday morning, June 25th at 8:03 a.m., the fax machine at his office fired up and began displaying the long-awaited order from the Presiding Hearing Officer, William S. Sewell.

Thaddeus was suspended from the practice of law for one year. Yet, Sheila's trial was scheduled to begin in thirty-five days.

Thaddeus hoofed it up Agassiz Street to meet with Shep Aberdeen. Time was of the essence. Shep called him right into his office without making him cool his heels in the waiting room. The older lawyer was buried under lawbooks at his desk. He looked up when Thaddeus walked in, removing his glasses and telling Thaddeus to take a chair.

"You saw?" asked Shep.

"I did. One year. I can't afford a year off, Shep. Too many people are counting on me for help. What can we do?"

"I've been doing some research," Shep said, indicating the law books strewn across his desk and open before him. "If the Supremes will accept our appeal, we can get it over and done in one month."

"How do we get them to take on an expedited hearing?" Thaddeus asked. He thought he knew the answer but wanted to hear Shep's version first.

"Exigent circumstances. Not yours, but someone who's counting on you and the exposure they're facing."

"Sheila Lowenstein. Scheduled to go to trial in thirty days and change. It's a death penalty case. Is that exigent enough?"

"Thaddeus, it doesn't come any more exigent than that. I'm thinking we demonstrate that a continuance in the trial for one year is unthinkable and impossible, of course, and we ride that pony."

"Exactly. All right. You need my affidavit?"

"Yep."

"I'll send it over in an hour or two."

Thaddeus walked the several blocks south to his office and disappeared into his private suite. Over the next hour, he drafted an affidavit setting forth client needs in several extremely serious cases where it just wouldn't be fair to force the defendants to obtain other counsel in lieu of Thaddeus's representation. When the affidavit was finished, he still didn't know if it would satisfy the court's requirements to take up the case on an emergency basis but, as so often happened in the practice of law, it was all he had to go on. So he walked it back to Shep's office while his signature was still drying and left it with the older lawyer's receptionist. That task done, he wandered over to Kathy's Koffee and ordered up a cup and a plate of scrambled eggs with ham. Time for a break.

Two police officers entered the cafe and took the next window table. One of them, quite young, blond, crewcut, swiveled in the booth and caught Thaddeus's eye. "Mr. Murfee, I was one of the first officers at the Russ Lowenstein homicide. No one from your team has asked to speak with me yet."

"Hey, how are you today? We've meant to get over to the station to talk to you, but it's been a bit hectic. But now is as good a time as any. What can you tell me?"

"I can tell you that I was the first one through the door. I had my gun out and ready to return fire. We had no idea if we had a live shooter situation there or not. Turns out we did, but her weapon was gone."

"Detective Snow said the same. No weapon was recovered. She wasn't still holding the gun when you came in?"

"That's right. We never did take a gun from her. Or from her daughter, either. I'm the officer who patted both of them down. I also searched backpacks and the mother's butt pack. Nada, no gun."

"So where did it go? What's your theory?"

"Somebody got it out of there before we arrived. That's all it could be."

"You're Bill Grayson, right?"

"Right. I've heard a lot about you."

Thaddeus laughed. "Try not to believe all of it. I'm quite a good guy."

"No, no, I mean—"

"I know. You were the officer giving Mrs. Lowenstein a drink of water when the detectives arrived, correct?"

"Yes, I was. She was about cried out and very dry."

"Did she ever slosh any of the water on her hands?"

"I know what you're asking about—the GSR test. No, there was no water sloshed, and I saw the gunshot residue test being administered. The dicks said it was inconclusive."

"What do you say?"

"Oh, no, I'm not about to disagree with the detectives."

"But?"

He sighed. "But the test was conclusive. She hadn't fired a gun."

Thaddeus's food arrived, and the waitress set it on the table in front of him. "Will you testify to that?"

The young officer looked at his partner. Then, "Of course, I have to tell the truth. I'm committed to being a good cop, Mr. Murfee. I'll tell the truth. I'll tell exactly what I saw."

"Fair enough. I'm going to add you to my witness list. We were actually about to call you for an interview. Turquoise, my daughter, had that on her list of to-dos."

"Well, now, she won't have to. Although I have to admit I've seen her around. I would much rather talk to her than you, Mr. Murfee, no offense."

"She is a gorgeous girl. We keep her tied up at home so the yahoos don't try to take her out for coffee."

"Do you think she'd go out to coffee with me?"

"Are you a yahoo?"

"Naw, I'm one of the good guys."

"Then call her mother's office and ask her out. She likes coffee, I've been told."

"And she used to be a cop?"

"Yes, but she wised up. Now she works for the defense."

He chuckled. "We won't hold that against her. She's still preferable to you, Mr. Murfee. No offense, but you're not my type."

"Well, I'll just have to go with that. Just call her, Bill. But be ready for her to pick your brain about this case. She's like her mother—it never quits."

"Fair enough, I've been warned." Bill turned back around and reengaged with his partner while Thaddeus finished with his eggs and ham and drained his coffee mug.

Thaddeus stood up, but before he left, he said, "Well, gents, back to work for me."

"So long, Mr. Murfee," said Bill. His partner only nodded, his coffee mug at his lips.

"Thaddeus, please."

"All right, Thaddeus. Have a good one."

"Thanks."

"Don't double-park, sir. We're watching."

"I've been warned." Thaddeus used the cops own words. "All right, then."

They laughed, and Bill gave a two-finger salute to Thaddeus. Thaddeus walked outside, loosened his necktie, removed his blue blazer, and headed east on Aspen Street toward his office.

20

Christine arranged seating at the deposition of Marshall Anders. They were meeting in the conference room of Christine Murfee and Associates in the same building she shared with Thaddeus. He was on the ground floor; she was upstairs on the second. The conference room was decorated tastefully with the bright hues of local Native American art. The carpet was a brick red and ochre melding, arranged in competing diamond shapes, which complemented Christine's art. In the center of the deposition table, her staff had arranged sandwiches, coffee, soft drinks, and water bottles since it was a one p.m. deposition so she figured some of the attendees might be hungry. All of this was lost on Marshall Anders, however, who glowered threateningly at everyone around the table.

Christine led things off as soon as the court reporter had her machine set up and primed with fresh paper. "For the record, we are meeting in the conference room of Christine Murfee for the taking of the deposition of Marshall Anders, who is present today with his attorney Marissa Huckabay. Mr. Anders, will you tell us your name for the record?"

Glowering at Christine like she was using up the last of his precious air, the man said through gritted teeth, "Marshall Anders. That's Mr. Anders to you."

"Mr. Anders, my client, Thaddeus Murfee, has been sued by the heirs of Mr. Russell Lowenstein. Were you acquainted with Mr. Lowenstein, sir?"

"No."

"But you know who he was?"

"What does that mean?"

"You knew who Russ Lowenstein was?"

"I didn't know him. Never met the son-of-a-bitch."

"I detect a note of antipathy, sir. Why do you call him that?"

"Because he was a cheater and a bastard, that's why. He cheated on his wife and tried to talk my wife into leaving me. Bastard finally got what he had coming. It should've come sooner."

"Someone should've shot him sooner?"

"That's my opinion. Is it illegal for me to have my opinion, lady?"

"No, not illegal. You're certainly entitled to whatever you choose to believe. If you choose to wish harm on someone, that's on you. Speaking of that, isn't it true that you encouraged Sheila Lowenstein to shoot and kill Russ Lowenstein?"

"Now who told you that? That's how lies get passed around this rotten town."

"A reliable witness told me that. She told me that you met with Sheila Lowenstein and even provided her with the gun used to shoot Russell Lowenstein. Would she be accurate about that, sir?"

"Lady, I don't know where the hell you're getting this bullshit. But just because you say it, don't make it so. Surely, you understand that?"

"You've already told us you wished Russ Lowenstein dead sooner than it actually happened. Why don't you tell us all the steps you took to make sure he died?"

"I didn't—I told the wife that he deserved whatever she decided."

"Okay, when was this?"

"She brought her Range Rover to my shop. We just happened to talk when I found out her last name."

"So you asked her whether she was married to Russ Lowenstein?"

"She told me when I was asking for the names of the owners of the car. It's SOP at my shop. We have to know who to invoice."

"When you told her Russell deserved whatever she decided, what did she say?"

"She asked me why I was so down on Russell."

"And you told him about your wife, that Russell tried to cheat with her?"

"I told her Russell had been snooping around. My wife's a waitress at the Flame Restaurant. Russell hit on her there. She confessed she'd stayed late for drinks with him one night. I asked her why, and she said it was because he was a great bar customer, and the owner encouraged the girls to fraternize with the whales."

"The whales?"

"The good ol' boys, the big spenders. The guys who spread the bucks around. That was your friend, Russell Lowenstein. Big spender in the barrooms and juke joints. Asshole, you ask me."

"So was that the end of it?"

"Nope, that wasn't all. Lucy Dee started talking about him to me. About how rich he was, what a great business mind he had, about his condo in Florida. I got sick of it."

"So your wife had drinks with Mr. Lowenstein, and the next thing we know you believed he deserved to die. Was drinks as far as it went between your wife and Mr. Lowenstein? Did they spend time together away from the Flame Restaurant?"

"I found them at Mormon Lake Lodge. My wife said she was only there to console him. He'd been crying and all that about his life. What a pussy. That's when I lost it. Man came after my wife. He didn't know who I was or he woulda gone sniffing someplace else."

"So, based on his sniffing, you wanted him dead?"

Marshall pounded the table. "He seduced my wife, the rat bastard!"

"So when you met *his* wife, you decided to give him back some poison, isn't that right?"

"She's the one asked me about my wife. She'd heard something about the two of them, too. I guess she knew all about his conquests. He didn't even try hiding it from her no more. Everything out in the open. He just didn't care who knew or how it made them feel. Asshole animal. Good effing riddance, Ms. Murfee."

"So, I've also been told you supplied the gun used to murder Russ. Any truth to that?"

"Sheila Lowenstein noticed I wear a gun in the shop. We do a large cash business so 'course I'm armed way over on the other side of town from the police station. You never know. She saw my gun and asked if I had any guns she could buy from me. I thought sure, why not, and I sold her a little Smith nine millimeter, an old Model 59. We went out back, and she shot a few rounds through it."

"A few? How many times did she fire the weapon?"

"She ran two boxes through it. She really got into shooting and took to it like a bird dog to water. Then she paid her bill and left my garage. Last I saw of her."

"Did you talk to her about shooting a man?"

"Not at all. I had no idea she would shoot a man."

"Let me get this straight. She was mad at her husband, knew he cheated with your wife, so you armed her, taught her how to shoot, and she went and shot her husband. None of that surprised you, did it?"

He scowled at Christine. "You know what? Nothing surprises me anymore, period. Was I surprised she shot her cheat of a husband? Naw, that wouldn't surprise anyone. He was the worst of the worst."

"Sure, but now she's charged with first-degree murder by using the gun you supplied to her. Now, do you see why the family will be adding you to the same lawsuit we're here for today? Does it make sense to you that they'll be asking for money from you to compensate them for their loss?"

"Talk to my lawyer. I'm done here."

"What do you mean, you're done here? What if I'm not done here?"

"Then lady, you have my permission to shove your questions right up your beautiful ass." His lawyer, Ms. Huckabay, laid her hand on his arm, but Marshall continued, ignoring her warning, "Shove away, but I'm done. D-O-N-E. Got it?"

"Counsel," Christine directed to Ms. Huckabay, "I'll be going to the court and asking for an order directing your client to answer the rest of my questions. I'll also be asking for attorney's fees for the trouble I'll incur in having to have a hearing and get that order. Please explain these things to your client while I step out of the room."

Christine walked into the hallway, a large smile on her lips. It was all she could do to keep a straight face when she went back inside the deposition room minutes later, only to find out Marshall Anders was still refusing to answer any more questions.

The deposition broke up—temporarily—while Christine would be filing for sanctions and orders to show cause.

Then they were done. She went downstairs and reported what she'd found out to Thaddeus, who hugged his wife and gleefully added the name of Marshall Anders to the list of witnesses he'd be calling at the Sheila Lowenstein trial next month.

Assuming he got to try the case, he told her. There was always the chance the Supremes wouldn't grant him relief from the administrative law judge's ruling in his bar complaint controversy.

Thaddeus took Christine out to dinner that night at the Flame Restaurant.

Lucy Dee Anders wasn't working that night, they were told by the hostess. In fact, she no longer worked there at all. So the Murfees ate the nightly special, bison burgers stuffed with blue cheese, and shared their tales of that day's events just like they did every night at supper.

When they got home to the ranch, the kids were already asleep, so Thaddeus led Christine by the hand to their room. He shut the door quietly and then wrapped her up in his arms. She locked gazes with him, a slight smile on her face.

Thaddeus gave her a soft kiss, just a peck, before he removed the pins that kept Christine's hair tied in a low bun at the nape of her neck, just enough messy to show her carefree nature. He ran his hands through her hair, massaging her scalp as he did, until it lay in waves over her shoulders.

Then he unhooked her dangling earrings, the ones Turquoise had bought her at the reservation with a bit of red in them and lay them on top of the dresser. He had loosened his tie at dinner so that she just needed to pull the tail through to remove it. She dropped it to the floor and began to unbutton his shirt. He stepped closer and sucked on her ear, now free of any ornamentation.

She moaned and lifted his tucked shirt from his trousers. At her insistence, her pushing the shirt off his shoulders, he removed it entirely and it, too, fell to the pile on the floor. Christine ran her hands up his bare chest, gently grazing his nipples.

He took her mouth with his, greedy for what she gave him, chasing her tongue with his own. He unbuttoned her shirt and slid it off her shoulders, then unclasped her bra. Her breasts finally free, he massaged them both, running his thumb over her nipples that pebbled at his touch. He pinched one then soothed it with his palm, then did the same to the other.

At her groan, his kisses turned aggressive and he pulled in her lower lip and sucked hard. He popped off the button on her pants in his urgency to slide them and her panties down her shapely legs. On his way back up her body, he took a nipple into his mouth. She arched back and dug her fingers into his hair.

His wife stood before him naked. Her hair mussed from their passion, her lips swollen from his kisses, he had never known such a beautiful, heart-wrenching sight. Thaddeus scooped her up in his arms and laid her on the bed. She scooted back and settled on the pillows while he removed his shoes, socks, belt, and work trousers. She was glorious with her flushed skin, her breasts splayed, her legs open and inviting.

Thaddeus crawled onto the bed, kissing up her belly, and nestled between her thighs. She arched up to him. "Please, Thaddeus," she begged, "I want you now."

So he slid into her, his gaze on hers, the love there surely reflected in his own. He stayed still, but she urged him by grabbing his buttocks and pressing her mound into him. He started sliding in and out, slow but then faster, her meeting his rhythm with her own thrusts. As her breathing turned to pants, he knew she was close, so he bucked into her, murmuring her name out loud over and over again until they both came together, the energy surging through Thaddeus's body.

He lay on top of her while the orgasm subsided, holding her close. When he shifted off her onto his side, she rolled to face him. She smiled and then gave him a slow lingering kiss. "That was lovely."

He tucked a strand of hair behind her ear. "You're lovely."

She sighed deep and closed her eyes, but he didn't let go, and they both drifted off before midnight. However, Thaddeus didn't sleep all that well. Tomorrow was the day the Supremes would hear oral argument on his attorney's motion to vacate the Court's suspension of his right to practice law.

At four a.m. he was still awake, tossing and turning, so he gave up, climbed out of bed and headed downstairs for the coffee pot.

21

The Arizona Supreme Court agreed to hear Thaddeus's appeal—made by Shep—on an expedited basis on July 18th, a Tuesday at seven a.m., less than two weeks before Sheila Lowenstein's trial began. The ungodly hour was an uncommon one for the court. It was designated only to accommodate an appeal that the Court evidently thought deserving ahead of the normal calendar. Thaddeus and Shep rode to Phoenix together on Thaddeus's Gulfstream. They touched down at Sky Harbor and made their way through the terminal then grabbed a taxi and headed for 24th Street. At Washington, the taxi turned west and sped to the Supreme Court Building on 15th Avenue.

At 6:59 a.m., the parties were assembled in the main courtroom, and the justices were in place, openly nursing cups of coffee and tea at the early-morning hour. It was Thaddeus's appeal so Shep went first with oral argument. It was now 7 a.m.

"May it please the court," he began. "My client is here today because he chose to obey one attorney ethical rule over a contrary ethical rule. He chose to keep a client confidence rather than expose a client's pronouncement that she was on the way to shoot her husband. Why did he do this? Because the client, at the end of their meeting, told him that he had talked her down—meaning she wasn't off to shoot her husband after all. Thus, my client's failure, if there was a failure at all, was that he chose to believe her statement to him rather than hop on the phone to the police department and reveal his client's name and her earlier comment about shooting her husband.

"The State Bar counsel has made much of the fact that the possible outcomes of the meeting far outweighed my client's choices. The State Bar has proceeded from the position that the threatened action of shooting the husband so outweighed the harm to the client that might possibly be caused by Thaddeus's remaining silent that he, as a matter of law, made the wrong choice. They would have it that my client's silence resulted in someone's death in and of itself."

Thaddeus heard these arguments in the light of day—arguments that he had made and re-made during the long, sleepless nights leading up to this morning's appearance before the Supremes— and wondered how he could have been so passive about Sheila's stated intent to shoot her husband. Thaddeus did, in fact, talk to Russ and try to warn him—though it was Russ who had called his office and not vice-versa. And he did, in fact, call Chief Meisner of the Flagstaff PD and request a visit for the purpose of heading-off a possible murder. But should he have done more? As he sat helplessly by and listened to Shep citing case law and opinions from Arizona and other states, he realized the entire thing was a subjective judgment call, pure and simple. There was no definitive rule that required a formal act in response to Sheila's comments one way or the other. Again, it all came down to judgment. When Shep had exhausted the subject at the end of his allotted time, Thaddeus felt the sweat break out along his back as the lawyer for the

State Bar took to her feet and began hammering him. He was, he realized, frightened, and the situation was, he feared, irredeemable.

Her name was Asissa Renfro and she was aggressive without seeming so, always maintaining a modicum of respect for Thaddeus, the subject, while cutting his heart out of his chest and stomping on it. She was rehearsed and succinct and wasted no time jumping all over the fact someone had died. Again, that was the State Bar's best argument, that someone had died due to Thaddeus's errors of omission. Someone had died due to the fact he ignored the weightier of the two ethical proscriptions Thaddeus had wrestled with.

The proceeding then shifted gears as the first Justice asked the first question.

"Counsel for the appellant, please comment on the prospective harm to Mr. Murfee's clients if the one-year suspension is allowed to continue."

Shep leaned hard into this first question. "It would be disastrous generally and could very well lead to under-represented defendants heading to prison specifically. For example, the case in point resulted in Sheila Lowenstein being charged with first-degree murder. Without getting into the facts and legal requirements to sustain such a charge, just let me say that Mrs. Lowenstein has chosen Thaddeus Murfee as her attorney and, over the past many months, Mr. Murfee has conducted his own investigation into the facts and arrived at his own tactics and strategies that he will employ at trial in the defense of Mrs. Lowenstein. It would be impossible for a substitute or replacement attorney to review the case and the witness statements and come away with the same depth of understanding that the front-line attorney develops during the months and weeks and days of doing their own investigation. At least not at this late date. To say it would be disastrous would not only understate but would also ignore the fact that sacrificing Mr. Murfee to some rule that could have been chosen over another rule is far outweighed by the needs of the client in this case alone.

"And there are many other cases that, during the next year, are scheduled for trial and at the same time are offering chances to resolve by settlement that only Mr. Murfee's incredible reputation as a litigator can bring to pass. While the District Attorney might offer Mr. Murfee's client a plea to possession of burglary tools, the same case, in the hands of lesser well-known attorney, might only bring in a step down in the charge of first-degree burglary to second degree burglary. These are only examples I'm making and not real cases, but the real cases are there, pending, ticking away while trial dates approach and settlement opportunities present themselves that only a lawyer of Mr. Murfee's standing and caliber might seize for his clients' benefit. In short, suspending him and allowing the suspension to run for a full year does much more harm to the legal profession and the needs of the citizens of our community than does allowing Mr. Murfee to keep his license in spite of the perceived wrongdoing by his choice of actions. I hope I have answered this question adequately. If I haven't, please advise and I will keep going. I will supplement."

"Ms. Renfro," said the same Justice, "what does the State Bar hope to gain by taking away Mr. Murfee's license? What is the desired result of suspending him?"

She was immediately on her feet and swinging. "Your Honors, Mr. Murfee has proven himself to be a danger to the community in his handling of threats against the public welfare. If this same case presented to him next week—and who's to say it won't?—we would possibly be right back in here looking at yet another shortcoming with another victim because Mr. Murfee hasn't learned the same lesson he will learn from a one-year suspension."

"And what lesson might that be?" asked a second Justice.

"The lesson that it is better to err on the side of public safety than on the side of one client's right to silence from her attorney. That is a key lesson and, because Mr. Murfee is so well-known, it is a lesson that literally hundreds of lawyers in our state and in other jurisdictions are watching with a great deal of interest because, as criminal lawyers, they are facing, almost daily, the same kind of choices Mr. Murfee faced. We are trying to encourage them to come forward when a crime is threatened by a client, even when the threat might not be a hundred percent intended. It's a fine line, but it's one Mr. Murfee fell far short of, and we want to let other attorneys know his choice to remain silent was not the proper choice."

Thaddeus listened half-heartedly as the back-and-forth continued. He could sense the justices leaning more and more toward the State Bar's position and leaning more toward allowing the license suspension to continue. He began to lose heart two-thirds of the way into the allotted time and, by the time the hearing concluded, he was all but certain he'd lost. The downcast look on Shep's face reinforced his own feelings.

It was time to prepare for the worst.

22

Just as Thaddeus and Shep were hailing a taxi to take them from the Supreme Court Building back to 24th Street and the airport, Christine, outside Flagstaff, was pulling onto the highway from the ranch property as she made her daily run from home to her office in Flagstaff. She failed to observe the gray Ford F-250 truck with the Canyon Classic Cars mud flaps. It sat on the side of the road with a spare tire propped against its rear fender as if repairs were being made. In truth, the repairs scenario was a ruse; the driver of the Ford truck immediately fell in behind Christine as she pulled away on US 180. The driver of the Ford left his spare tire lying on its side along the road's shoulder as his wheels kicked up gravel and dust, spinning to get up to speed behind Christine.

Driving south and east, Christine at one point looked up through the Ponderosa pine archway overhead and could have sworn she spotted Thaddeus's airplane in the pattern over the airport. He hadn't called her yet to let her know how it went, which meant either he didn't know anything yet or it had gone so badly he wanted to break the news to her in person. Were his suspension to continue, she would likely end up first-chairing the Sheila Lowenstein defense at trial. It would be a normal progression between their two practices for Thaddeus to refer Sheila to Christine to continue the defense.

She was so caught up thinking about the past few months, how hammered they were with new clients and new challenges, and how happy she was now that Turquoise had returned from L.A. to investigate her cases, that she failed to see the Ford truck creeping up on her bumper from behind. Maybe it was just that she was zoning out during her repetitive, everyday drive, or maybe it was she just wasn't looking, but when the bumper made contact with the rear end of her Mercedes, she just never saw it coming.

As it was, she had the speedometer pegged on 55, and the overtaking truck rammed into her at 95, spinning her rear end forward so that she lost traction and lost control. She spun off the highway into the pine trees lining the west side of the road, ripping out the entire passenger side of the 550 SL and easily flipping her car into the air, where it did two complete rollovers before slamming down hard on its right side and coming to a stop against a huge granite boulder.

Thaddeus's Gulfstream was on its downwind approach when the in-flight telephone erupted. Christine's cell phone was calling. He reached to the cabin wall, plucked up the phone, and answered.

"Payback," said a voice he didn't recognize. "You can scrape the bitch off a boulder."

Then the line went dead.

Thaddeus immediately called Christine's number. Her phone went to voicemail. He tried Turquoise's number. Hers went to voicemail too, which meant she was probably in the midst of an interview that was being recorded. So he called his office, the center of his life's operations. Surely, LaDora had heard something from Christine—if there was anything to be heard.

"LaDora, Thaddeus. Have you heard from Christine?"

"No, Thaddeus. She was due in here any moment but so far nothing. Should I have her call you?"

"Yes, please. And dispatch Turquoise to hunt down her mother."

"Turquoise is taking a statement."

"You'll have to interrupt her. This is urgent. Have her end the interview, walk out, and head for the ranch. Tell her to watch both sides of the road for an accident. Then call the State Police and alert them. Then call the Sheriff's Office and alert them. I just received a call from an unknown, telling me she could be scraped off a boulder. Sounds like a hit-and-run."

"Oh, my God. I hope not, Thaddeus." LaDora repeated, "Turquoise, State, County. Hanging up now."

SOMEONE'S ARM HAD SNAKED THROUGH THE WINDOW AND REMOVED her purse. Now that someone was talking. She knew the voice. Then it came to her: Marshall Anders.

She tasted blood. She knew she was alive because she could taste. Then she blacked out again. Five minutes later, she opened her eyes. She was dangling sideways in the front seat of her vehicle, seat belt ripping into her chest and waist.

She reached a hand up to her mouth. The air bag had all but exploded in her face, probably saving her life, but her mouth was smashed. There was an impact with something. Her mind was racing so she tried to slow it down. She needed her wits about her, needed to be able to think about what she should do.

Minutes passing, she finally realized she needed to get away from the car in case of fire. She gingerly reached for the seat belt release but the fingers on her right hand wouldn't work. So she reached across her body with her left hand. Except her arm was outside the steering wheel on the left side so she couldn't bring it across her body. She was stuck there, stunned, lapsing in and out of consciousness, bleeding from the mouth, unable to free herself.

No purse in sight, no cell phone, no way to call for help.

There was nothing else she could do.

Then she heard Anders' voice again, laughing. When she opened her eyes, he was standing at the front of the car, holding a BIC lighter. She knew he intended to set her vehicle ablaze. Christine reached down to her ankle and pulled free her Glock 43. Using her left hand, she slowly raised the gun until she had a clear shot. She knew she'd get only one before he set her afire.

She sighted down the barrel, held her breath, and squeezed the trigger twice in rapid succession.

Was it just a lucky shot? Or had the old combat soldier from Iraq had her day on the battlefield again? Either way, the second shot was perfect, catching Anders in the throat and knocking him backward off his feet. He was out of view, then, but she knew it had been a mortal wound as she had seen his throat blown away by the Hydra-Shok bullet. The jacketed hollow point had done its job —the man was finished. The gun slipped from her fingers, but never mind. The shock and blood loss swept her away on a deepening cloud of relaxation and escape from pain.

She didn't hear the sirens slow and stop where her vehicle had skidded and left tire marks before leaving the roadway. She didn't hear the voices of the men and women who came running to help.

"Is she dead?" asked a male voice.

The female EMT leaned inside the window and attached monitors to Christine. She shook her head. "Weak pulse."

The hydraulic rescue tool, the Jaws of Life, did its work, and she was pulled free and attached to a backboard before transport.

"What about the dead guy?" said a state police officer with very muddy boots.

"You remain here," said his corporal. "The detectives are on the way."

"Roger that."

Then she was loaded into the EMT's truck, and its sirens roared to life as the transport got underway.

She opened her eyes on the way to the hospital and said to the male EMT sitting at her side, "Got him."

Then she was unconscious again.

23

Two days later, Thaddeus finally left her hospital room long enough to order a grilled cheese and chicken noodle soup at the cafeteria and return to her room with his purchase. She was still coming and going. Her hip had been screwed back together and her dislocated shoulder tended to. Several front teeth needed crowns but, all in all, as the head swelling subsided, the doctors became increasingly hopeful for a full recovery. The thing was, Thaddeus told Shep, it was going to be months before the concussion and injuries would be healed enough for her to return to the office. In the meantime, Thaddeus's plan to refer all his pressing cases to Christine had evaporated. There wasn't an attorney experienced enough in the office by now to take on the cases left pending. There was Renny, and he would be awesome one day, but he wasn't there yet. Thaddeus's license was suspended and his efforts behind the scenes could only go so far. He couldn't appear in court and he couldn't do a jillion other things that lawyers do every day because they are admitted to the bar. He was stymied.

Shep couldn't help. He had his own practice. The idea of taking on even one of Thaddeus's heavyweight cases was too much to contemplate. He was underwater himself.

Coming into consciousness at one point on the third afternoon, Christine looked beyond Thaddeus with eyes yet unfocused and said simply, "Make a federal case out of it."

He was instantly innervated. Of course, that was it! His beat-up wife had given him the answer from some point in the recesses of her mind that had heard him making urgent phone calls from her hospital room in an effort to locate help. Make a federal case out of it, indeed.

The one person remaining in the world that he could represent as a lawyer was himself.

He would appeal the Arizona Supreme Court's ruling that upheld the license suspension. He would appeal it to the U.S. Court of Appeals. That afternoon and evening, still at his wife's bedside, Thaddeus balanced his MacBook on his knees and wrote his federal appeal. It was a *Sixth Amendment* appeal and, after doing some preliminary research, he knew he had the law on his side.

By noon the following day, he had his appeal on file and had a hearing date and time in San Francisco for the following week on Thursday the 27th of July. Thaddeus knew that his federal appellate case would be heard by a three-judge panel. The governing statute was 28 U.S.C. § 46(c), providing for a panel of not more than three judges. So he knew he had fewer judges to convince of the rightness of his appeal rather than a full court sitting en banc. He also knew that Ninth Circuit in San Francisco had a markedly progressive bent and that, because a defendant's Sixth Amendment Constitutional rights were involved, he stood a higher chance of success than if he were appealing a zoning case as the losing party.

He studied *Sixth Amendment* law by use of online legal research, reading cases, journals, and professional writings as well. By the following Tuesday, he felt he had a good grasp on the issues involved. He had an affidavit from Sheila Lowenstein attached to his opening brief, and he was ready to travel to San Francisco and set up shop in his hotel room. He took LaDora Canby with him, the senior of his two legal secretaries, and set her up in the next-door room, arranging for her husband and children to accompany her. The kids swam in the hotel pool while Mama worked Wednesday out of Thaddeus's makeshift office next door. He had arranged to leave Turquoise with Christine, who was now discharged from the hospital and home with round-the-clock nursing care and regular physician visits.

Turquoise called Thaddeus after lunch on Wednesday. "It's Mama Chris," she said, "I tried to take her into town for lunch, but she refused. When I pressed the issue, she admitted she was a little afraid to get in a car and go anywhere. So I dropped it. Is it just temporary, Dad?"

Thaddeus pursed his lips. He knew Christine as well as anyone ever had and knew her strengths. He also knew her fears, which were few and far between. She was more often gung ho and ready to take on the world than ever willing to admit she was afraid to go in a car. What was that all about?

"Try her again tomorrow, would you? And let me know?"

"Sure. I'll ease into a lunch party tomorrow morning and get her thinking along those lines."

"All right, Turquoise. Thanks for trying."

"We love that lady. Gotta get her up and going again."

"Did the detectives ever want to talk to her again?"

"Since the hospital? No, no one's called. But I'm going to tell them to talk to you if they do call, Dad. She shot Anders because he was going to set her on fire. They found the BIC."

"Any of us—or them—would've done the same thing," Thaddeus said. "No case, and there shouldn't be any more questions."

"Agree. Good luck tomorrow, Dad."

"Thanks, honey. I'll call after."

"Okay. I know Mama Chris is really worried."

"I'll call for sure. Goodbye."

24

Thaddeus walked inside the paneled courtroom and waited for his case to be called. Twenty minutes later, he was taking his place at counsel table. Then the judge seated in the center of three judges indicated he could begin his presentation. Thaddeus stood and crossed to the lectern. He carefully arranged his brief, his motion, and his notes, then began.

"Criminal defendants have a right to be represented by counsel of their choice. The remedy for erroneous deprivation of first choice counsel is automatic reversal. *United States v. Gonzalez-Lopez, 548 U.S. 140 (2006)*. There isn't a weighing of the harm in these cases. There is automatic reversal, period. The upcoming state court trial that I've referred to in my brief is *State of Arizona v. Sheila Lowenstein*. As the court is aware from Sheila Lowenstein's attached affidavit, I, Thaddeus Murfee, am her counsel of choice. But now the State of Arizona Supreme Court is preventing Ms. Lowenstein from having her choice of counsel by suspending my license to practice law. You know, Your Honors, even if the court today would simply order the suspension lifted to just those cases I had pending at the time of the bar complaint order in Arizona, that would be a result I could gladly live with. Leave the suspension in place, if you must, for all subsequent cases, of which there are none, but lift it and allow me to finish those cases that were already underway."

"Mr. Murfee," said Judge Ames, a black woman of maybe forty-five, who was also the judge sitting in the center of the three, "would the right to choose their attorney apply to new cases that might come into your office—just a theoretical question for you, sir?"

"Your Honor, as a matter of practice, there won't be any new cases. I am prepared to refuse all other work until the one year suspension is over. That could certainly be reflected in the court's order today."

Thaddeus had used the *assumptive close*—speaking as if there would be an order put in place that same day—an old trial lawyer's tactic. He wasn't above such things. He let a small smile spread his lips before he masked his expression once again.

"Mr. Murfee," said the judge on the right, "what would be the ramifications if the court were to lift the suspension as to the one case only?"

"Your Honors, my wife was just the subject of a brutal hit-and-run automobile accident. She has her own law practice and would ordinarily step right in for me and take over my remaining cases. But she's still recovering from that assault and can't help me. So it's me, or my clients all see their *Sixth Amendment* rights denied."

Thirty minutes later, the court ruled that the suspension of Thaddeus's license to practice law was lifted as to all cases registered in his office as of May 10th of the current year. His defense of Sheila— and many others—could continue. Thaddeus walked out of the courthouse and made the call to Sheila at the jail. She was ecstatic. Then he called LaDora, and she began phoning current clients. As to Christine's clients, who Thaddeus had wanted to help, those clients were outside his reach since he and Christine practiced separately in two different firms. Those people would need Christine to return to her practice very soon.

25

That Friday night at supper, everyone was home for a change. Every chair was filled at their extra-long farm-house-style table, and Thaddeus basked in the chatter and laughs as his family passed around the dishes of barbecued chicken drumsticks, rice, salad, and Turquoise's special corn bread, a Navajo recipe passed down from her mother, Katy.

The sun was slanting in from the west, and the room was golden in the evening hour.

All of the kids were present. On any given day, the family's schedule was little less than chaos, but today they were all home. No sports, no hobbies, no friends over, nor them staying at friends; no one was sick, fighting, or locked in their rooms. No one was working. All of them were rallying around the dinner table to try to get Mama Chris out of the doldrums.

"Mama Chris," said Turquoise. "Let's drive into town and find a quiet coffee house. We'll get a table and listen to some guitar."

"I don't think so," said Christine as she moved her food around her plate with a fork. Her appetite still hadn't returned from before the accident. "I still don't think I'm quite ready for that."

"Excuse me," said Thaddeus, "but your doctors have released you to full activity, Chris. You love to listen to music. Why not go?"

"I'm afraid you'll get lonely out here at the ranch, Thaddeus. You weren't invited."

"I'm fine. I have all the kids with me, and I might scare up a mean game of Monopoly." At the chorus of groans from the kids, Thaddeus humored them, "What? No Monopoly? Okay then, charades?" The younger ones liked that game, but the older ones booed.

"Or I might take an evening ride on Hearsay with some of them. You're probably not ready to ride Relevance yet."

"No, I can't imagine sitting a horse with screws in my pelvis. I'm far from that little exercise."

"Mom, you should get out of the house. It will do you good," said Jamie.

"Says the young man who is attached to his computer," she said with a smirk to their second eldest child.

Jamie motioned to his wheelchair. "I have an excuse."

Christine tsked. "That's never an excuse, young man, and you know it."

Jamie gave her a cheeky grin. "Okay, so I'm busy working. Not every kid can claim to have a contract with SpaceX for computer programming."

She held up her hand. "You're right, and we can't be prouder of you. But we'd still like to see more of you."

Celena, who was sitting to Thaddeus's left, tugged at his sleeve. "And we want to see more of you."

Aw, shoot. What could he say to the cherub? There weren't enough words to apologize for his absence in their life. "Well, how about this, Celena? How about we start over tonight? Family time every Friday. What does everyone say to that?"

The three young girls cheered, but Chad and Parkus groaned. Chad said, "That's when we usually hang out with friends. Ya know, the basketball and football games when school is in, movies in the summer. All that stuff."

Thaddeus couldn't win. At least not with a family this big. You couldn't please everyone, but he was going to try. "All right then, Sundays it is!" He hammered the table with his cutting knife like a gavel. "The verdict is in!"

Chad and Parkus gave each other a high-five across the table, knocking over a water glass. "Oops," said Parkus, who got up to get the paper towel.

"How about this?" said Turquoise to Christine. "We can take Dad's truck. It's big, and if it gets hit, we win. You can take a pain pill before we go. I'll help you up and down. We'll only be gone an hour. C'mon, now."

"I don't think so yet," Christine replied. "It worries me to even think about it."

"What do you mean 'worries' you?" Thaddeus asked. "You mean you're worried about your ability to travel?"

"No, I haven't said this—I'm just getting in touch with it—but I have this kind of generalized anxiety about going out. Like something's going to get me. I didn't say it was realistic. But there you are."

The kids quieted at her somber words, but he was proud of her for being so brave. Communication was hard, no matter what age a person was. "It takes a lot of courage to admit that," Thaddeus said to his wife. "Good on you for saying."

"We're only as sick as our secrets," Christine said. "And I don't like being sick. I won't accept it. Not at my age."

Thaddeus went into the kitchen and returned with the coffee carafe. He refilled his, Christine, and Turquoise's cup and then placed the empty carafe on a saucer. When the younger ones started to get antsy, he excused the rest of the kids from the table.

When Parkus left but forgot his plate, Thaddeus called him back. "And make sure to scrape and rinse and put into the dishwasher." While their other six formed a line at the kitchen sink to do just that with their own dishes, Thaddeus returned to the task at hand.

"Tell you what," he said. "We can take my truck. I'll drive, Turquoise can ride shotgun, and you can sit between us. My 40/20/40 will easily seat us. You have me and an ex-police officer to look after you. That's pretty safe. And all we're doing is going to listen to music for an hour. Not much risk there."

"Well..." said Christine.

"C'mon, Mama Chris," Turquoise pleaded.

"Give it a try, Chris," Thaddeus added. "I'll take perfect care of you."

"Well, it's against my better judgment, but I'll try. Let me go change and put on a sweater."

"Five minutes, Dodge Ram."

"Okay."

Ten minutes later, they had left Jamie and Parkus in charge of the younger ones and were pulling from the county road onto US 180, heading into Flagstaff. As planned, Thaddeus drove, Turquoise rode shotgun and Christine was buckled in between them. All was going well.

Then Thaddeus felt Christine stiffen beside him in the seat. She reached across and took his hand and began squeezing. "This isn't feeling so good," she whispered to Thaddeus and Turquoise. "I can't breathe so well."

Thaddeus slowed the truck. "Do you need to go back home? Go to a hospital?"

"I think I need to go back home."

"Okay, then."

Thaddeus found a turn-around and swung the truck back toward the ranch. He didn't understand what was going on with his wife but figured she was too tired to travel. Too much pain from the wreck.

"I'm sorry, everyone," Christine said. "I don't know what's going on with me.'"

"It's all right," Turquoise said.

"Oh, piss, I hate myself for this," Christine moaned. "I'm so sorry to do this to you, guys."

"Not a problem," Thaddeus said lightly. "We're still figuring out how you feel. Maybe we're hurrying things tonight."

"Maybe so," his wife agreed.

Two days later—Sunday noon—it happened again as Thaddeus was taking Christine to see some friends in Williams. Again, they got only three miles from home before the same feeling of light-headedness and shortness of breath overwhelmed Christine, and they had to turn back home. This time, Thaddeus remarked that he was going to take her to see Dr. Gorton on Monday morning. There was something going on that had him worried. Christine didn't argue, just remained huddled in the passenger seat, arms wrapped around herself, white around the mouth and looking ill.

The next morning, they called Dr. Clarisse Gorton, and Christine had an appointment for eleven. After waiting in the office reception area inside the Medical Arts Building on North San Francisco Street in Flagstaff, they were led to an examination room. The medical tech took Christine's vitals and asked about prescription changes. The preliminaries were entered into the network server, and the tech left after telling them Dr. Gorton would be in momentarily. Several minutes later, Clarisse Gorton breezed into the exam room. She brought with her the airy fragrance of body-wash and a pungent hand cleanser, probably mounted just outside the room in the hallway. She smiled brightly and asked Christine several questions. Then she had her hop on the examination table and did the head-eyes-mouth-ears exam, the heart and lungs, and an abdominal palpation. She asked Christine to describe the feel-ings of shortness-of-breath and dizziness and listened intently, nodding once or twice as Christine recounted her experiences. Dr. Gorton then listened to Christine's description of the hour or so of feelings leading up to the attempted trips away from home and then listened again to Christine's heart and lungs.

"At your age, we could do X-rays and maybe a CT scan, but I think we'd be wasting your time. I'm going to refer you for a psychological consult and see if we can get a clearer picture of your feelings that precede your sensation of drowning. Would that be agreeable, Christine?"

"Yes, if you think so. But I'm a pretty tough lady. I don't think it's a psychological problem. I think it's maybe an iron deficiency or something."

"Well, we're going to have you stop downstairs at the lab and do a blood and urine workup, so we'll rule out those kinds of things as we go. If the blood comes back suspicious, we can cancel the psych workup and proceed with hemoglobin attention. Fair enough?"

"All right. Who do I go see?"

"Randy E. Cummings. He's in this same building, and all the docs and their families use his service. So he comes highly recommended."

"You mean doctors have psychological problems?" Thaddeus asked, unable to resist.

She rolled her eyes. "Don't get me started, Thaddeus. Please."

"Just joking."

"I know."

THURSDAY AFTERNOON FOUND CHRISTINE SETTLING INTO DR. Cummings' inner office. She had gone into the office without Thaddeus. He had driven her into town and promised to stay by her side, but at the last minute, Christine had decided to speak alone with Dr. Cummings, so Thaddeus was left behind in the waiting room.

On the loveseat beside Christine, was an overstuffed bear with a red tongue made of felt. Christine arranged herself and waited for Dr. Cummings to begin.

The doctor looked up from his chart. He was about Christine's age, with short gray-black hair and round eyeglasses that gave him an owlish look. Then he smiled, and the room lit up. "Christine, what's going on? Thaddeus called and said you were reluctant to leave the house. Can you speak about that for me?"

She shrugged. "That's about it. I make a plan to leave the house, go out and climb in the truck, but then get short of breath all of a sudden. Then I feel dizzy and have to run back inside. I don't know what the hell it is."

"What's your normal ability to function outside the home?"

"Doc, I was a combat soldier in Iraq. Firefights and people shooting at me. No problem, understand? Then I came home and did college and law school despite my crappy grades from high school when I was working full-time at Dairy Queen and couldn't get much study time in. My husband was murdered in front of me, and I didn't hesitate to go on. I practically raised our child on my own. But then I'm coming from our ranch a few weeks back and some asshole rammed me from behind."

"I read about that in the paper. You actually shot the guy?"

"I did. He had a lighter out and was going to set my car on fire. It was either shoot him or burn alive. So I'm here and he's not. But now I've developed this shortness of breath, and I'm thinking it's anemia. Then I called Dr. Gorton back this morning, and they tell me the labs look good, including my iron levels and RBC. So now I don't know what the hell to think. I feel like I'm losing my mind."

Christine grabbed her head with both hands. "Tell the truth, sometimes I feel scared but I can't tell you what it is I'm scared of. I've killed lots of people, so it's not like I'm frightened by some fool out there. It's almost like it's my mind playing tricks on me, telling me stuff that isn't true. Trying to scare the shit out of me. And doing a pretty good job. I just can't quite put my finger on it. All I know is I don't want to leave home. I get physically ill even thinking about it. I want to go home right now, in fact. So...can we wrap this up?"

The doctor smiled. "Have you ever heard of agoraphobia?"

"Fear of open spaces?"

"Fear of crowded spaces, open public places. It has as much to do with fear of people as fear of place, we're learning. Does that resonate with you at all?"

"Well, I do worry about terrorist attacks at malls and movies. But is that irrational or a valid concern? I happen to think it's reasonable and rational both. There are terrorists and bad guys shooting up public places."

"Do your apprehensions come into your thoughts as images of people? Something that realistic?"

"Images of people? No. I feel this fear of the unknown, not people or places. That's what bothers me. It's not a fear of anything in particular. I'm pretty confrontational. If it was a fear of something real, I'd tackle it and resolve it. But this is just a generalized anxiety that settles over me like a cloud and brings me to my knees I'm so scared." Tears welled up in her eyes, and she felt inside her purse for a clutch of tissues and began dabbing and blowing her nose. "Sorry, Dr. Cummings."

"No need to apologize. Let me ask you this, Chris. If we referred you to a psychiatrist for some pharmaceutical help, would that be something you're open to?"

"Taking drugs for this? No way I'm taking medication, Dr. Cummings. This is fear, and the only way around fear is straight through it, as we say in the Army. Sometimes you just have to meet it head-on. If I can figure out which way to shoot or what I'm shooting at. That's my problem right now."

"Were you ever afraid of the dark when you were little?"

"Probably, but I really can't remember."

"Well, the fear syndrome you're dealing with now, Christine, is a lot like the fear of the dark one. The patient often has no idea what's lurking out there—in the marketplace, or the movies, or the mall. And that causes a fear response that some of us will say is out of proportion to the stimulus. Does this resonate?"

"That's just it. When I think it through, the logic gets me out into the car or truck. But then we go a mile or two, and all of a sudden the sky caves in on me, and I don't even have time to think through it. It's just BAM! And suddenly I'm a mush of fear. I can't even stop it from happening. I'm sorry. This probably isn't making any sense. I sound like I'm talking in circles, like I want help but the thing happens so suddenly, there's no time for help."

"Which is why I inquired about your willingness to visit with a psychiatrist and discuss a medication to help you through this time in your life."

She weakened—her face suddenly relaxed and the tension was gone. She had surrendered. She knew she needed help, probably more than talking-to-a-doctor help. She probably needed a medication. She was also realizing that it was her pride, her self-esteem and self-image, that were all tied in to how she handled these irrational fears. Being weak wasn't part of her inner view of herself. She didn't want to admit she needed help. But she did, so she did.

And just at that realization, Dr. Cummings spoke with the solution, "Dr. Kendra Issyat can see you at eight in the morning."

"Really? How do you know?"

"We have a system in place for acute sessions. She'll see my acute patients any morning at eight. I'll do the same for her. We don't abuse our little system, and so it works. Eight a.m. work for you, Christine?"

"It works."

———

THE FOLLOWING MORNING, CHRISTINE MET WITH KENDRA ISSYAT, M.D. She was Duke University with a residency at Bellevue and a fellowship at Stanford. The doctor was wearing a red silk dress, Western style, but followed Hindu custom and wore the red dot, or *bindi*, on her forehead. Christine knew that in India, a vermilion mark in the parting of the hair just above the forehead was worn by married women as commitment to the long life and well-being of their husbands. Dr. Issyat was married to Benjamin Issyat, a neurosurgeon in the same group as his wife. She was direct, to the point, yet soft-spoken and gentle, Christine found. Christine liked the doctor immediately and felt she had no agenda other than to help Christine get better.

Christine sat in a comfortable chair across from a large mahogany desk that was meticulously laid out. There was a small lamp on one corner that lended a soft glow to the room. No overhead lights. There was also one box of tissues aligned with the edge of the desk, one small Apple laptop in the center, a colorful coaster with a red mug, and a photo frame, but it faced Dr. Issyat so Christine couldn't see what picture it held.

Dr. Issyat began after she herself took a seat, "Mrs. Murfee, I hear you are experiencing anxiety?"

"I am. It comes and goes."

"Are you experiencing the anxiety right now?"

"To some smaller degree, yes."

"You came here from home?"

"From home, yes."

"Were you having the anxiety at home?"

"Yes. It started as soon as I woke up and remembered I had to come here today."

"What happened to reduce the anxiety to where you could leave home and come here?"

"My husband promised he'd protect me. I know him. He's one kick-ass body thumper. I'm good with him."

"But you can't always have him there with you, and so you want additional help? Is that fair to say?"

"It is. I can't be so dependent on my husband."

"I'm going to start you on a light dose of medication I find helps my patients dealing with generalized anxiety."

"Is it agoraphobia?"

"I don't want to put any name on it. For your sake, Mrs. Murfee, it will be going into your record as a generalized anxiety secondary to the assault you suffered in your car."

"You knew about that?"

"Dr. Cummings' remarks include that note."

"Good, so my insurance pays it or something? Oh, sure, so I can recover my costs of treatment from Marshall Anders' insurance company. Now I see what you're saying."

The doctor gave her a puzzled look. She seemed to be unsure why Christine was slow to get her rationale. Christine was a lawyer and should have come in here having already considered these insurance-coverage issues. Christine saw this uncertainty on the doctor's face and realized that she wasn't, in her thought processes, entirely herself yet. She became certain, right then, that she had no business being back in her law practice yet where her clients deserved the best thinking that Christine had long possessed, the thinking on which at least part of her reputation rested.

"Doctor Issyat," Christine slowly began, "I also need to confide in you that my cognition isn't its best since the assault."

"I'm glad you can share that. The type of physical and emotional trauma you suffered can cause slips in our thinking. Oftentimes, these things resolve themselves with the passage of time, but we can also refer you for neuropsych testing if that would make you more comfortable."

"Can we reserve that for last? I'd like to just let some time go by first."

"Have you thought about how you might structure your life if you take some time off from the office?"

"Not really. I'm not much of a hobbyist. But I do love horseback riding. That's not as scary to me as going into town. And, of course, there are the kids. I could fill my days by simply being there for them—running them to and from sports or clubs, all their school activities, even taking them for rides on the ranch. We have seven children, and there's so much to do with each one of them."

"That's a great idea, Christine." Dr. Issyat scribbled something on a pad she had pulled from her middle drawer. "Please take this prescription. You can get it filled right away. Just don't operate heavy machinery and stay away from that horse until we see how you're going to do with that med first, okay?"

"Okay." Christine took the prescription, folded it, and placed it in her purse.

"Nice to meet you, Mrs. Murfee." Dr. Issyat rose from her chair and came around her desk to hold out her hand.

"Thank you." Christine shook the doctor's hand heartily. When a person needed help, it was the best feeling in the world to get it.

She walked out to the waiting room to her Thaddeus, always steadfast and true. She couldn't have asked for a better husband. When she approached, he was reading an old *National Geographic*, deep into an article, she was sure. If nothing else, Thaddeus was the type of man to embrace exactly what he needed at that time.

He rose when he saw her and gave her a hug. That was exactly what she'd needed. And then he led her out of the building to his truck. While Thaddeus drove them to the Walgreen's to drop off the prescription, Christine wrestled with her feelings. She had come out of Dr. Issyat's office wanting desperately to just break down and cry, but she had been fighting that off. She wasn't willing to have Thaddeus see her as someone suddenly weak. She had been so strong for him for so long. She'd never been needy before and didn't know how to do needy now. But she did know this: she knew her choices were narrowed way down. She might not have any choice but to be weak around him when it was all said and done. She might have to let him in on how scared she was of her diminished thinking and her fears of leaving home. The altercation had changed her life in those milliseconds when Anders was going to light her on fire until she had shot him. Had she missed and the bullet gone off into the trees, she wouldn't be sitting here now, beside Thaddeus, on some random, wonderful tree-lined street, in some blessed parking lot, in the middle of a remarkable Flagstaff. No, she wouldn't be anywhere. Tears washed into her eyes, and she let out a small sob.

Thaddeus immediately picked up on it and, from the driver's seat, he reached over and took her hand and squeezed. "Let it out," was all he said and all he needed to say. The dam burst inside Christine, and then she was weeping in great inhalations and exhalations and wracking sobs. She couldn't have told him why she was crying, and he didn't ask.

It was just okay.

26

"How have you been feeling?" Thaddeus asked Sheila once they were seated in the attorney conference room at the jail. A uniformed deputy had just escorted Sheila inside the tiny room and removed her handcuffs. Remarkably, she hadn't cuffed Sheila to the table loop. The reason was that Sheila had become a model prisoner—the sheriff's words—once she began seeing an addiction doctor and began going to 12-Step meetings. Her entire attitude was changing from the previous weeks.

"I'm doing A-okay, Thaddeus," she replied.

The sentiment was behind the words, but she didn't look great. Her once healthy hair was now stringy and limp. Her blue eyes had lost their luster, and where she'd had an athletic build before, she was now too skinny, her muscles atrophying while sitting in her cell.

He was happy for her, still, that she was getting through her addiction, and she spoke a lot of gratitude. But then the cell got quiet after they finished their opening chit-chat. After a few moment's silence, Sheila contended again, adamantly, that she pulled the trigger of the gun that killed her husband. She wasn't going to budge from that position and so, as a legal professional, Thaddeus had to prepare for her trial on that basis.

Lawyers didn't get to force their clients to go along with the lawyer's version of the truth. It was the client's version of the truth that spoke, never the lawyer's. Lawyers could encourage their client to speak the truth, they can even threaten and cajole, but the client always had the last card to play. It was their call.

So, if Sheila said it was she who had wielded the gun that killed Russ, that was the theory of the case Thaddeus would present to the jury. It didn't matter that Thaddeus had decided it was PJ who'd pulled the trigger. His version of the facts would never see the light of day.

Thaddeus based the mother's defense—featuring the mother as the shooter—on two facts. First, Thaddeus had had the video examined at a crime lab in Los Angeles with film videographers who missed nothing. He had asked them whether the video had been doctored. Verdict: no doctoring, nothing unusual about the video itself. But there was something odd about the subject matter. After the shooting, the CCTV system had continued recording what occurred in Russ's office. Plenty of crime scene techs, cops, and detectives. Off and on, mother and daughter would come into or out of the scene. Essentially, they were recorded from front and back. The result? The person that had shot Russ had the same backside measurements as the mother's measurements in the subsequent, after-shooting video. The daughter, seen multiple times in the video and measured and re-measured, was nowhere near the proportions of the shooter. She was at least two sizes smaller. Only Thaddeus knew about this testing. At this point, because it pointed the finger at the mother, he decided to keep it under wraps as attorney work product, which a lawyer isn't required to turn over to the other side during discovery.

Sheila's version of the truth corroborated the video lab's version of the truth, and so it couldn't be shown to the jury because it tended to convict the mother. So Thaddeus didn't list the video test report as an exhibit because he didn't plan to use it at trial.

He discussed these matters with Sheila that day, especially elaborating on the testing done in L.A., which proved, almost indisputably, that the mother was the shooter.

She raised her hands in a type of supplication. "Well, I like what that bunch of L.A. propellerheads think! The shooter is the mother, and that's that."

"I thought you might say that," Thaddeus said. "So don't worry. I haven't turned the L.A. report over to the prosecution. Nor will I."

"No," she said, "I'll decide when we use it."

"Wait, Sheila. If you want us to use the report, then we need to turn it over to the prosecution now, while discovery is being finalized. We're filing an exhibit list in the morning, and this L.A. report must be on there if you're planning on us using it."

She smiled. "Like I said, Thaddeus, I'll decide when we use it. And no, there's no need to list it ahead of time. I'll get it into evidence. But only when I'm ready."

A storm was brewing inside of Thaddeus but he took a deep breath to keep calm. "Sheila, I don't work like this. You've got to tell me what you're planning. I can't go along with just anything."

She opened her hands palms up and shrugged. "I'm not planning anything, Thaddeus. You'll just have to trust me this time."

He shook his head. So contrite, yet so distrustful. "Not good enough. If we don't like the L.A. report as an exhibit, I won't allow its use. That can't be any clearer."

She chuckled and turned away momentarily before she looked at him again. "Thaddeus, I just love you. You've done wonders for me. How can I ever thank you?"

Such sarcasm, and for what? It wasn't like she was paying him. Any money for his long hours of work was to be kept into an account for PJ. Yet this woman still constantly played him. She spoke the words out loud, "thank you," but it had never felt real.

He rose from his chair at the table in the conference room. He wanted to tell her that he couldn't work this way, not knowing what she had planned at trial, but he wouldn't tell her he was keeping his options open to withdraw from her case if—if what?

She was fragile beyond everything else—her doctors had told him so. Even though it frazzled every nerve of his to work like this, she couldn't be threatened with a withdrawal of the attorney she was relying on. That just wouldn't work, wasn't fair, and he would avoid it.

He leaned on the table and met her gaze. "Just thank me by telling me the truth, always. That's it, right there. Just the truth."

A smug look adopted her face. "Of course, have I lied to you? I told you when we first met that I was going to shoot Russ, and I kept my word."

Thaddeus ground his teeth together. "You also told me I talked you down."

She waved a brush-off at him. "That didn't last. I was mad as hell as soon as I got outside that day. Mad as hell and ready to make Russell pay for molesting my little PJ. Let's never forget what we're troubled about here—a child molester, child sex assaulter, and a statutory rapist. My omissions pale in comparison."

He let "her omissions" slide. He was unwilling to pursue her or their discussion. There were days where "exhaustion" was too little to describe what he went through with his clients. And yet they took from him again and again, every ounce of his energy, every ounce of his goodwill. He had only ever wanted justice to reign triumphant, but too many times in his past, that line grayed until he wasn't sure who or what he was defending.

And, really, wasn't she absolutely right? Hadn't Russ deserved to be shot, or worse? In Thaddeus's world, the man had it coming. But in the world of man's laws, the state got to mete out all punishment. The injured only got to stand by and watch while the state dealt with the devil. That was what Sheila had been facing, that and forcing PJ to testify, when she picked up a gun. No, justice had been done. The case was over, as far as Thaddeus was personally concerned. But professionally, there was more to come.

Thaddeus took a deep breath, let it out slowly, and moved closer to the conference table to take up the topic of the trial itself. He reviewed with her what Detective Landis had to say, then went on to Detective Snow, Dot Marchant, the medical examiner, the crime scene techs, Russell's family, Carleen, and maybe—he had to bring this up—maybe Thaddeus himself, as the person who could testify about Sheila's state of mind when she left his office just eight minutes before gunning down Russ Lowenstein.

His own testimony had Thaddeus stumped. So far, the State hadn't listed him as a witness, and he didn't know why. He explained to Sheila why it was important. He told her it was an egregious tactical error the State was making. It was an error because Thaddeus could testify to premeditation and freedom from temporary sanity, even the absence of heat-of-the-moment rage, court language that would make the crime more serious than manslaughter. But the State hadn't listed him as a witness. The second, and even more important, reason why the State was making a huge error: listing Thaddeus as a witness would create a conflict of interest that would force him to withdraw as Sheila's defense lawyer. They could force her to lose Thaddeus by simply listing him. He told her this, and her eyes grew wide. But he wondered if it was because she would lose a lawyer that she could manipulate or if she was truly committed to Thaddeus and his defense.

"I would have to go to trial without you as my lawyer?"

"That's right. If they list me as a witness, I'm done. The judge won't allow me to continue."

"Who's the lawyer on the other side?"

"Jon Logan. He's a long-time DA, extremely experienced, and the fact he isn't listing me should be telling me something. It isn't a mistake, not by Jon."

"Who's my judge?"

"Still Judge Able M. Watertown. He's known for being very fair and very conservative with a small 'c.' He's been on the bench almost twenty years, and there isn't a kind of case he hasn't presided over. He'll follow the rules of evidence and won't sign off on oddball instructions to the jury. Everything is geared toward him making retirement so everything is by the book."

She laughed. "His retirement is at the bottom of how my trial goes? Jesus, spare me."

Thaddeus nodded. "Unfortunately, yes, but we can play it that way."

"Why hasn't this Jon Logan listed you as a witness and knocked you out?"

"Because he wants me there. Maybe he'd rather I wasn't a witness. A lawyer cannot be a witness in a trial he's defending or prosecuting. This is a law written in stone. Maybe Jon figures I could do you more good than harm by testifying in your defense and claiming, as a witness, that you were just going to visit with your husband, that he'd said something at the office, *once you arrived*, to provoke you into a sudden shooting that wasn't premeditated and was done in the heat of passion so you get convicted only of manslaughter. That's an easy charge to beat, and he doesn't want that. So maybe that's why I'm still on the case. We'll have to hope that doesn't change, though, because I don't think, legally, you're guilty of anything. I'm going to raise the issue of defense of another by the use of deadly force, Sheila. I'm going to claim that you shot your husband as the only way of protecting your daughter by stopping him from committing another felony by having sex with her again. I'm going to claim it was the same as self-defense. Except they call it 'defense of another,' and sometimes it allows the use of deadly force in defending another person."

"Wow. Will that work?"

"I don't know. But it's all I have. I don't have a lot of faith in it, no. Too many moving parts—too many things can go wrong that can bite us in the ass."

27

The court room was jam-packed, every seat taken, some standing at the back against the wall. A case like this, especially one that might carry the death sentence, always drew the crowds and media. Even with the air conditioning on full blast, it was warm in the room. Although Thaddeus felt uncomfortable in a full business suit, a dampness already gathering at his armpits, Sheila Lowenstein looked as cool as a cucumber.

When Thaddeus asked how Sheila was, she leaned in and whispered, "God will take care of everything. I have faith in him." She sat back upright, but then leaned over to him again. "I have faith in you, too, Thaddeus. God led me to you."

Thaddeus didn't mind such faithfulness. No, not at all. But what Sheila Lowenstein didn't seem to understand was that her life was on the line. And sometimes even God wouldn't step into a courtroom for a case as one-sided as it was now. Thaddeus took a deep breath, wiped his glasses of the sweat, and then readied himself mentally for the day ahead.

At 8:00 a.m., the court clerk quieted everyone down and then asked everyone to rise for Judge Able M. Watertown, presiding.

Detective James Landis was the first witness called at trial by Jon Logan, the Deputy District Attorney. He testified he was the first detective to enter the scene of the shooting. When he entered into Russ's office, Officer Bill Grayson had the defendant off to the side, giving her water. He also said the defendant confessed to him, confessed to Detective Snow, and confessed to her daughter. He heard it all.

At the time, when the defendant talked to the detective, she had allowed him to switch on his digital recorder. So now today, Jon Logan snapped the button, and the confession began with Detective Landis setting the scene:

"My name is Jason Landis, and I'm meeting here in the office of Russell Lowenstein with his wife, Sheila Lowenstein. Mrs. Lowenstein, are you aware I'm recording our conversation?"

"I am. It's fine."

"So, I'm recording our conversation with your permission?"

"You are."

"You know you have the right to remain silent?"

"I know."

"And you have the right to speak to an attorney at point?"

"Yes."

"And you have the right to refuse to talk to me?"

"I want to talk to you. I want to tell you what happened."

"So you waive your right to remain silent and waive your right to an attorney?"

"Yes, I shot Russell. He was having sex with my daughter, and I shot him."

"So you're telling me this freely and voluntarily?"

"I am."

"Why don't you take us through what happened this morning?"

"I woke up, and Russell hadn't come home overnight from the sale barn. This was common and was part of doing his job. No problem. But that morning, I heard PJ crying in her room."

"PJ is your daughter?"

"Yes. She's fourteen years old."

"So, you heard her crying?"

"Yes."

"What did you do?"

"I knocked on her door and went in. I've never seen her eyes so red and her cheeks so wet. Even her pillow was wet. I asked her what was wrong. She said Russell had seduced her and had sex with her in the barn many times, and now she feared she was pregnant. She had missed two periods."

"How did that make you feel?"

"Really? You want to ask how it made me feel? Did you hear what I said? I'm her mother. How do you suppose it made me feel?"

"Probably very angry."

"It threw me in a rage. I couldn't see straight. I threw on some clothes and went up to Mr. Murfee's office."

"I see you're wearing a holster. Did you wear that to Mr. Murfee's office?"

"I did. It had my gun in it."

"Where did you get that gun?"

"I bought it. A man sold it to me for one-hundred dollars."

"You kept it loaded?"

"It came loaded. I looked it up online. It holds, like, fourteen bullets."

"Is that the gun you shot Russell with?"

"Yes."

"Where is that gun now?"

"I don't know."

"What do you mean you don't know where your gun is? What did you do with it after you shot Russ?"

"I'm telling the truth, officer. I don't remember what I did. I was crying and out of control. I just shot my gun. I think I might've dropped it somewhere."

"So far, the officers can't find it. But we'll come back to this." There was a moment's pause, and then Detective Landis' voice came back on. "Did Russell say anything to you before or after you shot him?"

"Nope. Just slumped over in his chair. At that point, when it was over, I was like, 'Oh, God, I've shot my husband!'"

"Mrs. Lowenstein, is it fair to say you planned out how you were going to kill your husband?"

"I don't know. I just put on my gun and drove uptown. I knew I was going to need a lawyer so I went to see Mr. Murfee."

"Did you have an appointment with him?"

"I made an appointment that morning before I left home. I told his receptionist it was urgent. They don't usually take appointments last minute like that."

"What happened at Mr. Murfee's?"

"He tried to talk me out of it. I lied and told him he'd talked me out of it. But he hadn't. I didn't budge. I was going to kill that no-good Russell Lowenstein if it was the last thing I did."

"Now, you said your daughter had missed two periods. Is it possible it was someone besides Russell who might have gotten her pregnant?"

"No, she's only fourteen. She isn't allowed to date or anything of the sort."

"What is your work?"

"I'm a church counselor. I counsel people enduring hardships."

"Did you think you needed counseling?"

"I wasn't thinking. I just wanted Russ dead. Period."

"Is there anything else I haven't asked you this morning?"

"Not that I know of."

"Okay, I'm going to turn off my recorder now. What you've told me on here is freely given with all rights waived?"

"Yes."

The District Attorney snapped off the recorder and stepped back from the witness. "Detective Landis, did you also encounter the daughter, PJ, at the scene?"

"Not at first. She wasn't there at first. At least I didn't see her."

"What is the daughter's full name?"

"Patricia Jean Walston. She's Jim Sam Walston's daughter with Sheila Lowenstein. Patricia Jean goes by 'PJ.'"

"Did you take PJ's statement?"

"No. But I took one later."

"Was that a written statement?"

"Yes."

"The statement of Patricia Jean Walston, marked State's Exhibit 22, Your Honor, has been stipulated into evidence. May I present it to the witness?"

Judge Watertown nodded. "You may."

"PJ wrote these words in this statement, 'I knew my parents were having trouble before the shooting.' Do you see that?"

"Yes."

"Mr. Murfee is going to ask you whether it's possible the daughter pulled the trigger and the mother's covering up for her. He's going to ask you if that' s maybe why the mother is so anxious to confess. What will you answer me when it's suggested the mother is covering up for the daughter?"

"The mother can be seen on the closed circuit video, pulling the trigger and shooting Russell Lowenstein."

"You've seen this video?"

"Yes."

"And on it you can see the mother shooting Russell?"

"You can see the back of her head and maybe the waist up."

"What about the gun? In a holster?"

"Can't tell. It's the way she's standing."

"What is the shooter wearing?"

"Shorts and T-shirt."

"What was the mother wearing?"

"Shorts and T-shirt."

"What was the daughter wearing?"

"Shorts and a navy T-shirt that said 'Patagonia.' The writing was on the front."

"Did you ask the daughter about the gun?"

"No. The mother confessed."

"What did the mother say? We're talking about Sheila Lowenstein when you first walked in?"

"As soon as we walked in, she raised her hands. 'You caught me,' she says. 'I shot Russ.'"

"You did a gunshot residue test on the mother's hands at the scene?"

"Detective Snow did one."

"Test result?"

"Inconclusive. GSR wears off in hours sometimes. We didn't talk to her until after she had been given water. It might've sloshed so there wouldn't be any gunshot residue."

"At the scene, did you ask PJ if she was having sex with Russ?"

"No."

"Why not?"

"It just never came up."

"Did you test the daughter for gunshot residue?"

"Like I said, the mother was confessing. We saw no reason to test the daughter for anything."

28

I t was to be a special day: Christine was driving into town to meet Thaddeus for lunch on the second day of trial.

That morning, the crime scene techs would be testifying for the prosecution, and Thaddeus was already prepared for the after-noon witness, Detective Linus Snow, so a leisurely lunch would be just the thing. She needed it; he wanted it. The last week had been extremely busy as Thaddeus and Turquoise made last-minute adjustments to their witness list and exhibits list and prepared jury instructions and pre-trial motions as usual.

Christine's offer to drive into town for lunch had come as a surprise to Thaddeus, but she had been meeting with Dr. Issyat, taking her medications as prescribed, and felt finally ready to try a drive on her own.

She pulled away from the ranch house, leaving the property line to edge out onto the northbound county road before turning east toward Flagstaff. One mile breezed by almost effortlessly for her.

There was no straining, no self-talk, no cold sweats. She was growing more thoughtful by the mile as she picked up speed and looked forward to meeting the man of her dreams, Thaddeus Murfee. Then, five miles out of town, she had to jerk the wheel suddenly to dodge a chicken hawk sitting in her lane as it ate the innards out of a roadkill squirrel. As she jerked the wheel right, the right side of her new Mercedes dropped off the asphalt down onto the shoulder, a distance of about four inches. When her tires caught the gravel, they threw up a tremendous whirring noise and a cloud of dust that climbed up the passenger window before blowing back alongside the vehicle. But with the sudden drop-off and loud noise came an overwhelming realization: she was about to run off the road and end up in the trees yet again.

Christine swallowed hard and backed off the accelerator. She fought down the knee-jerk reaction of pulling the car over, stopping, and calling for help. It was all she could do to keep going, but she did. Finally, she was a mile outside of Flagstaff with her eye on the prize of the city limits sign.

Meanwhile, inside the courtroom, Thaddeus was just beginning his cross-examination of Amanda Gallegos, a beautiful young woman with a master's degree in forensic science who was testifying about the crime scene, especially those moments when she first arrived at the sale barn. She was dark-skinned and flaxen-haired and wore Invisalign retainers that day as she did her job professionally and thoroughly, recalling all key details of the case.

Thaddeus asked, "Ms. Gallegos, you testified that you saw PJ Walston outside the offices at the bike rack, reaching inside of her seat bag, correct?"

"Yes, I did."

"And you testified it looked to you like she was placing some kind of tool inside the bag, correct?"

"Yes."

"So you would like the jury today to believe she was hiding the murder weapon. Isn't that what you want?"

"I don't think—"

"Whoops, yes or no. Calls for a yes or no answer, Ms. Gallegos."

"Please repeat the question."

"Do you want the jury to believe you saw PJ hiding the gun inside her bicycle bag?"

"No."

"No, you don't want them to believe that?"

"No, I don't want them to believe anything but the truth."

"As do we all, Ms. Gallegos, I can assure you. Now, let me ask you something. If PJ had been hiding a gun in the bicycle seat, wouldn't it stand to reason you would have gone inside the office suite and told the detectives you thought you saw a gun?"

"Yes. I did try to tell them."

"What happened with that?"

"Detective Landis was busy with Mrs. Lowenstein, and then Detective Snow took the lady and her daughter who had re-entered the office into another room. When I turned back around, Detective Landis had stepped into the outer office. I stuck my head out there to tell him, but he was talking to the lady from outside, who was now sitting at the receptionist's desk. So I didn't get to tell him about the gun then."

"What happened next?"

"I turned around, opened my bag, prepped my camera, and began memorializing the scene."

"Taking pictures?"

"Taking pictures, yes."

"So when did you tell Detective Landis about the gun you thought you saw?"

"I didn't. I never did get the chance. Don't forget, I had my job to do, too. Plus, after he met the lady in the outer office, then he went into the smaller office, and I could hear him recording the defendant's statement in there. I knew better than to interrupt a confession."

"If you thought you saw the daughter with the gun, then I'm sure that was so important, so uppermost in your mind, that sometime that afternoon or by the end of the day you called Detective Landis or Snow on the phone and reported what you saw, isn't that correct?"

"I did. They went to the home of the Lowenstein daughter and tried to view the bicycle, but it was gone. I know now she had ridden the bike to her father's house, Mr. Walston's house, and was staying there from that point on. So no one knew where the bike had gone. By the time they did catch up to it at the high school where she rode it to class, the bag was searched, and it was empty."

First, it was interesting to Thaddeus that PJ had gone back to school after her step-dad was killed and her mother hauled off to jail. If she'd been so traumatized as Detective Snow has suggested in his interview, she should have stayed home with her dad, Jim Sam. What kid did that? Went to school when there was a very good reason not to attend? Any school administrator would clear the absence, no questions asked. But, for now, Thaddeus tucked that information away for later.

"So you want the jury to think the gun was in the bag but missed?"

"Like I said, Mr. Murfee, I don't want the jury to believe anything but the truth. That's why I'm telling the truth."

Thaddeus walked alongside the lectern, back to counsel table. He picked up his laptop and placed it on the lectern. "Has anyone played for you the video taken kitty-corner from the sale barn, the video from Kinsman's Pizza?"

"No. I didn't know there was a video from there."

"Objection, Your Honor, if counsel is preparing to play some video, it hasn't been disclosed on the exhibit list."

The trial judge eyed Thaddeus sideways. "Counsel? Is there an unlisted exhibit in my courtroom?"

"Impeachment exhibit, sealed and filed with the Clerk, Your Honor. That would be Defendant's Impeachment Number Four. Defendant requests permission to voir dire the presenting witness prior to asking the witness questions about the exhibit."

"Who would your presenting witness be, Mr. Murfee?"

"My investigator, Turquoise Murfee."

"You may call Ms. Murfee to the stand. The witness will stand down, but you're not excused from the courtroom."

"The defense calls Turquoise Murfee."

Turquoise was seated at counsel table with Thaddeus as his investigator. She stood and was sworn in and took the witness seat. Today she wore gray slacks instead of her normal jeans, and a white blouse. With her hair down and her cherished turquoise pendant around her neck, she was so beautiful, a person couldn't help but look at her.

After a preliminary examination was provided, disclosing her name, training, work history, and role in the case, Turquoise was then asked, "Were you instructed in this case to canvass the business owners in the strip mall across the street from the sale barn?"

"I was so instructed," answered Turquoise. "You instructed me, Mr. Murfee."

"What did I ask you to do?"

"Go to the stores across the parking lot and investigate whether any of their private CCTV cameras had recorded anything from the day of the shooting."

"Did you talk to the management of Kinsman's Pizza?"

"I did."

"Tell us what you found out."

"On the day of the shooting, their video system was recording all the day. Among other things, they recorded the witness, Amanda Gallegos, coming outside the sale barn after the shooting."

"Has the video been confirmed by you for its accuracy as to date, time, and place and the accuracy of the camera system?"

"It has. The video is legitimate, it was made the day of the shooting, and the camera and recording system are all accurate and truthful."

"You may step down. Defense recalls Amanda Gallegos to the witness stand."

Ms. Gallegos returned to the witness stand as Turquoise rejoined her father at counsel table.

"Now, Ms. Gallegos, I'm going to ask the clerk to play the video marked as Defendant's Impeachment Four. Please view it with me and with the jury and judge."

The video was then played. The selected portion lasted all of three minutes. In it, the witness, Amanda Gallegos, wearing the coveralls of the Coconino County Sheriff's Crime Scene Investigators, was seen coming outside the sale barn from inside and proceeding directly to the bicycle previously identified in the State's photographs as belonging to PJ Walston. The witness is seen to bend over and unzip the bicycle's saddle bag just behind and below the seat. Clearly, she unzipped the bag and put her hand inside. She came away with nothing, rezipped the bag, and went back inside the sale barn.

"Isn't it true, Ms. Gallegos, that you previously testified you saw PJ Walston putting a gun into that same bag?"

"I said it looked like a gun."

"Was it a gun?"

"I didn't find a gun there."

"So isn't the truth of the matter, the real reason you didn't tell the detectives about a gun in the bicycle, was because you had seen no such thing?"

"I—I don't remember when I saw what. It was all so chaotic."

"Really? There was chaos outside by the bicycle when you were alone with no other person in view? Is that what you're saying was chaotic?"

"Not that. I—I mean inside the building."

"Why didn't you tell the jury today that you looked inside the bike bag?"

"Honestly, I forgot I'd done that."

"You forgot? Seriously?"

"I must have forgotten. I made a mistake."

"How much of the rest of your testimony is a mistake?"

"I don't—it's all accurate."

"Except there was no gun ever seen in the daughter's hands."

"No, there was no gun."

"Now...you helped search the sale barn?"

"I did."

"Tell us about the gun you did find."

"I didn't find a gun."

"Did you ever see any gun from that day?"

"No."

"Have you ever seen the report of a gun test fired as the murder weapon?"

"No, there is no gun."

"That is all."

At that point, the court broke for the noon recess. Thaddeus and Turquoise walked out together, intending to meet Christine for lunch.

LaDora was waiting outside the courtroom. "I didn't want to interrupt. Christine has been taken to the hospital. She's having a terrible time, Mr. Murfee."

Thaddeus broke into a run for the stairs, Turquoise on his heels. He took the stairs two at a time and then ran for his truck across the street. They flew into the truck and roared north on San Francisco Street toward the Medical Center.

29

They had moved her to the psych ward in the east wing of the hospital. She was decompressing, having been given a relaxant injection, when the institution had called Thaddeus's office. The panic attack still had her hyperventilating, and they had fitted a paper bag on her mouth and were making her breathe in and out using the bag's atmosphere. She kept complaining of chest pains so they were monitoring her heart with electric leads as well.

They found her inside a curtained area with low lights and very little outside noise beyond the low tones of health-care worker conversations. Thaddeus entered through the curtain and went to her bedside. He took her hand in his.

Her eyes blinked open when he touched her hand.

"I'm sorry this happened," he said gently.

"Hello." Christine's voice was groggy, scratchy.

"Hello to you. I'm glad you're in a safe place."

"I'm sorry I missed lunch. I want to go home. Will you take me?"

He nodded. "Sure. As soon as they say you're ready, I'll take you in my truck."

"What about your trial?"

"I'll have to ask the judge for an afternoon recess. LaDora has Renny McAdams headed to court now. He'll speak with Judge Watertown and Jon Logan. I'm sure there won't be a problem."

"I'm so sorry. Please tell Sheila it's my fault."

"Let's leave the fault stuff alone for now. It is what it is. You were violently assaulted, and there are remnants of that hell still pressing on you. No fault there, Christine. You're still my number one lady."

Turquoise stuck her head through the curtain. "Hi, Mama Chris."

"Hello, Sweetheart. I didn't know you were out there. Come in."

"I'm going to stay with you and dad this afternoon. Your varsity team will be with you."

"Thank you." And then after a moment, "Oh!" she exclaimed, pressing a palm to her face. "I keep imagining I can't breathe! What the hell, Christine?" Chris was talking to herself she was so mad. And he understood. Christine was always in control, so she was spiraling at the moment. And probably scared to death.

"Hey, go easy on my lady," Thaddeus said. "You feel what you feel."

"Please don't talk like that," Christine shot back. "It feels like you're patronizing me."

"Okay, I'm sorry." He stroked her forearm with his fingertips. She didn't pull away.

"No, I'm sorry. It's passing now. Just another aggravation. Sorry, everyone."

A nurse pulled the curtain open and came inside. She checked the vitals screen and placed a hand on Christine's forehead for just a moment. She nudged Thaddeus aside. "How are we doing?"

"Not good. The attacks are coming and going now."

"Your heart strip looks like a good sinus rhythm. Your temperature and pulse-ox are normal. Is the medicine starting to work?"

"I'm feeling drowsy."

"That's a good sign. How would you feel about staying over tonight?"

"I want to go home."

"I think Dr. Issyat might want you to remain with us and let us follow you a little more closely. She wants the heart leads left in place. Plus she wants to do some blood workups. What do you think, Thaddeus? Can you spare her tonight?"

"Sure, we'll be right here with her. In fact, I'm staying this afternoon."

"Probably no need for that," said the nurse. "Didn't I hear on the news you're in trial today on the Lowenstein murder case? Don't you need to be there?"

"We can make arrangements around that."

"No need. We're going to keep Miss Christine a little drowsy this afternoon. You can get back to your trial."

"Yes," said Christine, "go back to court, Thaddeus."

He considered seriously what he should do. When he looked into his wife's eyes, he couldn't bear to have her in the hospital without him. But if the tables were turned, he'd want Christine to take care of what she needed to as well. It was a hard call for him, but finally he turned to Turquoise. "Go head-off Renny. Call him and tell him we're going to go ahead this afternoon after all."

"Done," said Turquoise, already making her way out of the curtain.

"And tell him I want him to second chair just in case I have to leave."

"Will do," she said over her shoulder. And then Turquoise was gone.

Thaddeus turned back to Christine. "You're sure about being here this afternoon while I'm in trial?"

"Positive. You go back to court. I'm getting drowsy so I'll probably doze off."

"All right, then. I'll see you as soon as we adjourn."

"I'll be right here, it seems."

"It won't be long."

Christine closed her eyes. "Just go, please."

"Okay," Thaddeus said and kissed her on the forehead. "Sleep well."

30

D A Jon Logan called Detective Linus Snow to the witness
stand. After ten minutes of stops and starts, trying to reha-
bilitate the testimony of Amanda Gallegos, they saw it was going
to be impossible to patch up her failings and so they decided to
move on with what Snow himself had to say about the shooting
and its aftermath. When it was all said and done, he'd mainly
rehashed what Detective Landis, his partner, had said, and Thaddeus laid off any cross-examination. He worked from the trial
lawyer school of thought that if a witness hasn't hurt you, don't
cross-examine. The possibility of bringing out something harmful
on cross was just too high to go there. So, he left it alone, forcing
the State to immediately call its next witness.

Who happened to be Dot Marchant, the receptionist/secretary at
the sale barn. Dot told the jury what she'd told Thaddeus, that
Russ had many girlfriends and jilted boyfriends. Angry husbands
sometimes came looking for Russ. The morning of the shooting,
PJ was the first to arrive, followed by her mother, maybe ten
minutes later, and the shooting occurred maybe two minutes after

that. The police arrived in under five minutes from the time of the shooting. She had no idea who called the police and had found out she still had her job. Things were going to go on as usual at the sale barn but with a new auctioneer, of course.

Logan next called to the witness stand Melina Dillard, the owner of Redrock Security, which was the video CCTV provider that provided all the camera and video storage for the sale barn, interior and exterior. Videos were introduced and played for the jury. The courtroom was darkened for the showing and, because it was just after lunch, many of the jurors became drowsy and some might even have nodded off. None of the video they showed was of the mystery head and shoulder that appeared briefly the morning of the shooting.

Following the video show, the lights came back up, and the prosecution called the medical examiner, who proved the cause and mechanism of death. Dr. Winwood testified as expected. Turquoise had interviewed him, and there was nothing new there. Following testimony of little value from the other police officers and crime scene techs mentioned in the police reports, the prosecutor then called two members of Russell Lowenstein's family. Their job was, ostensibly, to talk about Russell and how much he would be missed, yes, but their real value to the prosecution was to paint Russell as a good guy who didn't deserve to die merely because he was guilty of stat rape with his stepdaughter. It was a hard sell, but they did all right. However, Thaddeus didn't cross-examine since there was no point in it. It was their opinion of Russell.

Then the State rested its case. Thaddeus had Renny present to the court the Defendant's motion for directed verdict, the motion that's always required in criminal cases at the close of the State's case, which is also the motion that is never granted. When that little chore was out of the way, the court turned to Thaddeus. It was his turn to present the Defendant's case. It was time for the defense to speak up.

He had already discussed with Sheila what would happen at this point in the trial. There had been complete agreement that the defense would present no witnesses except the jail psychiatrist and Sheila's treating psychiatrist, who had been coming to the jail for visits ever since her incarceration. Dr. James F. Mangrum, the treating psychiatrist, was called to the witness stand by Thaddeus. The doctor was a tall, lithe man with a thatch of silver hair, black eyeglass frames, and a carefully cultured silver mustache. He was wearing a light blue suit, white shirt, and gold necktie that reminded Thaddeus of a northern Arizona sunset. He spread a few papers before him on the witness desk and folded his hands. He turned to the Jury and gave them a curt nod of his head before he shifted his focus to Thaddeus.

Thaddeus gave a quick smile, but then he wasn't smiling. "Please tell us your name."

"James Fred Mangrum."

"What is your profession?"

"Medical doctor."

"Where do you live?"

"Sedona, Arizona."

"Do you still practice medicine?"

"Not actively. I do some consulting now and then."

"You're a psychiatrist?"

"I am. Educated at the University of Arizona College of Medicine and residency and fellowships at Arizona State Hospital and UCLA, respectively."

"Did you consult on this case?"

"I did. You called me two months ago and asked me to visit with your client, Sheila Lowenstein."

"Did you do that?"

"I did. All in all, I've seen Mrs. Lowenstein a total of six times now."

"Describe what else you've done on this case."

"I've administered some basic tests on Mrs. Lowenstein and done some clinical tests as well. I've spoken with her at length, prescribed medications, and made my clinical observations. All of my records have been turned over to you, and the prosecution has those records as well because Mr. Logan called me last week and interviewed me by telephone. Which I was happy to do."

"You've been paid for your services?"

"Handsomely, thank you."

"Who paid you?"

"You did, Mr. Murfee. I can only assume the funds were your own."

"Now, as a result of your visits, tests, and observations of Sheila Lowenstein, do you have an opinion about her state of mind when she shot and killed her husband, Russell Lowenstein?"

"I do."

"Please state that opinion."

"Objection. Foundation."

"Overruled."

"Please tell us your opinion, Doctor," Thaddeus asked a second time.

"I have concluded that, at the time she pulled the trigger, Sheila Lowenstein was suffering a psychosis brought on by the decedent's sexual assault of her daughter and she did not know the shooting was wrong. I believe the psychosis was so great that she was, at that exact moment, incapable of knowing right from wrong."

"Would you say she was insane?"

"Objection! Leading."

"Sustained. Please rephrase."

"Is there a common term that describes her state of mind?"

"Some might say she was suffering from insanity."

"Doctor Mangrum, let's back up. Can you give us a brief summary of the issues you're looking at after examining and applying medico-legal standards to such a patient?"

"Yes. In Arizona, a person may be found guilty except insane. This is commonly known as GEI. GEI requires the doctor to find that, at the time of the crime, the person was so ill they didn't know the crime was wrong. This would be a finding of a mental defect or disease that wouldn't include alcohol abuse or drug abuse. It also wouldn't include character defects or psychosexual disorders. Legal insanity also doesn't include temporary conditions such as extreme pressure from what another person has done, and doesn't include passion growing out of anger, jealousy, revenge, hatred, or other motives in a person who does not suffer from a mental disease or defect or an abnormality that is manifested only by criminal conduct. That last part is a mouthful, but it is taken from Arizona's insanity statute, so the words are key."

"Objection. Doctor testifying to legal standards."

"Overruled. It's within the scope of his training and experience that he know of such standards. Plus, for the record, the court will instruct the jury on all legal questions of insanity and criminal conduct. Please continue, Mr. Murfee."

"Well, let's take apart what legal insanity is not. First, voluntary drug or alcohol consumption can't cause legal insanity?"

"No, voluntary intoxication is never a defense."

"It also doesn't include character defects or psychosexual disorders. Is there any indication in your workup that Sheila was suffering a character defect or psychosexual disorder when she pulled the trigger?"

"None whatsoever. That has never been a part of my findings."

"Directing your attention to mental disease or defect. These can form the basis for insanity in our state, correct?"

"Correct."

"Please relate your findings regarding Sheila Lowenstein's mental defect or disease, if any."

The doctor leaned forward and addressed his answer to the jury, "At the time of the shooting, Sheila Lowenstein believed Russell Lowenstein was about to injure her child yet again with another sexual assault. The child was underage and unable to consent to sex. Sheila was under the belief that she had to take matters into her own hands in order to protect her daughter. In some circles, she might be said to be suffering a mental defect by believing she had to take matters into her own hands. But, in other circles, she might be seen as totally sane in shooting Russell to end his sexual assaults on her daughter. The psychosis becomes apparent in Sheila where she cannot see any other course of action other than shooting. There were several other things she might have done, including going to the police and having them arrest Russell for sexual assault on a minor, statutory rape, battery, and the whole litany of other things his actions might have gotten him arrested for. But Sheila was incapable of seeing this, her psychosis was so strong. It is my belief that she suffered an overwhelming mental defect at the time of the shooting."

Thaddeus turned to the judge. "Judge Watertown, Dr. Mangrum's direct testimony ends at this point. I'm sure the State wishes to cross-examine."

Jon Logan was immediately on his feet and passing Thaddeus on his way to take over the lectern. "Dr. Mangrum, the defendant has a duty to prove to the jury by clear and convincing evidence that the defendant is guilty except insane. Do you believe your testimony is that strong that it rises to the level of clear and convincing?"

"I do."

"You are aware that Dr. Twyla Gilliam has also examined the defendant?"

"I'm aware that happens in all cases where the defendant has raised the insanity defense."

"And have you seen Dr. Gilliam's report?"

"Yes."

"Turning your attention to her report, do you see, on page two, under 'impressions,' where she states, 'I see no evidence of psychosis in this patient. She was aware and alert at all times and understood that what she was doing was wrong as evidenced by her visiting the office of Thaddeus Murfee and paying him one-hundred dollars to tell her what she should say to the police after she shot her husband. This clearly indicates she knew what she was about to do was wrong. There is no psychosis. There is no mental defect or disease.'"

"I see those comments, yes."

"Well, wouldn't you agree she did stop by Mr. Murfee's office and ask for his help?"

"Yes."

"And wouldn't you agree this amounts to a demonstration that she knew right from wrong?"

"It is some evidence. But I don't think it's conclusive, no."

"But it is enough evidence that the defendant cannot prove by clear and convincing evidence that she was insane, correct?"

Thaddeus stood. "Objection. The witness is being asked to invade the province of the jury."

"Yes, sustained. Please continue."

"You would agree that there is enough evidence of knowledge of right and wrong that it would rise to the level of your same certainty that she didn't know right from wrong?"

"I don't understand."

"Don't you believe that Dr. Gilliam's opinion cancels out your opinion?"

"Well, they're both opinions, certainly. Psychiatry isn't like other parts of medicine. There are no X-rays or CT scans or gauges capable of measuring our findings. So yes, in that sense, we physicians operate by our impressions and, in that sense, two doctors can certainly disagree."

"Which doesn't, of itself, make one doctor right and another doctor wrong, does it?"

"No."

"Tell the jury why Dr. Gilliam's findings are every bit as compelling as your findings."

"I didn't say they were."

"But you didn't say they weren't, either. We're exploring here, doctor. I want to know why you believe Dr. Gilliam's findings are incorrect."

"Because she says there was no psychosis at the moment of shooting. I happen to believe there was."

"So she says no and you say yes, and that's all that separates the two of you?"

"That's overly simplistic, but yes. We both have opinions only."

"Thank you, doctor. That is all."

With that, Jon Logan returned to counsel table, a satisfied smile on his face.

Thaddeus knew the damage was done. In fact, he had expected it to be done. But the point of Dr. Mangrum's testimony was to give Thaddeus a fact the jury could use in finding Sheila not guilty merely because they believed Russell Lowenstein got what he had coming to him. It gave them a way to do that. Which was all the lawyer needed. It was just a way out.

It was 4:40 p.m. Judge Watertown announced the court would stand in recess. There wasn't time to begin with another witness and only get down twenty minutes of testimony before stopping for the day. He stated he hated to bifurcate witness testimony, and they would begin fresh in the morning with the defense's next witness.

Thaddeus was given ten minutes to speak with Sheila before she was taken back to jail. It was good; he wanted to discuss with her where he saw things standing.

"Well, we haven't proven insanity by clear and convincing evidence," he told Sheila. "What we have is a pissing match between experts. That never wins cases."

"Yes, but they only offered me second degree murder when you met with Mr. Logan. I can't do that. Russell got what he deserved for raping PJ."

"I don't disagree that second degree murder is out. You're not guilty of second degree murder at all. Maybe manslaughter. According to ARS Section 13-1103, manslaughter is committed when a second degree murder is committed in the heat of passion due to provocation by the victim. It carries a sentence of three to twelve years of imprisonment in many cases. I've argued with Jon for manslaughter, but he stood firm on second degree. We might try manslaughter again with him now that Dr. Mangrum has testified. Except the doctor was pretty weak alongside Dr. Gilliam. So I'm stymied, truth be told. I don't want the jury to get this case because it's going to be hard for them to find you not guilty of anything since someone was shot and killed. If we can get a manslaughter plea with a recommendation of three years, that seems to be your best bet."

"I don't want to do any more time in jail. I can't stand it when I was justified in shooting the bastard. I did the State a favor."

"You've changed. At first you felt like you deserved to be in jail. Now you want out."

"I've gotten past my original guilties. The man had it coming, Thaddeus."

"I know your thinking, Sheila. I really do. Let's do this. Let me call Jon yet tonight. We can talk again and see where he is. Maybe he's come around somewhat."

"All right. But credit for time served."

"There's no such thing as credit for time served when the range is three years minimum, not that Judge Watertown is going to go along with that anyway. That's something Logan won't agree to and Watertown wouldn't allow. You're looking at three years, Sheila."

"What about defense of another? I thought we were going to claim I was defending her?"

"I think that's what the guilty-except-insane angle gets you. It's based on defense of another. I'm going to ask for an instruction based on 13-406, which says you're justified in using deadly physical force to protect PJ if you would be justified in using deadly physical force to protect yourself against the physical force the jury would believe is threatening PJ. That's called defense of another and it's a good defense, except you used deadly force to repel less than deadly force by Russell. The wrong jury could look right past this and still find you guilty on the basis you overreacted. And maybe you did. As you'll remember, Sheila, I wanted to call the cops and swear out a complaint against Russell. But you went ahead with deadly force where a warrant for his arrest would've stopped the sexual assaults.

"Don't rub my nose in it, Thaddeus," she said forcefully.

"I don't mean to throw this up in your face, but it's what you're facing because of your actions."

Her anger turned into a sigh. "No, I know you're not. I know you're only trying to guide me."

He pushed back from counsel table where they were sitting. "Absolutely. I'm just analyzing the case and sharing my thoughts out loud. This is how I spend my days, and today is your turn in the barrel. I think I need to call Jon Logan."

"Yes, emphasize the defense-of-another angle, please."

"I will, believe me. We've pled it as an affirmative defense so it won't be anything that isn't keeping Jon up worrying about. But there's one more thing. If we're going ahead with this defense-of-another, we'll need you to testify. I don't like that. In fact I always advise against it, but in this case, I think the jury needs to hear from you."

She smiled broadly. "Yes, they do need to hear from me. They'll get the surprise I promised you a long time ago, Thaddeus. Let me at them."

He leaned forward and lowered his voice. Guards were standing at the courtroom doors, and he didn't want them to hear what she was about to divulge. "What are we talking about, Sheila? And keep your voice down."

"We're talking about Russell's death. About how he died and why he died. Just put me on the stand and ask me why I did it. You're my attorney, and I'm instructing you that's how I want it done. Let me bare my soul to them. I'm only asking for my chance, Thaddeus."

"I can't argue with that," he said. "Will do." But there was something very wrong the way Sheila would hop from one side of the fence to another. He couldn't keep things straight and in parameters with Sheila. First, she was happy to stay in jail to do the time for the crime, but now she didn't want to be on the inside. And this "surprise" she had. That worried Thaddeus more than anything.

They broke off then, and Sheila was taken by the guards back to jail while Thaddeus headed for the hospital. Renny told him he'd be back to assist in the morning, and Thaddeus told him he'd see him then.

The court day was finally over.

31

Christine's heart was looking perfect, and her blood tests were all within normal limits. The medical staff was satisfied her hospital stay was secondary to Dr. Issyat's diagnosis of panic disorder. But it was decided a night in the hospital was warranted when the patient was less than stable, so they kept her overnight. Thaddeus dropped by after court and had supper with Christine in her room. Turquoise went home to make dinner for the younger kids. She would be bringing Christine home in the morning, anyway, and she had job-tasks to get done before then. After supper, Thaddeus went down to the family area and placed a call to Jon Logan's cell phone. It was answered on the second ring.

"Jon Logan, Thaddeus.

"Thaddeus. How's Christine tonight?"

"She's better, but they're keeping her over."

"Do you need time off in the morning? Is that why you're calling?"

"No, I'm calling about the case itself. I'd like to talk about a plea."

"I think my last offer was second degree. I'm pretty good with that still."

"I'm thinking manslaughter capped at three years. We've got a fairly good chance based on 'defense of another,' but I'm calling because it's the right thing to do, to try to settle before a jury gets the case and does Lord only knows what."

"There's always that, sure. I might be inclined to talk manslaughter but with a minimum of eight years. She did the deed, Thaddeus, and we know she wasn't insane at the time. Your Dr. Mangrum did you no favors today. I was watching the jury. They weren't taking notes and some of them looked like they were snoozing. I know Judge Watertown was paying very little attention once your witness brought up psychosis. Nobody's going to believe that, Thaddeus. So I'm thinking eight minimum."

"Give me five, and I'll talk to her."

"No can do, my friend. Eight minimum, and I'm not budging. You're already getting manslaughter down from second degree. At least let me save face around the office."

"I'm at five, maybe. You're stuck at eight. I'll talk to her first thing in the morning and get back to you, Jon. Fair enough?"

"Sure. Talk then."

The call terminated. Thaddeus slipped his cell phone back inside his suit pocket. He wondered what Sheila had in mind. His thoughts raced as he paced back to Christine's room, chewing his cheek in consternation. There was something about Sheila's readiness to testify. Most defendants were scared to death of testifying, but not Sheila. She was almost begging to get on the witness stand. He decided he never would understand Sheila Lowenstein.

But he wasn't going by the jail that night. She'd had his whole day; Christine got his whole night.

So he never left Christine's side.

IN THE MORNING, TURQUOISE BROUGHT A CLEAN SUIT, SHIRT, underwear, and a razor. Thaddeus prepared for court in Christine's bathroom. His head ached and his joints were crying out for activity since he had spent the entire night in an upholstered, non-reclining chair at Christine's bedside. If there was any sleeping, he couldn't remember when that might have been. After showering and dressing in a clean outfit, he was feeling more refreshed than he probably deserved, he had to admit. He kissed his wife, told her he'd see her at home after court, and left her with Turquoise, who was ready to pack up and leave when she was discharged.

THE DEPUTIES WERE LATE BRINGING SHEILA TO COURT. BUT WHEN she did arrive, Thaddeus passed her a note just before court began. It read: *I've got manslaughter + 5. Interested?* She read the note, took it in her right hand, balled it up, and tossed it into the wastebasket. Then she waved him off. There was his answer.

Today she was wearing a business suit with a blue pencil skirt and matching jacket and a lavender blouse underneath. She'd been dressing up for her trial as Thaddeus had instructed, but today her hair was clipped back in a barrette and she was wearing makeup.

As much as she drove him crazy with her own crazy, he couldn't blame her for not taking the deal. Five years was an entire lifetime in prison. She preferred to roll the dice, and he couldn't argue with that.

Judge Watertown took the bench, and the clerk called court to order.

"Mr. Murfee, please call your next witness."

Sheila elbowed him in the side. Her meaning was clear. But just then, just as he was about to say her name, PJ came into the courtroom, and Sheila touched Thaddeus on the elbow. "Call PJ," she said. "She wants to clear up what happened."

"What?" he whispered. "I thought you didn't want her to testify!"

"I changed my mind."

Of course, she did. That had been her *modus operandi* ever since he met her. "But, Sheila, that's the reason you tried to kill yourself. To keep PJ from having to go through exactly what you want her to do today."

Again, in that laissez-faire way of hers, she waved Thaddeus off. "Teenagers want to be heard these days, Thaddeus. Let PJ have her say."

Thaddeus couldn't delay another second. The judge was impatient as well as the jury. In his strongest voice, he announced, "The defense calls Patricia Jean Walston to the stand."

PJ, head held high, walked boldly to the witness stand and seated herself. Her long blond hair was in a French braid down her back and she was wearing a light blue A-shaped dress with a thin black belt around her middle that matched her flat shoes. She placed both hands on the desk before her and looked at her mom, then at Thaddeus.

"State your name."

"Patricia Jean Walston."

"How old are you?"

"Fourteen."

"Are you related to the defendant, Sheila Lowenstein?"

"I'm her daughter. Jim Sam Walston is my dad."

"Are you in school?"

"SF Fees High School. I'm a freshman."

"Were you present in the office of Russell Lowenstein the day he died?"

"Yes."

"What was Mr. Lowenstein to you?"

"My stepdad and my rapist."

A collective gasp went up from the jury. All eyes were fastened on the witness. This wasn't at all what they were expecting.

"Your stepdad was raping you? How many times did he rape you?"

"I didn't count. But it would be ten at least."

Thaddeus counted slowly to ten. He wanted her number to sink in with the jury. Ten rapes? Surely, they understood the hell she'd been put through by Russell Lowenstein.

"How did you feel when Russell Lowenstein died?"

"Happy. Free."

"Did you see him die?"

"Of course, I did."

"What do you mean, 'of course?'"

"I mean, of course I saw him die. I shot him."

This time the jury gasped out loud. Several dropped their Spiral steno books. Two ladies broke into tears and smiles; they were nodding. It looked like they might even break out in applause.

"Ladies and gentlemen," intoned Judge Watertown. "If we could all just relax and let the testimony come out. Let's try not to react out loud, shall we?"

A million thoughts flashed through Thaddeus's mind. But one key thought took root and blossomed up through his being: double jeopardy. The jury had been sworn. If the charges against Sheila went away, she could never be tried again. Just then, Thaddeus got it. He understood everything perfectly. He had been used.

But he didn't mind. If not him, someone else. This was their whole game coming to a head.

"You shot Russell Lowenstein?"

"I did. I can prove it, too."

"How can you prove it?"

"I have the gun, and it has my fingerprints. It doesn't have my mom's prints, and I'm betting everyone here it doesn't have her DNA, either. You've got a gun with my prints, my DNA, in my possession where no one else can find it, and you've got my testimony. You've got me, Your Honor, and ladies and gentlemen. Now please let my mom go. You've got the wrong person."

"Patricia Jean, where is the gun right now?" Thaddeus asked.

"At home in my dictionary on my bookcase in my room. I cut out the pages in a long rectangle and hid the gun there. It's waiting for the police to come get it."

District Attorney Jon Logan struggled to his feet as his chief investigator, Jason Landis, tried to pull him back down for a whisper. Logan said, "Your Honor, the State claims surprise. This is an undisclosed witness. A—a—"

Thaddeus didn't hesitate. "The witness was disclosed. The State chose not to talk to her. We still don't know why that was. In the same vein, though, I had no idea what the witness was going to say until she took the stand, either. I haven't failed to disclose anything because I didn't know anything. Now, I suggest the State send an officer to the witness's home and retrieve the dictionary from her bedroom. We can all wait here, Judge, and once the dictionary is brought here, I'll question the witness about its contents."

Judge Watertown took charge of his courtroom. "The court is sending the courtroom deputy to the witness's home. He will seize the dictionary and its contents and bring those, without delay, to this courtroom. He will not open the dictionary but will preserve its contents unseen until the court orders further. We'll stand in recess pending his return."

The courtroom turned into a mob scene as media reporters hauled out iPads and cell phones and began linking up to their outlets. The reporter from the *Arizona Daily Sun*, Flagstaff's own paper, made her call to her editor. The story would be held open right up to the time of publication. What was known then would be published then, right on page one.

Thaddeus needed air. He broke for the courtroom doors and bolted downstairs and outside. There, he stood on the top step and waited for Renny to catch up. Renny was Thaddeus's heir apparent, the lawyer tagged with taking over more and more of Thaddeus's daily duties with an eye that Thaddeus would retire from the practice of law in five years. At least, that was the plan.

Renny approached, running a black hand across his black beard. "Whoa, Nelly," he said. "Never saw that one coming."

"I know," Thaddeus said. "I know."

"First thoughts?"

"I'm like a Stradivarius, Renny. I've been played by the best."

"Ouch! Well said."

"As I've heard you say, Renny, that's gangster."

"Gangsta. But never mind. So what happens now? Does Sheila walk?"

"If the gun is what PJ says it is, they have to dismiss the charges against Sheila and go after PJ. Justice cries out and all that."

"Indeed."

"This is why we never believe our clients. We can like them, even love them, but we can never believe them. All statements are subject to investigation and verification. All of it."

"What would you have done differently, Thaddeus?"

"Seriously? I can't think of anything, Renny. Not a blessed damn thing."

ONE HOUR LATER, COURT WAS CALLED INTO SESSION BY JUDGE Watertown. The courtroom deputy sent on the errand was back, holding a battered black briefcase in his left hand. His right hand rested on the butt of his gun. He eyed anyone with great suspicion who might venture within five feet. Then he heard the judge directing him to deliver the briefcase to Detective Landis, seated beside DA Jon Logan. Detective Landis, said the judge, would open the briefcase and the suspect dictionary. If there was a gun, he would know how to handle it to preserve any trace and transfer evidence for the crime lab.

The deputy did as ordered, handing off the briefcase to Detective Landis, and then took a seat at his desk. His face had remained unchanged. However, his hand no longer hovered near the handle of his gun.

"Please, Detective, open the briefcase and the dictionary."

Landis did as ordered. Out came the thick book, red and white with bold black lettering. He opened the cover and stared down at his find. Ever so carefully, he lifted the dictionary and held it aloft for the judge and jury to view. There, exactly as promised by PJ Walston, was tucked the 9mm gun that, Thaddeus knew, would prove to have fired the bullet that killed Russell Lowenstein. Thaddeus also knew the gun would give up the fingerprints and DNA of PJ Walston, but that neither her mother's prints nor DNA would be found there.

"Ladies and gentlemen," said the Judge, "the clerk will mark the item as *Court's Exhibit 1.*"

The clerk went to the DA's table, took the dictionary/gun combo from the detective, and returned to her desk and her press-on exhibit labels. While she did her work marking and recording, the judge said for the record, "Detective Landis will resume custody of *Court's Exhibit 1* and transfer it without delay to the Arizona Crime Lab with a court order commanding the crime lab to cease all other work and test the exhibit for any and all forensic evidence it might contain. The exhibit and the crime lab report will be returned to the court by eight a.m. tomorrow morning. We stand in recess until nine a.m. Remember the court's admonition."

Thaddeus stood up from counsel table and began angrily slamming his law books and files into his briefcase while Sheila waited for the guards to come take her away.

"You're lucky I didn't know about this scheme ahead of time," he bitterly exclaimed to Sheila Lowenstein.

She smiled. "You did know, Thaddeus. You were told I had something up my sleeve."

"You're very lucky, Sheila."

"I am, Thaddeus. Which is why I came to hire you. I needed more than luck. I needed you."

He suddenly calmed down. "Soothe me with your words, would you?"

Sheila smiled at him. "See, I know much more about you than you do about me."

"Spare me."

They had her up now, on her feet, fastening the handcuffs around her wrists from behind. "Before we forget, Thaddeus, let's remember how we got here. Child sexual assault? Of my child? And what, I'm just going to go away? We're here because Russell raped the wrong daughter of the wrong wife. Now tell me there's any other kind of justice in this case than where we're headed now. I thought not. Go home, Thaddeus. Go take care of your wife and kids. If you don't, someone else will, and you don't want that. Take it from someone who's learned."

With that, she was taken away.

Thaddeus was at a loss for words. Even Renny seemed preoccupied with the task of packing four briefcases and managing them back down the street.

He went downstairs and fled the courthouse, jogging across the street to his truck. He climbed in, slammed the door, and jabbed the starter with his forefinger. The big RAM roared to life. He laid ten feet of rubber before coming to his senses and applying the brakes. Then finally he edged around the corner within the speed limit. He was sure Turquoise had Christine home by now. It was time to go there and be at peace.

Only God knew what was coming in the morning.

But Thaddeus reserved the right to guess.

32

"Defense calls Matthew Grayson."

A young, blond crewcut police officer—in the uniform of the Flagstaff PD—strode forward into the courtroom and took a seat in the witness chair.

"State your name and occupation."

"Matthew Grayson, patrol officer, Flagstaff Police Department."

"You were on duty the day Russell Lowenstein was gunned down?"

"I was."

"Tell us what you observed that day regarding the gunshot residue test performed on Sheila Lowenstein."

"I was one of the first officers on the Russell Lowenstein homicide dispatch. I was the first one through the door of the sale barn. I went inside the Lowenstein office with my gun out and ready to return fire. I didn't know—nobody did—if we had a live shooter situation there or not."

"Was there a live shooter?"

"Sheila Lowenstein said she was the shooter, so yes, there was a live shooter, but there was no gun. I helped search inside and out for it."

"Back to the gunshot residue test. Sheila had no gun when you came in, and her daughter had no gun?"

"No. I'm the officer who patted both of them down. I also searched a backpack and the mother's fanny pack."

"You were giving Mrs. Lowenstein a drink of water when the detectives arrived?"

"Like I told you before, Mr. Murfee, she was completely cried out and very dry."

"Did you see any of the water get on her hands?"

"I was standing two feet away. No water ever got on her hands. I saw the GSR test administered. It was negative."

"The detectives said it was inconclusive."

"They're wrong. She tested negative. I saw the whole thing."

"So she hadn't fired a gun?"

"Not from the GSR test she hadn't."

"GSR is the gunshot residue?"

"Yes. The test was conclusive. She hadn't fired a gun."

"Did the District Attorney or his investigator interview you?"

"Yes. I told her the same thing."

"Which was the test that would rule out Sheila as a shooter?"

"That's right."

"But the State didn't call you as witness?"

"No. You called me, sir."

Jon Logan was then given his opportunity to question the witness.

"Officer Grayson, you weren't there when the shooting occurred?"

"No."

"Do you know anyone who was?"

"Yes, the decedent, the defendant, and the daughter."

"Immediately after the shooting, isn't it possible the mother went into the bathroom and washed her hands?"

"Anything's possible, sir."

"Well, do you know she didn't?"

"She would have to know about GSR. But I guess everyone does now with all the CSI TV shows."

"So, she might've been the shooter?"

"So could the daughter, sir. Nobody tested the daughter."

The courtroom was silent, only breathing could be heard. Thaddeus had purposely not asked the question about the daughter. He left that for Logan to stumble over.

"You mean no one tested the daughter that you saw?"

"That's correct, sir."

"Did you view the daughter the entire time you were there?"

"Yes, sir, and nobody did GSR testing on her hands or clothes."

"But they were taken into another room?"

"I accompanied them, sir. I was the arresting officer. No testing in the second room, either."

"Did anyone test Sheila Lowenstein's clothes?"

"I don't know, sir."

Logan turned from the lectern, "That is all, Your Honor."

Judge Watertown: "Officer Grayson, you're excused. Thank you for coming."

33

The judge had added a court's witness, the representative from the crime lab, who performed the tests Judge Watertown ordered. DA Jon Logan was selected to present the witness's testimony, even though, it would turn out, the testimony and evidence severely damaged his case against the mother, Sheila Lowenstein. The court required that this be done nonetheless because the court, as the judge put it, was on a fact-finding mission, not a fact-obscuring mission. Judge Watertown wanted the truth more than he wanted a conviction.

Corie Hertzenrather from the Arizona Crime Lab had done more than just a workup on the outer surfaces of the Model 59 Smith. She had also worked up the outside—and inside—surfaces of the Merriam Webster dictionary the gun was found lodged within. She gathered all of her 5-2 frame, dressed in a pair of khaki trousers and pink polo shirt, pulled herself upright in the witness chair, and launched into her testimony with the aplomb of someone who had been testifying for years whereas, in truth, she was a newbie to the entire courtroom task.

She clasped her hands in front of her in her lap. "First off, I removed the firearm from the dictionary where it was lodged. I examined the weapon for both DNA and fingerprints, all trace and transfer."

"What did you find out about the gun?" asked Jon Logan.

"I compared the oils found on the gun to DNA from the hair sample supplied by Patricia Jean Walston. There was a match. The mathematical probabilities of the match being another human are so impossibly small as not to even register, not a number with enough decimal places to tell us anything useful."

"Were there fingerprints?"

"Some portions, some partial prints. I compared what I could to the fingerprints of Patricia Jean Walston and determined the partials—those I could verify—were all hers."

"What about analysis of the gun to the gun that fired the fatal shots?"

"Same gun. The firearms identification analysis matched the fatal bullet exactly."

"So this was the gun that killed Russell Lowenstein?"

"Beyond all doubt, it is."

"In summary?"

"In summary, the gun was handled by one person, and that was Patricia Jean Walston. In summary, the gun killed Russell Lowenstein."

"But you didn't stop with the gun, correct?"

"That's right. I also examined the dictionary itself. The interior of the book had been removed in a rectangular fashion. Who did this work? We located a Swiss Army knife in the subject's bedroom desk, third drawer down, right-hand side. On the largest cutting blade of the knife, I was able to locate particulates, pieces of paper, that matched the composition and striations of the dictionary pages removed."

"So you're telling us someone used the knife in PJ's bedroom to remove the pages where the gun was hidden?"

"Exactly. Whoever owned that knife had used it—or allowed it be used—to remove those pages."

"Anything else?"

"Yes, I located two complete girl scout uniforms in the closet in that bedroom. I didn't draw conclusions from those uniforms."

"But you might have thought perhaps the girl scout owned a Swiss Army knife?"

"That would have been one avenue of thinking had I been so inclined to conjecture, but I wasn't so inclined."

"Let me make sure I understand then, Ms. Hertzenrather. The gun and the dictionary where it was hidden were both covered with body oil—DNA—and fingerprints belonging only to Patricia Jean Walston—PJ?"

"That is correct."

"Was there any testing done to learn whether the mother's DNA or prints were on the book or the gun?"

"Testing, yes. Did I find any? None."

"By the way, what is the length of the pages in the Merriam-Webster dictionary?"

"9.9 inches."

"And the length of the Model 59 Smith and Wesson nine millimeter gun?"

"7.55 inches."

"So the gun easily fit inside the book?"

"Yes, easily."

"That is all, Your Honor."

Judge Watertown told Thaddeus he could cross-examine.

"Ms. Hertzenrather, I appreciate the thoroughness of your workup, but tell me this. Was there any possibility the gun had been scrubbed to remove the mother's DNA and fingerprints altogether?"

"I found no cleaning substance residue. I tested."

"So nobody had washed the gun with a chemical cleaner?"

"No."

"But still, it could've happened, and you might not have detected it?"

She shrugged. "Anything is possible, Mr. Murfee."

"So you have ruled out my client, Sheila Lowenstein, as a person who handled that gun."

"There is no evidence from the crime lab to support any claim your client handled the gun."

Which was exactly the testimony Thaddeus was after. He decided to leave it right there. It didn't get any better than that. "No further questions."

"Nothing further," said Jon Logan.

The courtroom was very silent, very still, after Corie Hertzen-rather climbed down from the witness stand and left the court-room. Then Judge Watertown asked a question of District Attorney Jon Logan.

"Mr. Logan, does the State have a motion to make?"

Logan, pale and not his usual hard-charging self, climbed to his feet and said in a shallow, impossibly small voice, "Your Honor, the State dismisses the indictment against Sheila Lowenstein. I don't do this lightly. While it might be possible to take this matter to the jury and perhaps even get a conviction, the State doesn't believe justice would be served by doing that. Clearly, by her own admission and by the findings of the Arizona State Crime Lab, Patricia Jean Walston was the shooter here. The mother, in her confessions to the police, was simply covering for her daughter. For these reasons, we dismiss the charges and ask the court to dismiss the jury."

"Mr. Murfee?" said the judge.

"It's the right thing to do," said Thaddeus.

It was all said and done.

"The court dismisses the jury. All charges against Sheila Lowen-stein are dismissed. Jeopardy has attached, and so the charges cannot be refiled since double jeopardy now prevents that. The defendant is free to leave at this time. Thanks to the jury for its service. Court stands in recess."

Standing there, receiving hugs from Sheila Lowenstein, Thaddeus couldn't help but think about the video testing he'd had done. That testing had measured the size of Sheila and the size of PJ. Sheila was ruled in as the shooter; PJ was ruled out. He was already wondering whether he would use that video in the upcoming defense of PJ Walston. But then he remembered: his license was suspended as to new cases. He wouldn't be defending PJ; it would be someone else's problem. Maybe Shep's, if Thaddeus had a say in it.

He could work with Shep.

34

S he looked tiny, maybe a size two, thought Thaddeus when PJ answered the door.

"C'mon in, please," said the high school freshman. "What happened at the grand jury today?"

"You were indicted. You'll remain free until the initial appearance tomorrow."

It was a new case, but Thaddeus had called the State Bar Counsel. Thaddeus had said he was considering going to the media and telling them about his suspension, that it was preventing him from defending the daughter of his client. The Bar had wisely decided it didn't need the negative publicity and had, without comment, signed the stipulation to allow Thaddeus to defend the PJ Walston case because it flowed out of the Sheila Lowenstein case and was the same family. It was a smart move on Thaddeus's part; the State Bar certainly wasn't required to do it.

Thaddeus took the beige wingback offered in the formal living room. It was covered in mauve peacocks and was tall enough to accommodate his frame. PJ sat across from him in a bentwood rocker. She kept both feet flat on the floor to prevent rocking. *Or,* thought Thaddeus, *she's trying to make her world stand still. Massive changes for her.*

"Mom!" she called toward the connecting room, "Mr. Murfee's here!"

In the next instant, Sheila was walking in, drying her hands on a paper towel. She approached Thaddeus and hugged him. "My hero, right here."

He smiled and took a step back. "I don't think I'm anybody's hero. I'm still in shock the case against you went away like it did. Bam, and we were done. That was quite a show you two put on."

Sheila took a chair beside Thaddeus. She looked at him quizzically. "Show? That wasn't a show, Thaddeus. A mother trying to protect her daughter is liable to tell the police anything. That's all it was."

"Yes, but then PJ coming in and blowing the lid off the trial—I have to admit I didn't see it coming. Neither did Jon Logan. Neither did Judge Watertown."

"It didn't surprise me," said PJ. "I knew all along I had to get up and tell the truth. It was my shooting. I owed mom."

He sat back. With PJ to his left and Sheila to his right in an easy chair, he felt like he could be caught up in a crossfire, situated between them as he was. He smiled at the notion. "How about we get down to the real deal?" he said. "Let's start by telling me who really did shoot Russ?"

PJ didn't miss a beat. "I shot him. Bastard had it coming. Excuse my French, Mom."

"I shot him," Sheila said with a laugh. "Maybe we both shot him."

And even now, they both treated it like a game. He gritted his teeth so he wouldn't tell both of them off right here and now. "Seriously, I need to know."

"Me," said PJ.

"Listen to PJ," said Sheila. "It's her turn. She got herself into this now." And with those words, the caring, protective "Mom" character flew out the window. In all his years as a trial attorney, he'd met his share of characters, but none of them compared to these two.

"PJ, tell me what happened that day," Thaddeus said. "Don't leave anything out. Incidentally, I'm going to record your statement. I don't want to be in the middle of any further surprises down the road."

He switched on his phone and began recording. "All right now," he said to PJ with a nod.

"Russ caught me in our barn early that morning. I was haying Susie when he came up behind me and squeezed my breast. I kicked backward, but only caught him in the leg. Then he threw me down on the hay and screwed me. It wasn't the first time he'd caught me in the barn. I never knew when it was coming next."

Thaddeus knew for a fact from the video that Russ had been at the office that morning, so if he had caught her at the barn, it would have to have been much earlier in the morning, only for him to return to the office so he could be caught on tape.

"Did you ever tell your mom about the rapes?"

"No, because he said it would kill her. He said she would shoot him and go to prison for the rest of her life. I definitely didn't want that because I felt like I was doing something wrong. I didn't want mom paying for my sin."

Again, completely contradictory to what Sheila had said, which was that she found PJ crying that morning.

"You viewed it like a sin?"

"I did. My mom is a pastor at our church, and I'm very familiar with the doctrine in the Bible. I've been taught what is right and wrong. I thought I was at fault somehow. He made me think that, too, telling me how I was always posing around the house and provoking him. Especially a year ago when I was thirteen. I believed him then. Talk about gullible!"

"Take us on through the morning you shot him."

"When he rolled off me, I felt dirty. So I pulled up my shorts and gave Susie her oats, then went back into the house and took a shower. I still had school that day. I was still planning on going by his office first and getting my 4-H check. Once I got it into the bank, I was going to get my own apartment. I know, nobody's going to rent an apartment to a fourteen year old, but I was desperate. If I told my real dad, he would kill Russ and go to jail. So I was thinking if I could only get away, get my own apartment, I could solve the problem and still keep my mom and dad. I was going to try to find some NAU students sharing a house who wanted to take in a roommate. That would have been perfect for me."

"Okay, you took a shower, then what?"

"I climbed out of the shower, wiped the steam off the bathroom mirror, and looked at myself. I had a bright handprint on my boob where he grabbed me and wouldn't let go. I started crying. Then I slumped down on the floor and just let it all out. I cried without making a sound for about five minutes. Then I reached over to the toilet paper and started wiping my nose and blowing and wiping my eyes. All of a sudden, I was done. I felt strong then, but I don't know why. I'd never felt strong like that before. I don't know where it was coming from. So I sat there and thought and thought. Then I remembered. Mom had brought home a new gun. I saw it in her bedside table when I was looking for batteries. I decided to take her gun and go in and shoot Russ. So I did. I went to the sale barn, and he started writing out my 4-H check. I was going to wait—"

"Excuse me, PJ, but wait for what or when?"

She raised her shoulders to her ears. "I dunno. Wait for a better time I guess."

Thaddeus made some notes. "Sorry, please continue."

"All of a sudden, I needed to shoot him like it was the most important thing I was ever going to do. I unzipped my backpack, reached in, and jerked the gun out. He had his head down looking at the check on his desk. I said, "Hey, Russ!" and he looked up. The last thing he saw was me shooting him."

It appeared from PJ's testimony just now that Thaddeus wasn't going to get the truth from the daughter either. Either her mother hadn't told her or her mom didn't know either, but Thaddeus was on the other end of the phone when Russ was shot, and that wasn't how it went down at all.

"What happened next?"

"My mom came in. She jerked the gun away and told me she was going to say she shot him. I told her he raped me. She said she knew all about it. I don't know how she knew, and I don't know why she never did anything if she did know."

Again, their stories didn't agree. Sheila had told Thaddeus she'd found PJ crying in her room that morning, that she'd had no idea what Russ was doing to her daughter. And it was interesting to Thaddeus that her mother wasn't defending herself now.

Thaddeus didn't interrupt this time, and PJ continued, "I was just lost all of a sudden. I took the gun back and said I would hide it. I put it in my backpack and took it home with me that day. I washed it with soap and water and carved out a hiding place in my dictionary."

"Why did you wash it?"

"CSI. All those shows about DNA. I didn't want Mom's DNA on the gun."

"What about the police? Didn't they search your bag?"

"Not right away. I took my bag outside and strapped it to my bike with a bungee cord. I re-locked my bike lock around the bag. Then I slipped the gun out of the bag and hid it."

"Where did you hide it?"

"Dot's car was parked right in front of the sale barn like always. I took the gun and hid it on top of the tire and went back inside. I knew her car wasn't going anywhere."

"Wow. Very clever."

"Hey, I've been watching crime shows since I was three. You're bound to learn something. Then, when they let me go, I grabbed the gun and rode my bike home. That was how it happened, Mr. Murfee."

"Thanks, PJ. I know how tough it is for you right now. But there is work we need to get after. One thing I don't quite follow. He just raped you that morning. Yet you went to his office where you were alone with him? Who would do that?"

"I had to have my money so I could move out. All I could think of was getting away. I didn't even think about him. Besides, I knew Dot and other people were around the office."

"Dot said there wasn't anyone else there that morning other than herself. Did you see someone else?"

She hesitated, just a brief moment, and he knew he'd caught her off-script. She hadn't practiced this part. "No, but there are usually other people there."

"I see. Go on."

" The whole point is I didn't feel alone with him. I had the gun. I knew I could protect myself."

"Pretty damn hard, nevertheless."

PJ lifted her right foot then immediately put it down. "Not really so hard. He got what he had coming to him. I knew I would shoot him if I had to."

"Let me ask you a couple of specifics. He was writing you a check?"

"Yes. I netted over twelve-hundred dollars on my cow."

"You must be proud!"

"It was okay. Except Russ caught me in the barn a lot. I never want to go in a barn again."

"What were you wearing that day, PJ?"

"Jeans, Patagonia T-shirt, and shell."

"Did the coat have pockets?"

"Pockets for your hands? Yeah."

"You're sure the gun came to the office inside your coat and not your mom's?"

PJ leaped to her feet, placed her hands on her hips, and bent forward. "What's the matter with you? Mom said you were here to help us, not get her in the middle of my fight."

"Sorry, PJ. Please sit down. It's just my job to ask everything I can think of. I'm going to write down that you brought the gun. By the way, do you know where your mom got the gun?"

"No. There was one in the chamber, too."

"One in the chamber? Are you a shooter, PJ?"

"Russ taught me to shoot. He did stuff with me like that. Sometimes I didn't hate him, not before it started happening."

"So you knew where the gun was kept, you were angry at Russ, and you were going to his office that morning to get money for the cow he made you sell. Is that about right?"

"Yes."

"When did your mom find out Russ was sexually assaulting you?"

"Sunday night. I broke down crying. She finally got it out of me."

"You sure it wasn't Monday morning?"

She made a face at Thaddeus, the kind only a teenager had the capability of making with lots of venom and spite. "I should know!"

"Okay," he placated PJ, "what was her reaction when you told her?"

"She got very quiet and her mouth was hard. When Mom goes quiet, you want to look out. And when her teeth are clenched like that, you've had it."

"Did she confront Russ that night?"

"No, it was a sale day and he slept on his couch at the sale barn because he waited until everyone got paid."

"So if he raped you in the barn the morning after the sale, he must have left his office early to get home to find you there. Am I right?"

She shifted in her chair. "Yeah, maybe he only came home to get his rocks off and then went back to the office. I dunno."

Thaddeus nodded and jotted another note onto his pad. "So he didn't come home that night, and you went out there for a check the next morning after he raped you. If everyone got paid the same day as the sale, why were you not getting paid until the next day?"

"Because my check was coming from the sale barn itself. That's who bought my cow. And Bernice has to sign the checks and wouldn't be there until Monday morning. So I waited on my check. Mom went to see you, then she came in after I shot Russ, and that was the end of that."

"Did you ever get your check?"

"I did. Bernice mailed it to me."

"Has your mom ever told you what she discussed with me as her lawyer?"

"She told me she told you she was going to kill Russ."

"She did? What did I say to do?"

"You said she should try counseling. Something lame, excuse me."

"Did I try to stop your mom?"

"She said that was the funny thing. She told you she was going to kill Russ, but you didn't try to warn him. I wonder why…" She smirked, but tried to hide it behind her hand.

"So what did you think after you shot Russ?"

"The sound was real loud, but no one came in. Then my mom got there."

"Did she say anything?"

"She said, 'I'll say I did it. It's all I know to do to protect you, PJ.' Something like that."

"Like she did it to protect you?"

"Yes. Who can blame her for protecting her kid?"

Thaddeus nodded. "Exactly. It's called defense of another, and it's an affirmative defense. I think it was working until you confessed."

"Sorry to ruin your trial, Mr. Murfee."

Thaddeus stood up. He dropped his phone into his jacket pocket. "Well, thank you."

"We're done already?"

"For now. If the case goes to trial, then we'll spend several days getting you ready, PJ. In the meantime, please don't talk to the cops. You don't have to talk to them if you don't want."

Thaddeus went to leave but turned back around. "By the way, did the police ever swab your hands for gunshot residue?"

"No."

"Not even after you told them you handled the gun?"

"I didn't tell them I handled the gun."

"Did you handle it?"

PJ sighed. "Are we finished here?"

"One thing. I got the DA to agree you'd remain free and report to court tomorrow with me. With any luck, we'll get bail tomorrow, and you'll leave with me, too."

"I'm glad."

"Thank you, PJ." He turned to PJ's mother who hadn't said one word since she'd sat down. "Thanks, Sheila."

He held out his hand to his new client.

PJ gave him a brief, weak handshake, and then Thaddeus was gone.

35

That afternoon, Sheila got hold of Thaddeus on the second ring.

"Thaddeus, Sheila Lowenstein here."

"Hey, what's up?"

"Tomorrow you have PJ's initial appearance. When the jail sets her bail, I want you to know that I've got the money to bail her out. I can do a million with a call to the bank."

Thaddeus was glad to hear the news, if not a little surprised. He hadn't expected the family of Russell Lowenstein to have that kind of money within easy reach. Given Russ's dalliances and their inevitable cost, he would've guessed Russ had his sale barn assets and not much more. But now here was Sheila saying she was easily liquid. With her own bail, money had always been a concern. It was good to know, if not a little puzzling.

"Well, we'll soon know what her bail is going to look like."

"Here's something I wanted to ask this morning. Tell me the truth. Were you surprised they prosecuted PJ as an adult? She's only fourteen."

"No, our statute is pretty clear. Fourteen and over go in as adults for first and second degree murder. Or any other violent felony. It's not hard to be tried as an adult in Arizona, Sheila."

"Well, she's got the money for bail. Just wanted you to know. Also, she's not guilty. You've never let me testify, but I can prove it was me, Thaddeus."

Thaddeus was floored, even when he shouldn't have been. "You can prove it was you who shot Russ?"

"Yes."

"Don't get me started, Sheila."

"I dare you, Thaddeus. Just put me on the witness stand, and my daughter goes free."

He sighed. The gamesmanship was terribly top heavy. "All right. I'll keep that in mind. But in the meantime, I think I'll put together her self-defense case and see where that goes."

"What of self-defense? Is that what you're trying?"

"Self-defense in Arizona is very clear. Let's say PJ walked into Russ's office to get her 4-H check. Let's say she's waiting, having been raped that morning by Russ, and she believes he's going to rape her again at any minute."

"What about the CCTV? Doesn't his office video have to show he was coming after her? What they showed during my trial didn't have any of that."

"The argument is that she knows what body language precedes a rape. Maybe it's how he suddenly starts to get up or looks at her with an evil intent. The point is, when the jury hears about the earlier morning rape, they're going to forgive her for shooting him if there's even the slightest indication he was about to do it again. She can say what she needs to say, and the State can't beat her because its witness is dead. PJ wins."

"How do you prove the earlier rape? She took a shower and washed herself. There's no medical workup, no DNA."

"I know. It gets tricky."

"Did you ask her what else he did to her?"

There was a moment of silence. "What do you mean, what else he did to her?"

There was a moment of silence on the line, and then, "I'm still so enraged over this I can't even think straight. Russ injured a college girl. We had to pay her out of our homeowner's insurance for what he did to her."

"What did he do?"

"He bit her."

"Bit her? Where?"

"On her vagina. Left teeth marks. Even broke the skin. She went to the college infirmary and a pre-med nurse took pictures and video. Then her lawyer had a forensic dentist make casts of the bite marks and photographs. They made Russ give a sample of his bite and compared them. It came back 99% it was Russ."

"Where was this?"

"In Phoenix last year. We were on vacation. He had a late night down at the hotel bar. The girl's boyfriend found our room the next day. I thought he was going to kill Russ, but she was able to talk him down. But her family sued us."

"Why hasn't anyone told me this before?"

"I just found out that Russ bit PJ last night, Thaddeus. So I'm telling you now."

Thaddeus's words came quickly, spilling out. "Find out if Russ bit PJ the morning of the murder or even the week leading up to the shooting. Ask her now, please. Then call me right back."

"All right, Thaddeus."

Fifteen minutes later, she called back. "He did bite her that morning, the frigging animal!"

"Okay, I've got an odontologist for her to see. When I get her out on bail, you'll take her there."

"What's an odontologist?"

"A bite mark specialist. If I can show the jury that PJ had bite marks and prove they were from Russ, I can prove self-defense by showing an imminent threat. That he had just raped her that morning and would again now that they were alone."

"All right."

"It's very important, Sheila. I need bite mark impressions, and I need the name of the lawyer who represented the first bite mark girl. Can you get me his name?"

"Yes, I know it's in the file. Can I bring it tomorrow to court?"

"No, go look it up and call me back. This is critical for PJ's defense."

She called back thirty minutes later. "Okay, the girl's lawyer is Shelly Hansen out of Peoria, Arizona. She's a domestic violence specialist but got involved in the Phoenix case against Russ because the girl who was bitten was her sister."

"Her sister? Ouch! That made it hard for Russ to dodge that bullet. How much did they settle for?"

"The whole policy. I think it was five-hundred-thousand."

"Do you happen to have Shelly's phone number?"

"No, but I checked the state bar directory. She's still in Peoria."

"Good enough. I'm going to call her right now."

"Call me back, please."

"Will do."

Thaddeus dialed the Peoria number. There was a wait, but he was told Ms. Hansen would be on the line momentarily.

Several minutes later came a female voice. "This is Shelly Hansen."

"Hi, Shelly, Attorney Thaddeus Murfee, Flagstaff. I've got a case where the same man who bit your sister bit my client."

"That fucking animal! Someone needs to euthanize that bastard."

"Uh, someone did. His victim this time shot him in the face. He's dead."

"Good riddance! Well, how can I help, Thaddeus? Need Russ's old bite marks?"

"I do."

"All right, but they'll cost you."

Thaddeus held the phone out and made a face. "Really? How much."

"Just kidding! I'll drive them to you myself if it'll help your girl."

"Well, she's been charged with murder. I'm going to allege self-defense, that she'd been bitten and knew it was imminent again. But I need to show the rape from earlier in the day and need the bite marks to prove it was his teeth that left the marks on her vagina."

"Got it. Let me put together a package and FedEx it. You'll have everything tomorrow. Does that help, Thaddeus?"

"Honestly, that would be great. Even better if you forward the records directly to Dr. D.E. Eamons on Camelback."

"Oh, I know Ellison Eamons. He's fantastic. We used him for my sister's case. I'll have someone hand deliver a release today. Then he can use Russell Lowenstein's records right out of my sister's file. It's probably the same bite mark unless someone wants to claim his bite mark's changed."

Thaddeus said, "If they do, I'll dig the son of a bitch up and take another impression. I'm dead serious."

"I like you already."

"Thanks so much for your help."

"Consider it payback to the bastard. Your girl deserves a medal with a big pink ribbon on it. Call me if you need anything else."

"I will. So long, now."

They disconnected the call. One down, thought Thaddeus. That would cover the biter's evidence. Now he needed to cover the bitee's marks. He dialed PJ's cell.

"Hi, Thaddeus. Mom said I could use your name. Hope that's okay."

"Are you at school?"

"Cafeteria. We're having advanced English class here. It's the only available space."

"Can I get you to drive down to Phoenix with me tomorrow after court?"

"Can my mom go, too?"

"Of course. I need you to see an expert witness."

"Who?"

"A doctor who will measure the bite marks Russell Lowenstein left with you."

"They were gross. I looked with a mirror. But they're barely there anymore. I shot him three months ago."

"We'll let the doctor still take a look, okay?"

"Yes. We'll be leaving after court?"

"We will. I'll probably have my wife along, too. She needs to get out for a drive. Plus your mom. So there's plenty of female company along."

"Don't worry. I'm not afraid of going alone with you if we have to. I trust you."

"Thank you. But I want your mom there, and Christine could use the air. So we'll leave after court. I'll write you an excuse for school."

"Cool. So you think I'll get bail tomorrow?"

"I'm pretty confident, yes. I already have the District Attorney agreeing not to object, so it's a pretty good chance you'll walk out when we're finished before the judge."

"Oh, thank you!"

"No problem. See you outside courtroom 201 before nine a.m."

"See you then, Thaddeus."

36

Thaddeus was right. Judge William J. Stormont set bail in the amount of $100,000, and Sheila immediately posted so PJ remained free. After court, mother and daughter, joined by Thaddeus and Christine, piled into Thaddeus's truck with crew cab and hit the road for Phoenix. Christine had been accompanying Thaddeus on short drives in and around Flagstaff, and the meds were working, so slowly but surely her fear-cycle was losing its grip. Today's trip would be the longest she had made since the onset of her symptoms, but she and Thaddeus were hopeful.

Dr. D.E. Eamons' forensic dental practice was located in north Phoenix, just off Camelback and 19th Avenue. It was inside a medical building complex and easily accessed from the freeway. The Flagstaff visitors found the elevator and headed up to the second floor.

First, Thaddeus met with Dr. Eamons and told him what he wanted and why. He explained that PJ had been bitten by Russ Lowenstein three months ago but that Thaddeus was hopeful there would still be enough impression or bruising to compare her bites to the bite mark sample of Russ possessed by Dr. Eamons from the prior forensic case for Shelly Hansen. Dr. Eamons said he would be happy to help. He would need to examine PJ with her mother present in the examination room.

Thaddeus and Christine found themselves alone in the reception area while PJ and Sheila were off to the exam room. He held her hand, sitting beside her on a loveseat, and she returned his squeeze.

"How we doing?" he asked.

"I'm holding up," she said. "A little twinge when we left Flag city limits, but I reframed that fear like my doctor said to. That was easy enough. It's just fear that someone is after me or my family. I can't shake the panic. Even being home with the kids now, when they are right in front of me, I have visions of them being hit and run by a car or stalked by an angry client. And you know I've had some of those in the past." She hooked her arm through his and nestled her head on his shoulder. "I've started to hate the idea of spending my days in a law practice that makes people so wildly angry. I might be ready to hang it up, Thaddeus."

"Really? What would you do?"

"I haven't gotten that far. Maybe something charitable, something like Lodzi did with his charity."

"Makes sense. Tell the truth, I could give it up myself."

She snapped upright and met his gaze. "Law? You could give up law?"

He never thought he'd be saying this but, "Sometimes I think about it. Maybe I'll get into raising quarter horses."

"Or thoroughbreds."

He smiled down at her. "Churchill Downs, here we come."

"I know," she said, getting into the spirit of the conversation, "What about derby winners?"

"Sure, why not?"

When he squeezed her hand, she rested her head once again on his shoulder. She sighed. "For some reason, I can't picture you doing anything but law. It's so much an essential part of what makes you my man, Thaddeus."

"Well, maybe some kind of public service law practice then. Maybe something on one of the Indian reservations," Thaddeus said thoughtfully. After Sheila and PJ, the daughter and mom duo with all the planning and scheming, he was about ready to move on. They didn't understand enough to fully appreciate all the work he did for them. Oh, they smiled and said thanks at the right times, but it wasn't in their hearts. He could tell. And there had been so many other clients who had been the same way. Just wanted to squeeze everything out of Thaddeus, but with no equivalent appreciation in return. Yes, perhaps he would go work with Turquoise and Katy's people, do some good there.

"That would be something I could get behind," Christine said with a nod. "I could help out with the admin end of it, anyway. Or maybe it's best if I do horses with you. I don't know."

Thaddeus cast a glance around the room. The sliding glass window separating the office staff was closed. He said in a low voice, "So, what are you thinking about PJ's case? These two have me a little baffled."

Christine tossed her head in a laugh. "I think they're getting away with murder. I think Sheila shot Russ, she got off when PJ confessed, and now PJ's going to trial and you're going to get her off somehow. Which is all right with me. Russ Lowenstein had it coming."

"He did, didn't he? And I'm thinking you're right about how it's going to go down. I think they're playing with more cards than me. I feel like I'm their tool," he said. "Somebody isn't always dealing me in."

"Lots you don't know, Thaddeus."

"Exactly."

Fifteen minutes later, the doors opened. PJ, with Sheila close behind, appeared in the waiting area. "Ready?" asked Sheila.

"Let me talk to Dr. Eamons for a second," Thaddeus replied. Just then, the doctor appeared in the doorway and curled a finger at Thaddeus.

They went into his private office.

"Well?" said Thaddeus when they were seated. "Any preliminary thoughts?"

"No doubt, you've got yourself a self-defense case. The incisors are a dead giveaway—no pun intended."

"That close?"

"Oh, yes, Russell Lowenstein was up to his old tricks when he bit the girl. I could testify to that comfortably right now."

"Even after all this time?"

"The sensitive tissue of the labia majora and minora area is easily bruised. The blood and nerves are quite close to the surface. And he must have bit her so hard that there is still enough formed marks that I can connect the two, with very little doubt."

"So glad to hear. I had a hunch we were close."

"What made her think he was about to repeat when she shot him?" the doctor asked.

"I haven't come up with that yet."

"Here's an idea. PJ's bite marks were so deep they broke the skin. I've got that documented now. But my guess is, she was in so much pain when she went for her 4-H money that even the slightest movement by him frightened an already-hurting girl. I can testify how existing pain telescopes down the fear of more pain. 'Once bitten,' as they say."

"You can testify to that?"

"Sure, as a dentist. Once you hit a nerve with a drill, your patient's trust quotient flies out the window. You won't be trusted again. That's where PJ was with her attacker. A bite attack is the absolute worst because it's disgusting and beyond what any of us ever imagine another human is capable of doing. These things were working on PJ definitely."

"That kind of testimony would be very helpful."

"Plus, she said an interesting thing to me," Dr. Eamons said.

"What's that?"

"She said the morning that she shot him, Russ had a toothpick in his mouth and kept playing it between his teeth. She felt like he was sending her a message with it. How's that for terrifying?"

"Wow, first I've heard of that. Thanks for the tip. That's very compelling, Doc."

"I know. That will put your jury on edge."

"Disgusting."

"It is. So, long story short, I can bring it on this case. We can make good things happen for your client."

"By the way, I'm going to have her examined by her family doctor, too. Just in case any other precautions need to be taken."

The doctor smiled. "Such as rabies shots?"

"Really?"

"Just joking. But there is always the risk of infection. It would have been better if she'd had herself treated at that time, but there are still things that can help the bruising there now. Get her to a family doctor for their concurrence of the pain and bruising and get some cream for treatment. It might be as simple as that, or it might be more. You might have her mom inquire if there is any lasting impact from a bite like that on the genitalia. Her mother agreed to the photos I've taken just now for use in the trial, so at this point, we want her to heal."

Wow, that was a lot of new info. Could it impact sexual activity later on in life? Could the bite have spread disease? Russ was more than promiscuous. "Will do," Thaddeus said. "As soon as we get back."

37

PJ's trial was set for September 4th, a Monday, in Flagstaff Superior Court. The judge was Cecily Van Meter, a U of A grad with history of public service law. She had served on the bench eleven years, three of them on the criminal calendar. She was known as a hard-nosed sentencing judge with a pronounced interest in the rights and protection of young people—a history not lost on Thaddeus. He was happy she'd drawn the case and was hopeful they would catch the fifty-fifty issues on PJ's side. The prosecuting attorney was again Assistant District Attorney Jon Logan, who evidently had inherited the case because he'd prosecuted the mother on the same set of facts. Before trial, Thaddeus met with Jon Logan to see if they might arrive at a plea agreement.

"You know I'm looking for manslaughter with no time," Thaddeus told Jon. "I've listed Dr. Eamons, you've seen his report, and you know PJ was attacked by Russ Lowenstein the same morning she shot him. You really need to settle this case, Jon, and give this young person the break she deserves. If not, I'm going to walk her out on self-defense. That's my promise to you."

Jon Logan's office was small, but his mood was expansive. "You know, I'd like to deal with you, Thaddeus, but I'm getting lots of heat from the Lowenstein family and the various service groups Mr. Lowenstein belonged to."

"Such as?"

"Oh, the Rotarians have been up in my face. They want a lynching. And his sale barn partners, Bob Shipley and Anderson Harmon— they're out for blood. I also know the Lowenstein family is suing them for not having a secure working environment, which allowed for someone to bring a gun right onto the premises without an alarm or something going off."

"Okay, so you've got Rotary and business partners up in arms. That doesn't seem like a showstopper to me."

"It's not. But I've also got a boss who's up for re-election in two years. Off the record, he's expecting a mass uprising within his own party and sees at least one, maybe two, tough primary challengers. This is not the time for him to be seen as soft on crime. If the jury wants to take the case and turn the girl loose on self-defense, that's one thing. But for him to turn her loose on a plea to a lesser-included, I'm afraid my hands are tied. I think we'll be going to the mat on this one. Unless you want a second degree plea with ten years."

"Get serious, Jon. The local high school civics class could get her a better result than that. No, if you can't do a weapons charge or greatly reduced assault, then I think you're right. I think we're done here. Well, I tried. At least I can tell my client and her mother I tried."

Thaddeus took the news back to PJ and Sheila. "Sometimes politics reaches out and twists law cases. That's the situation here where we've got a District Attorney facing re-election.

"Doesn't worry me," PJ said lightly. "I trust you a hundred percent, Thaddeus. You're going to walk me out a free girl. I know you will."

Thaddeus gave her a studied look. "You know, sometimes I feel like the two of you have a card up your sleeve. If you do, I'd sure as hell like to know about it now. This case is keeping me up at night."

"Get some sleep, Thaddeus," Sheila told him. "Go ride your horse."

Which is exactly what Thaddeus decided to do. Just as soon as court was through for the day.

38

The prosecutor, Jon Logan, went first. As expected, Logan called detectives Landis and Snow, then he called the crime scene techs and the uniformed police. He then read to the jury PJ's testimony from the first trial where she confessed. The jury, the new jury in this second trial, heard the same testimony the jury in the first trial heard:

Logan: "Were you present in the office of Russell Lowenstein the day he died?"

PJ: "Yes."

Logan: "What was Mr. Lowenstein to you?"

PJ: "My stepdad and my rapist."

Logan: "Your stepdad was raping you? How many times did he rape you?"

PJ: "I didn't count. But it would be ten at least."

Logan: "How did you feel when Russell Lowenstein died?"

PJ: "Happy. Free."

Logan: "Did you see him die?"

PJ: "Of course, I did."

Logan: "What do you mean, 'of course?'"

PJ: "I mean of course I saw him die. I shot him."

The State then rested its case against PJ.

The judge decided at 4:35 p.m. there wasn't enough time left in the trial day to proceed with the defense's case. She announced the court would be in recess until the following morning.

"It makes me feel like I've already lost, Mr. Murfee," PJ said in reference to the State's case she had heard all day long. Thaddeus had to admit that, as always, at the end of the State's case, he felt like his client was 100% guilty. It happened every time he went to trial, and this time was no different. Still, he tried to put PJ at ease.

"It always feels bad when the State finishes with its case," Thaddeus told the girl. "Just remember, you haven't heard any of your defense case yet, and that always puts things in a very different perspective once we start doing our work."

"I'm just feeling like I should give up and go to jail. That's where they want me for shooting Russ."

Sheila came forward from the spectators' seats and heard her daughter's comment. "I don't know how you can say these things," she said. "You didn't shoot Russ. I shot Russ."

PJ shook her head. "Thanks, Mom, but there's no need to continue playing the game. They've got me fair and square, and they should just put me in jail for ten years and let it go at that. Is that still possible, Mr. Murfee, that I can go to jail for ten years and just get it over with?"

"It's possible," said Thaddeus, "but I'd strongly advise against it. Even if you shot Russ, you were under terrible duress. You felt like he was about to attack you again, and you were just protecting yourself."

PJ leaned in close to her mother and Thaddeus. "The truth is I wasn't scared at all. I was mad. He raped me. You'd be mad, too. This was payback, like they say on TV. I got my payback."

Thaddeus had a quick look around to see if there'd been any ears listening. Luckily, most everyone was out of the courtroom at that point. "All right, well, we're done for the day so let's leave it right here," Thaddeus said to the girl. "Let's come in tomorrow and hear what the video experts that I hired have to say. Maybe after they have their testimony on the record, we'll know more about what we want to do."

"I want to plead guilty and get it over with," PJ repeated. "It's horrible to be trying to go to school and have a life with this mess. Plus, I'm starting to feel sorry for shooting Russ. I should've told Mom and got some counseling. Or told my dad and let him handle it. Russ might still be alive, and I wouldn't have this hanging over my head."

"Sure," said Sheila, "but your dad would be in jail if he ever found out about Russ. He would've killed the bastard himself."

Which was the very moment Jim Sam Walston came forward and hugged his daughter. "How you holding up, honey?" he said to PJ. Jim Sam was a burly, ape of a man who worked as an HVAC installer and troubleshooter. He was in his forties with the frame and musculature of a man who spent his days moving heavy equipment and tools around. Thaddeus saw that he was the kind of man who liked bass lakes and trout stream weekends, who filled pickup trucks with supplies from Home Depot, who took care of their families and homes while showing up for work day after day in not very pleasant jobs lots of the time. He liked the man right away.

"I'm holding up okay," PJ told him, leaning against her dad for support. "I just wish I had come to you before I shot Russell."

Jim Sam looked at his ex-wife. Sheila gave a quick shrug while PJ wasn't looking.

"Honey," said Jim Sam, "I think you're a little mixed up. I don't think you shot Russ, did you?"

"What? I've told everyone I had the gun that had my prints and DNA. What else is there? Of course, it was me."

"Okay, honey," Jim Sam said, but there was a hint of resignation to the fact his daughter was holding onto a version of what happened that was believed only by her. "I still wonder why your mother didn't straighten this out at her trial and come forward and tell the truth." He looked askance at his ex-wife.

Thaddeus spoke up. "Because I didn't want her testifying. That's why nothing further came out," he said. "A courtroom is some-times the worst possible place to pursue the truth. Particularly in a case like this. It would've done no one any good for PJ to confess to the shooting and then have Sheila take the witness stand and contradict her. It would've resulted in Sheila getting convicted."

"But you let a young girl testify," said Jim Sam to Thaddeus. "Didn't you know my girl was going to lie?"

"I thought she was going to say something completely different," Thaddeus told the father. "I only put her on the witness stand to talk about the rape in order to show why Sheila was crazed by it when she shot Russ. Your daughter suddenly confessed without any knowledge on my part that it was going to happen. Let's try to keep our facts straight here."

"I'm in a mess," PJ said meekly. "I've ruined everyone's life."

"No, honey," said Jim Sam. "Mr. Murfee is going to get this all straightened out."

"We're your mom and dad, honey," Sheila said. "You can't ruin our lives. We'll never turn our backs on you. We'll always be fighting for you no matter what you do. Besides, you've done nothing wrong. You just need to talk to someone. We're going to see a doctor who can help us all understand what you're thinking. We all know you didn't shoot Russell. Now we need you to know that, too."

"Un-uh. I've ruined your lives," PJ repeated. "I feel like running away before I do anymore damage."

"Nonsense," said Sheila. "You're not going anywhere. Dad and I are working on this, and we'll get it sorted. Just give us some space to do our work. Mr. Murfee is going to make it all right. Isn't that so, Mr. Murfee?"

"Yes," said Thaddeus. "We're going to hear some testimony coming up, PJ, that will tell us it was your mom with the gun. It will help you remember what happened better."

For his part, Thaddeus believed the girl was under a mountain of shame from the rapes and actually believed she had lashed out against Russell Lowenstein to stop him from hurting her. Thaddeus believed she needed to see a professional, talk it through, and come to understand she hadn't actually done anything.

It was contrary to what he had first believed. When PJ told her mother's jury that she had shot Russ, Thaddeus had felt used. He had felt like mother and daughter had conspired to shoot Russell and then get each other off by claiming the daughter had done it when it was the mother's trial and claiming the mother had done it when it was the daughter's trial. But more and more, he now wondered if PJ actually did believe she was the shooter, and there hadn't been any conspiracy at all. PJ had created the whole spectacle at the first trial by claiming she was the shooter. He had to admit he had been giving them far more credit to be clever and slippery than they ever deserved. They were just mother and daughter trying to muddle through what had been a horrible time of betrayed trust and sexual abuse. The guilty party was six feet under, but his actions had left behind a family of ex-spouses and their daughter fighting to come to grips with what had happened and how they had reacted to it. If they could just let Thaddeus have it his way, he felt confident no one would go to jail. But it had become increasingly difficult to do it his way.

"I want to go. Daddy. Would you take me home with you?"

Jim Sam looked at Sheila, who shrugged. "Why not? Just have her back here by eight tomorrow morning."

"Is eight okay, Thaddeus?" asked Jim Sam.

Thaddeus smiled. "Eight o'clock is perfect. See all you good people then."

Then they were gone.

Renny had come over to court and was now helping Thaddeus gather books and briefcases and lug them back down the street to his office.

"Long day?" asked Renny. Today he wore pinstripe pants and vest with a white shirt underneath. His shoes were polished to a shine, always polished. There was no one like Renny who could pull off pinstripes and a vest like he did. He always kept his hair cropped tight to his head and was young enough he didn't need reading glasses yet so his handsome face was on display at all times, unless he wore a beard, which he was liking to do lately. Now, a look of concern colored his fine features.

"You wouldn't believe," Thaddeus said as they trudged down the street, pulling their carts behind. "I'm so ready for this one to end."

"One more day? Two?"

"Two days of testimony. Half day of closing arguments and jury instructions. Then a half day of deliberations—if even that."

"You think they'll find her not guilty that fast?"

"I don't think there's any question about it. PJ did nothing wrong."

"I heard some of what was being said just now. It sounds like she thinks she did something wrong."

"She needs counseling. I don't think it's anything that a capable doc can't straighten out."

Jim Sam and PJ honked from Jim Sam's Ram truck as they swept past the two lawyers. Thaddeus saw the look on his client's face just for a brief moment. She reminded him of a woman he once saw in a movie, a woman who claimed everyone around her was dead.

Except this time there was family, and they weren't letting go.

39

PJ was lucky. It was Dorothy and Paul Rand who picked her up on the freeway on-ramp at one in the morning. Jim Sam was back home asleep. Sheila was on the other side of town asleep in her house. Only PJ was awake, and she had made the decision she would rather go to Las Vegas and enter the skin trade than wait to be convicted of murder in a Flagstaff court and then go to prison. As she told Dorothy, "I've got no skills, but I've got young flesh and men like that. I'm not going to lie to you and tell you I'm going to school or anything like that. I'm going to do what I can. Change my name, dye my hair, forge a new birth certificate—I'm not going to prison because my stepfather raped me. I don't deserve that."

Dorothy and PJ were sitting across from each other in the dark at a small dinette table in Dorothy and Paul's motorhome, drinking old coffee, while up front Paul guided the motorhome down the freeway, away from Flagstaff, headed for the Riviera RV Resort in Las Vegas. They expected to check in just before sunrise. They had decided to stop and give PJ a ride because she was alone, had no bags, not even a backpack, and looked cold in the high mountain night. She was all goosebumps and chattering teeth when she climbed the steps and came aboard.

Dorothy was a sixty-year-old retired home economics teacher from Southern Illinois, the town of Perry. Paul, her husband of forty years, was a retired systems engineer with the State of Illinois in Springfield. They had sold everything last year, bought the twenty-nine foot Coachmen Mirada, and so far had decorated the end cap with no less than twenty-seven decals of the states they had visited. The motorhome was their lifelong dream: outside kitchen, outside flat screen, double awning, and a queen-size bed. They were guileless people with low expectations of the world. Stopping for PJ in the middle of nowhere just made good sense to them. So far, Paul had only said, "Howdy," to PJ before Dorothy had collected her up, swaddled her in a Perry High School sweatshirt, and set a cup of evening coffee before her on the dinette.

For her part, PJ was running on automatic. She paid little attention to her thoughts and had taken more and more to acting on feelings alone, particularly that old friend called FEAR.

"Honey, how old are you?" asked Dorothy.

"Eighteen. I can legally vote."

"You look like one of my freshman students. Sure it's eighteen?"

"Well, I just turned eighteen."

"Do your mom and dad know where you are?"

"They're dead. My sister is waiting for me in Las Vegas. She has a place."

"What's the address? We can take you right there and drop you off."

"I've got it written down. If you could take me to where the casinos are, that's close enough."

"What's your sister's name?"

PJ kept her hands wrapped around the hot mug of coffee and didn't bother sipping. "Gosh, why do you want to know?"

"Because I'm trying to help you. Can I be honest about something?"

"Yes."

"You look to me like you're fourteen, you're a runaway, and you're about to go to Las Vegas and make the biggest mistake of your life. Am I getting close?"

"My stepfather is raping me."

"I know. You said as much when you first got in and, honey, I can't tell you how much my heart hurts to hear that. I'm so sorry for you. How about this? I can have Paul turn this thing around right now, and we can go to the police and report him. Would that help? Paul?" she called to her husband.

"What's that?"

"Find an exit. We may need to turn around."

"No," said PJ, "I can't go back. He's waiting for me. I really do have a sister, and she's waiting for me. Her name is Sheila."

"Sheila?"

"Yes, Sheila."

"What does Sheila do?"

"Do like what?"

"How does she pay her rent? Does she have a job?"

"Sure, she's a waitress. I'm going to waitress, too."

"You told me when you first got in you were going into the skin trade."

"Well, I've changed my mind."

"Do you have a driver's license I could check?"

"No."

"Why no driver's license, honey?"

"I lost it. I lost my whole wallet."

"You'll need a driver's license and Social Security card to work. Do you have a Social Security card?"

"Can we talk about something else?"

Dorothy sighed. At least the girl was safe with them for the time being. "Sure. What else would you like to talk about?"

"How far is it to Las Vegas?"

"A few hours. We'll pull in about dawn."

"Can you drop me at the iHOP?"

"We can, but a minute ago you wanted us to drop you to the casinos. Is the iHOP where she's waiting tables? Your sister Sheila?"

"Yes. She works there."

"Which iHOP in town? There are a few of them if I remember correctly."

"The first one we come to."

"Does your mother know you're going to live with your sister?"

"She thought it was a good idea when I told her about Russell raping me."

"A good idea?"

"Yes," said PJ. "She said it would make things easier all around."

"Uh-huh. Would you like to stretch out and sleep for a bit?"

"I don't think so. I'm very excited."

"Yes, I can see you are," said Dorothy.

"Oh, yes."

"Honey, are you getting ready to sell your body to survive?"

Tears clouded PJ's eyes. "I don't—I don't—"

"It's all right. I won't try to stop you."

"I don't—maybe. He wouldn't stop raping me. So I shot him."

"You shot Russell?"

"I killed him."

"Goodness. Do the police know?"

"Yes, they're having a trial for me. They're trying to put me in prison."

"All because you shot Russell after he was raping you?"

"Yes."

"Do you have a lawyer? Do you have a good lawyer?"

"His name is Thaddeus Murfee—but don't call him, please. He might get angry."

"Why would Mr. Murfee be angry? You're the one who got raped."

"Because I'm going to miss my trial today. I'm not going because I don't want to go to prison."

The dam burst, and PJ started crying. Dorothy pulled down a paper towel and passed it to the girl. PJ cried, dabbed, and blew her nose. Then she cried some more.

"I hate Russell Lowenstein. He raped me so bad!"

"Of course, you do. And do you know what I think?"

"What?"

"I think that jury is going to send you home a free young woman. They won't send a nice girl to prison for protecting herself."

"They won't?" asked PJ.

"Gosh no. I'm pretty sure they love you already. And you've got a good lawyer. I think you're going to be just fine. Let's do this, PJ. Let's turn around, head back to Flagstaff, and get Mr. Murfee out of bed. I'll talk to him and make sure you're going to get off. But if he says you might not get off, I'll make Paul take you to Las Vegas. Would you like me to talk to him while you listen?"

"Ye-ye-yes."

"All right. Paul, whip it around eastbound, honey, we're going back to Flagstaff."

They could hear Paul mumble, but several miles later they lumbered down an off-ramp and turned around, heading back toward Flagstaff.

"How would you like a pimento cheese sandwich and some chicken noodle soup, PJ? I have it all the time when I'm blue."

"Okay. But not too much. I'm feeling funny. Just a half."

"One-half pimento cheese coming up. Just sit tight."

Dorothy busied herself in the kitchenette. PJ heard the microwave beep-beep-beep and roar to life. Dorothy set half a pimento cheese sandwich before her on a saucer. A cup of chicken noodle soup followed. PJ tasted her food, slowly at first, then all but inhaled the offering.

"Would you like some more?"

"Yes, please."

"Coming right up."

Dorothy kept up the chatter with PJ about school, her classes, her hobbies, which inevitably came back around to her 4-H cow and caused her to burst into tears anew. So Dorothy tried again with other topics, telling the girl about her and Paul's travels, which seemed to excite the girl a bit more. She fed PJ another half of a pimento cheese sandwich and some potato chips and even convinced her to eat a banana, all the while talking calmly.

Thirty minutes later, they finally entered the Flagstaff city limits.

"Do you have Mr. Murfee's phone number?" asked Dorothy.

"I have his cell memorized. He gives it to all his clients."

"Well, say it slowly, and I'll punch it in my phone."

PJ carefully recited the number, and Dorothy initiated the call. Within seconds, a voice came on the line, male.

"This is Thaddeus."

"Thaddeus, my name is Dorothy. I'm in an RV at a Little America Hotel off of Interstate 40 with a client of yours named PJ."

"Okay, how can I help?"

"Paul and I picked PJ up on the freeway. She was going to see her sister, Sheila, in Las Vegas. She said you might be mad at her if you knew."

"No, please tell PJ I'm not mad. Tell her I'm happy you called."

Dorothy covered the phone and said to PJ, "He says he's happy, honey. That's good news." Then she said into the phone, "Mr. Murfee, could we meet with you and discuss PJ's situation before she leaves town?"

"Of course. Where can we meet?"

"How about the Little America hotel where we're at? We'll be in the maroon Coachmen Mirada. I'll have Paul pull right up to the front of the parking lot so you can see us from the road."

"See you in thirty. Tell PJ I'm very happy you called."

"All right. Thank you, Mr. Murfee."

"Thank you, Dorothy. Goodbye, now."

THIRTY MINUTES LATER, THE FOURSOME WERE SEATED AT THE Coachmen dinette. Paul was puffing on a cigar while Dorothy fired up the exhaust fan she'd mounted in the open dinette window up against the screen. The smoke floated flavorfully above the dinette table before the exhaust whisked it out into the cool night air of Flagstaff.

"So, Mr. Murfee," Dorothy began, "PJ here is worried sick she's going to prison. What can you tell us about that?"

Thaddeus waved a hand through the smoke, slicing it horizontally. "PJ is getting a very fair trial. Tomorrow we have an expert witness to testify that the measurements of the woman who fired the gun matched the exact measurements of PJ's mother, Sheila."

"You mean PJ's sister, Sheila?"

"No, Sheila's her mother. Am I right, PJ?"

She looked sheepish before she looked down at the mug she still strangled in her grasp. "Uh-huh."

Dorothy's brow furrowed. "Oh, I must have misunderstood. I thought she said Sheila was her sister. What other witnesses are we looking at, Mr. Murfee?"

"Sheila is going to testify. I just found out about video that I expect will end the trial when it's shown. I don't think the case will even make it to the jury."

Paul said, "I had a DUI once, Mr. Murfee. After a Christmas party in 1996. The jury turned me loose because the cop didn't show. Any of that possible for PJ?"

"I don't think so, Paul. The police have already testified in PJ's case. Of course, they weren't there when the shooting occurred, but both of them testified Sheila confessed to them that she was the shooter. So we've even got the police testifying for PJ. Once the evidence is in, I don't see the jury getting to decide. I think the judge has to throw it out and dismiss the charges."

"What happens if PJ runs for Vegas. What happens if she boogies?"

"They issue a warrant and come arrest her. Then she goes to prison because the court will find her guilty if she goes missing. That would be the worst possible thing. Paul and Dorothy, you've actually saved PJ from a terrible ending by bringing her back home. I've got this under control."

"Can you promise she gets off?" asked Dorothy.

"Never any promises," Thaddeus said. "The law doesn't even allow me to make promises of results. I could lose my license if I did that."

"Well, that's good enough for me. So, PJ, how are you feeling by now, honey?"

PJ stared into her untouched coffee. "Better. I trust Mr. Murfee. I'm tired. I think I want to go to bed."

Dorothy suggested, "Why don't we do this? Paul can drive us around back, you can sleep here in the motorhome, and we'll drop you at the courthouse in the morning. Don't worry about a thing. We've got an extra toothbrush, and we can run you by home when the sun comes up so you can shower and change. Does that work for everyone?"

"Works for me," Thaddeus said.

"I guess so," PJ said. "My dad will be pissed, though."

"I'll talk to your dad," Thaddeus told her. "Jim Sam and I already have an understanding. I can promise you he won't be mad. That much I *can* promise."

"All right. Then I'll stay with Dorothy and Paul."

"Now we're talking," Dorothy said. "The dinette makes up into a bed. We'll get you set up as soon as Thaddeus clears out."

"My cue to leave," said Thaddeus. "See you in court, PJ. And Paul, Dorothy, how do I say thank you enough?"

"Just set our girl free, Mr. Murfee," Dorothy said. "We'll drop her off, and then we're off to Las Vegas ourselves. There's an AA convention underway. We're both in recovery."

"Well, you're angels," Thaddeus said and gave Dorothy a hug. He shook Paul's hand heartily and headed for the door and the stepdown.

Then he was gone.

Fifteen minutes later, PJ was asleep behind the Little America Hotel. At last the duress of the shooting, her mother's trial, her stepfather's death, her father's criticism of Russ, and all the weight of her own trial lifted from her shoulders. As she drifted off, she remembered about the shooting of Russell Lowenstein.

It hadn't been she who had pulled the trigger at all.

At last she remembered the entire thing, and she was ready to go free.

40

Almost immediately the judge turned to Thaddeus to present his defense of PJ Walston.

Thaddeus decided to try the shotgun approach. He would shoot several different theories at the jury and see which one got legs. Then he would follow that one down its path.

As his first witness, he called Estil Morse III, the owner and chief technologist of L.A. Video, the videographers and enhancement professionals on Sunset Boulevard in Los Angeles. Mr. Morse was a hip, thirty-something-ish technologist with a background in film studies from USC and ten years at Disney. He knew everything there was to know about video, as he had demonstrated to Thaddeus, so the lawyer was quite comfortable in calling him to the stand.

"What is your occupation, Mr. Morse?"

"I'm officially a videographer. In practice, I do everything at LAV from sweeping the sidewalks to signing the paychecks. Plus I'm in charge of all the technologists."

"What kind of work does your company do?"

"We are a high-end video company. We make videos, shooting them and editing. We do post-production with lots of Southern California clients and many studio jobs. We do forensics, such as what you've requested and for the Los Angeles Sheriff's Department and the LAPD. We do thousands of hours of video a year for lawyers and medical schools. Just about everything, sir."

"Did you receive a work request from me earlier this year?"

"We did."

"Please relate what that was."

"You sent two videos and asked me to establish measurements for two of the people appearing in the videos."

"For the record, can we call those two people Sheila and PJ?"

"Yes, that's how we wrote up our study."

"Tell us what the video portrays."

"There's a picture of two women, I know now a mother and daughter, and they are portrayed at a crime scene. In the video, we have anterior and posterior shots—front and back. So we have plenty of opportunity to establish body measurements. We have located common objects in the background of the videos and have obtained measurements for those objects in the real world. We have then derived ratios and arrived at the relative sizes of the people in the video. For example, we were able to compute the height of Russell Lowenstein even though he was sitting at his desk. We compared computations to the measurements of the body as recorded by the medical examiner. Our figures were an exact match to his. So we proved our methods and our numbers. We have also done the same thing with the measurements of the real women we see in the videos. Their present measurements match the measurements of the women in the video. Not almost match, mind you, but an exact match."

"Please tell us what those measurements reveal."

"Sure. In the second video, the post-shooting, we've established the woman named Sheila at a median body width of twenty-one inches and the daughter named PJ at a median body width of eighteen inches. A three-inch difference."

"Could that difference be attributed to the clothing they were wearing?"

"No, and when we play the video, I can demonstrate how we can tell."

"What else does the video portray?"

"At the moment, the arm sweeps up and the gun is fired in the first video, so we can measure the backside of the shooter and we can report to you, beyond any doubt that, as to the two women, it is the larger woman, Sheila, who is wielding the gun."

Thaddeus was watching the jury out of the corner of his eye. At this testimony, that the shooter was Sheila, he saw them scribbling furiously in their notepads.

"What other identifying characteristics can you find in the video, if any?"

"That was pretty much it. The focus is such that we can't make out any identifying characteristics along the viewable portion of the arm, or of the fingers, so there isn't anything there to shed light on our inquiry."

"What about hair or clothing?"

"Since the video is only black and white, we can't validate whether a person is wearing a blue shirt or a black shirt. You might have variants of darker gray, but it's not exact. Same with hair color."

"Your Honor, I'm going to ask my assistant to cue the video and play it now with the court's approval."

"The court approves. Please proceed, Mr. Murfee."

The video then played. It was the same video coverage that had been played at Sheila's trial. By the video timer, at 8:31 a.m. a figure wearing shorts and a tank top was seen from behind. The figure went up to Russ's desk and raised a pistol. Without hesitation, the figure then leaned across the desk and shot him point-blank in the face, right between the eyes. He flew backward in his chair, and the figure came around the desk and shot him multiple times. Without ado, she stood upright, turned left, and then crossed the room to the back wall. She pulled open the door, walked through, and closed it behind her.

The second video then began playing, and the jury watched as Sheila and PJ came into the frame, both wearing T-shirts and shorts. They approached Russ's desk and then froze there, as if suspended in mid-air, while the video chugged along. He could be seen lying crumpled on the chair. There was no sound and their backs were to the camera, so it was impossible to detect what they were saying or if they were even talking at all. People then began arriving, including uniformed police officers. The place was then swarming with crime scene technicians in coveralls, a still photographer and a videographer, and men and women wearing suits and dresses. Midway in, Sheila and PJ were seen being escorted by Detective Snow out of the room. That was the last of them in the courtroom video.

Thaddeus then continued his examination of the witness, Estil Morse III.

"Mr. Morse, what is a median body width of twenty-one, such as you say is the mother's measurement?"

"We've taken three measurements across the back, across the shoulders, the thoracic spine at T3, and across the buttocks at S1. The median width of the three measurements in the mother is twenty-one inches. In the daughter, it is eighteen inches. The certainty that the shooter is the larger woman is in the ninety-fifth percentile."

"So you're telling the jury that you are certain, within ninety-five percent, that the shooter was the mother, Sheila Lowenstein. And that the chance of the shooter being the daughter is only five percent?"

"That is correct. Beyond almost all doubt stands the mother with the gun in her hand."

"That will be all my questions, thank you."

It was then Jon Logan's turn to cross-examine. He asked questions that tried to prove false the methods used by LAV and Estil Morse III. The dead end he kept running into, however, was that Mr. Morse had, in each instance, proved his video measurements with real measurements from the real world. The median width of the shooter exactly matched the median width of the mother. Logan didn't stumble around, but he ultimately succeeded only in re-proving Thaddeus's case a third time—the mother was the shooter. Then he sat down.

So, Thaddeus went for the jugular. He called Sheila Lowenstein to the stand.

41

Sheila Lowenstein walked to the witness stand with an ease not many of his other clients could attest to. She wore the same blue skirt suit and lavender blouse as the day of PJ's testimony in her own trial. She wore her long, blond hair back in a barrette. Again, the same as her own trial. After the witness was sworn and seated, Thaddeus wasted no time.

"Sheila Lowenstein, do you recall the first time you visited my office?"

"I do."

"And do you recall removing a three-inch barrette from your hair?"

"I do.

"And what did you tell me that barrette actually was?"

"A video camera."

"Was it a video camera?"

"Yes."

"Where is that barrette today?"

"Right here in my hair." Sheila reached to her hair and removed the barrette, holding it in place. A substantial comma of hair fell forward, which she gamely ignored, instead concentrating on displaying the barrette to the jury.

"Sheila, in just a moment I'm going to have your barrette marked as an exhibit and passed around to the jury. But first, let me ask you, were you wearing that barrette at the time Russell Lowenstein was shot?"

"I was."

"And did that barrette record on video the actual shooting?"

"It did."

"Did the police locate that barrette and video on your person after they arrived and searched you?"

"They did not."

"Please tell us why they didn't find it."

"Because I went out the back door of Russ's office, pulled a pre-addressed Fed-Ex envelope from my fanny pack and dropped the barrette into the envelope. I then put the envelope into the Fed-Ex mailing bin that was in the courtyard. The police never looked there. The barrette was delivered by Fed-Ex to my home the next day, and then I had the video I took of shooting Russell."

"Do you have that video today?"

"I do."

"Your Honor," said Thaddeus, "I amended my list of witnesses and exhibits this morning before court. I've marked the exhibit as an impeachment exhibit. Which means Mr. Logan has never seen it. I did this in order to impeach the testimony of PJ Walston, whose confession at the first trial was read into the record by Mr. Logan. If the court will allow, I'd ask leave to play that video now for the jury."

The Court said, "Mr. Logan, what is your position?"

"We object, Your Honor. We claim surprise and claim this is no impeachment exhibit but a simple exhibit that should have been turned over to the State prior to trial. Mr. Murfee has misled the court and counsel with this fraud of his, and I plan to turn him in to the State B—"

"Hold it, Mr. Logan!" cried the judge. "That is an entirely inappropriate argument, and the court will order the jury to ignore the comments made by Mr. Logan. Further, the court will grant counsel's request to play the video for the jury at this time. Mr. Murfee?"

"Thank you, Your Honor. I happen to have the video cued on the court's video system and am ready to roll it now. Please play the video."

What the jury saw lasted all of fifteen seconds. The screen was black then erupted in living color as a hand holding a gun came into focus. On the ring finger of the left hand holding the gun were the wedding and engagement rings that, the jury would eventually decide, were the same rings being worn right then in court by Sheila Lowenstein. The gun barked once, and the face of Russ Lowenstein erupted in a red blossom between the eyes, spreading outward. The video then followed the hand and arm as it circled Russ Lowenstein's desk and then fired off seven bullets into his dead body.

Then the screen went black.

"That was all of it?" asked Thaddeus.

"Yes," she said simply.

"Did any police officer or detective or anyone from law enforcement ever ask if you had video of the shooting or its aftermath?"

"No."

"Did they ever search your home?"

"They did. They came with a search warrant. The barrette was lying in plain sight in my jewelry box. Obviously, they didn't seize it."

"When they came with their search warrant, did anyone ask whether you had video?"

"No."

"Why did you make the video?"

"Because I didn't want to see PJ falsely accused of shooting her stepfather."

"Did that in fact happen?"

"Yes, this trial happened. It happened because PJ was worried about me and came into my own trial and said she did the shooting. I didn't show the video then to prove her wrong."

"Why not?"

"Because I wasn't going to testify about anything. You and I had already decided that."

"So was PJ lying when she told your jury she shot her stepfather?"

"I really don't know her state of mind. She could have honestly believed she did shoot him if she were suffering enough from the trauma of his repeated rapes. She's only fourteen—she could be thinking any number of things, for all I know."

"Have you discussed these things with her?"

"I have."

"And what does she say about that day?"

"She says she shot Russell Lowenstein."

"Do you mean she believes that?"

"Yes."

"What is your judgment about that?"

"I believe my daughter needs to see someone. A psychiatrist. I wish the court would order a psychiatrist to examine her."

"Are you asking Judge Stormont to appoint a psychiatrist to examine your daughter's mental state?"

"I am."

"Are you asking the court to examine her for the purpose of finding out why she insists she's the shooter?"

"Yes. I think she's imagining things."

"As her mother, is she fit to stand trial?"

"Objection!" cried Jon Logan. "Foundation."

"Your Honor," said Thaddeus, "I'm not seeking a medical or expert opinion. I'm simply asking the child's mother whether she's behaving erratically."

"Then phrase it that way, counsel," said the judge.

Thaddeus rephrased the question. "Is your daughter behaving erratically?"

"Yes."

"Please describe in what way."

"She believes she shot her stepfather. She came into my trial and said so. She still believes it now when I talk to her. In all other respects, she's fine. She's attending school, hanging out with her friends, texting day and night with her buddies, all the things she did before the shooting. But she actually believes she shot her stepfather."

"Your Honor," said Thaddeus, "I move for the court to appoint a psychiatrist or other medical professional to examine my client, PJ Walston, and then come into court and tell us whether she is capable of standing trial."

With a sigh, the judge removed his eyeglasses and rubbed the bridge of his nose. "Mr. Murfee, why wasn't this issue raised pre-trial?"

"Because, Your Honor, I didn't know the truth about what she believed. I was operating from the premise she was raising a legitimate, fact situation that had her as the shooter. At that time, before trial, I wasn't aware Sheila Lowenstein had her own video."

The judge asked, "When did you find out about the video?"

"Within the past twenty-four hours when the mother came to me and said she wanted to testify. I had her listed as a witness anyway, so I called her to the stand. I'd only seen the video an hour or two before she testified."

"Gentlemen, I'm going to excuse the jury from the courtroom. Then we'll discuss the video before proceeding."

The jury was then led from the courtroom by the bailiff. When they were gone, Judge William J. Stormont turned his attention to Thaddeus. "Sir, I feel like I've been misled by this whole video issue. I find it hard to believe you've just learned of its existence."

Thaddeus climbed to his feet to respond. "Your Honor, I feel equally misled by the entire experience. But the truth is, I, like all law enforcement, failed to ever ask Sheila Lowenstein whether she had video of her own. In the age of Go-Pro cameras and miniature recording devices, I should have known better and asked." *Especially since Sheila had pointed out the device in his office that very morning.* "I've learned my lesson about the new world. From now on, I will ask clients whether they have their own video of the alleged crime. I know that in more and more auto accident cases, one or both of the drivers have their own dashboard-mounted video of the intersection and traffic light than ever before. It's an explosion in technology as the world arms itself with cheap, extremely good video cameras capable of recording their lives. Like I say, I have learned my lesson. This is no more an effort to mislead the court than a prior recorded statement held in abeyance as an impeachment exhibit is. It happens every day in court that a recorded statement is found that blows a case wide open. Well, now it's happening with video as well. I'm a smarter man, a wiser lawyer, than I was coming into this case."

The judge turned to Jon Logan, who simply continued to claim surprise and claim that Thaddeus had purposely misled the court. "Further," he added, "I intend to report counsel to the State Bar of Arizona for misleading this tribunal and for misleading the office of the district attorney by failing to notify law enforcement of the existence of the video. I don't believe that it happened only because Mr. Murfee wasn't astute enough or learned enough to ask. I believe it was done consciously, with forethought, to defraud counsel and the court. For this reason, the entire video should be thrown out and the jury ordered to disregard it as unreliable."

"A bell once rung cannot be unrung, Mr. Logan," mused Judge Stormont. "You know that—you deal with evidence issues every day of your life. It's too late now to withdraw or cross off the video. It's in evidence. Gentlemen, one thing is for sure—the video doesn't lie. Whether we like the video or hate the video, whether we believe it was used to mislead the court or the district attorney, the video is accurate and clearly portrays the shooter as Sheila Lowenstein. The other side of the coin is that Ms. Lowenstein has already been put on trial for the murder of Russell Lowenstein with jeopardy attached before the charges against her were dismissed with prejudice. She cannot be retried for the same offense now that we know about the video. She shot and killed her husband, but the state cannot bring those charges against her again. I believe it is that fact, that unfairness, that is working in this case and making the district attorney so angry. In a way, the DA dropped the ball by neither asking about video nor finding video. But maybe the state will start doing a better job of evidence collection as a result. I don't know. But the video is in, and it stays in. The trial will continue."

Jon Logan stood up again. "Then the State at this time has no option but to dismiss the charges against PJ Walston. We so move. There is no case against her given Thaddeus's evidence of the median width of the shooter and given the video evidence. The charges are hereby dismissed."

"Very well," said Judge Stormont. I will dismiss the jury. The defendant is free to go, and her bail will be returned to the posting party."

"Your Honor," Thaddeus said, "let's be clear. The charges are dismissed with prejudice and cannot be refiled. If not, I have to object to dismissal."

"The charges are dismissed with prejudice," Judge Stormont confirmed. "Your client cannot be charged again with this crime."

"Thank you, Judge," said Thaddeus.

"Ladies and gentlemen, counsel, the court stands in recess."

With that, the judge stood and left the astonished spectators and participants with nothing further to do or say.

Thaddeus tried to shake the hand of Jon Logan. Logan brushed him aside, renewing his vow to "report Thaddeus to the authorities," as if he had masterminded the result in the case.

Which he had not. That was all Sheila Lowenstein, a woman he had severely underestimated. As much as he had hoped for otherwise, and had believed once, it was pure manipulation and the threads of humanity were not there all along. And there were still questions unanswered to Thaddeus's satisfaction.

Which Turquoise vocalized as much once they were out of the courtroom. "So if PJ didn't do it, and Sheila *did* do it, then who is that smudge in the video we thought could be the head of a person?"

Thaddeus walked around to the passenger side of his truck and opened the door for his daughter. After she climbed in, he stayed by her side, one hand resting on the car door. "That, Turquoise, is something we might not ever know."

"But doesn't it drive you nuts *not* to know?" She buckled herself in with a loud clip. "I mean, I almost want to investigate it further, but there's no point now."

"No, there isn't any point, and sometimes we just have to let some things go." He shut her door and walked around to the other side where he got into the driver's seat. "I just don't want to go there. That's a can of worms I'm not going to open."

"So you're pretty sure Sheila did it, right?" Turquoise could be relentless when breaking things down. It was another element that made her such a good cop, and now private investigator.

"Now *that* I do know. Sheila killed her husband. It was already written by the time she got to my office."

"Really, Dad?"

"When I look back, I think so." He turned the truck and eased into traffic, heading in the direction of home.

Turquoise commented, "What a strange couple cases."

Thaddeus chuckled. "I hear you on that."

"And no one went to prison for first-degree murder. The crime of the century." Turquoise rolled down her window and let her hand ride the air current. She never did like the air conditioning, even when it was as hot as it was today.

"I don't know if I'd go that far..."

"After all that work and money, it seems like we should have more closure or something."

"I agree. But you could look at it this way." Thaddeus took a right onto US 180, a long stretch of open road in front of him. "Everyone pretty much agreed that Russ got what was coming to him." The skies that had been threatening rain finally let loose a few sprinkles, so Thaddeus turned on the wipers. "And, really, that's kismet at its best. Everything came full circle. It's done."

42

J on Logan was true to his word: he reported Thaddeus to the
State Bar of Arizona, filing a bar complaint in which he
claimed Thaddeus had manipulated two jury trials to result
in two dismissed cases by "creating an opportunity for a mother
and daughter team to lie and defraud the court and jury and
police about the facts and circumstances surrounding a fatal
shooting." Logan went on to say that Thaddeus himself had "sub-
orned perjury, lied to a jury, and influenced witnesses by paying
for testimony from a Los Angeles, California video firm, which he
knew wasn't supported by the facts."

All in all, Logan made it sound like Thaddeus alone had masterminded the defense of Sheila Lowenstein and created a landslide
of falsehoods to achieve her freedom. Logan made it sound like
Thaddeus did it in such a way that Sheila, the actual murderer,
had been allowed to walk free because Thaddeus had manipulated an impressionable minor child. Logan warned that Thaddeus did, indeed, manipulate a minor child to come into court and
lie about her role in the shooting, which led to the death of her

stepfather, to the detriment and permanent harm to the child herself. All in all, Thaddeus sounded like "Jack the Ripper" by the time the District Attorney of Coconino County had filed its heavy-handed complaint with the Bar.

The Bar this time was represented by Demetrius Demosthenes, a Flagstaff criminal law attorney whose brother was a U.S. Attorney in Phoenix. Demosthenes was connected to all the right people in all the right places. Plus, as a competitor with Thaddeus for criminal work in Flagstaff, Demosthenes would be ever so happy to see Thaddeus permanently lose his law license and his flow of clients.

Which was just the point. This time the Bar wasn't out to suspend his license. This time around, the Bar was out to permanently take away his license, also known as a disbarment. Disbarment would mean Thaddeus couldn't practice law anyplace ever again. He would be finished as a lawyer.

"In a way," Thaddeus told Shep at their first meeting, "the two cases do stink to high heaven. I couldn't have dreamed up this scenario even if I wrote pulp fiction for a living."

Shep, his feet resting on his desk and a Winston cigarette poking out between his fingers, nodded and allowed how he'd never heard of such a bizarre set of events himself. But he did agree to represent Thaddeus on the bar complaint.

"First thing we need to do is take statements. I'm thinking Sheila and PJ need to be nailed down so the Bar can't get ahold of them and try to get them to say the wrong thing. I'll notice their depositions for next week."

"All right," Thaddeus said. "And we need to hit Estil Morse III in Los Angeles and get him pinned down on the video research he did for his testimony."

"What did he do again?"

"Measured mom and daughter by using the video. Told the jury whose back they saw when the gun came into the camera frame."

"Oh, right, right. Who else did you use at trial?"

"Police officers, detectives. Nothing there, really. They heard Sheila confess and administered a GSR test on her hands. No chance for me to twist their words, so nothing to do."

Shep's brow furrowed. "You know who else we need? Both judges. Able M. Watertown and William J. Stormont. We need to get their stories boiled down to whether they felt misled by you or not. Their testimony is critical. If they're on your side, Thaddeus, you can't have a better witness. But if they're against you, look out."

"I think they'll both be pretty straightforward witnesses without an ax to grind. Both of them have been sitting judges since forever, and by now they've seen and heard everything. Neither one is going to admit he was taken in by some lawyer's shenanigans. First, they weren't. Second, even if they were, they'd never admit it. Too much pride to admit you got snookered. So yes, let's nail them down but make it short and sweet."

"Sounds good. My idea, too, Thaddeus. Which one do I start with?"

"Well, how about we keep in the order it happened? Watertown heard Sheila's case; Stormont heard PJ's case."

"Last question. Do you want to attend these statements?"

"Not necessary."

"But you do want to attend the hearing itself because you have to." He finally lit the cigarette he'd been playing with the last five minutes and turned to crack the window. When he pivoted back on his chair, he continued, "Okay, then, I'll contact some people. By the way, the demon has been sending me all kinds of threats and offers for you to voluntarily surrender your license for five years in return for not turning you into the district attorney for suborning perjury, etcetera."

"The DA already knows what happened because he was there so that's a non-starter. As far as turning in my license, tell the truth, Shep. What chance do I have? I'm about ready to give up law altogether. I don't need this crap anymore. Christine's going to bow out of the practice and take care of herself. Maybe I should do the same and mail them my license."

"You don't mean that. You're too much of a fighter to just surrender your license. But if you do actually mean it, then you don't need me. You need a postage stamp and an envelope."

"Let's proceed to defend. But don't be surprised when it's all said and done if I finally just give up and ride away into the sunset. I'm pretty tired by it all."

"I get it. You just had that terrible thing with that FBI agent. What was his name?"

"Donnie Francisco. I can't take another one of those ever. I might be about ready to move on from Flagstaff, Shep. I do want to protect my license in case I ever have need to venture into a courtroom again for someone else. If it's just me, I don't need a license. But who knows? Maybe one of the kids gets himself tossed in the clink or Turquoise does this or that. I'd like to have my license intact just in case. Ya never know."

"All right, then. I'll proceed."

43

The State Bar hearing began on a Monday in October, a cool day with the Autumn colors at peak and clouds so low the San Francisco summits were shrouded.

At nine a.m., in the borrowed city council chambers, the three judges in charge of the hearing called the proceeding to order. The court reporter arched her back and cracked her knuckles in readiness. The large room was a hearing room, and their seating arrangement up front was a curved row of chairs where the council would ordinarily sit. Name plaques adorned the front of each chair's placement at the bar, but they were the names of city council members, not the names of the three-judge panel. The hearing officer flanked by the two other officers began speaking.

"Good morning, counsel and parties. My name is William S. Sewell, and I am the presiding hearing officer on the case entitled *In the Matter of Thaddeus Murfee.* The case is brought by bar counsel of the State Bar of Arizona through counsel Democritus Demosthenes appearing for the Bar. Appearing with the respondent, Thaddeus Murfee, is his counsel, Shep Aberdeen. Gentlemen, are we ready to proceed?"

"Ready," said Demosthenes.

"Ready," said Shep.

The hearing officer read the usual preamble. "No agreement has been reached between the parties, so this contested hearing is held before this hearing panel, which includes the Presiding Disciplinary Judge, a lawyer member, and a public member. At the conclusion of the hearing, the panel will issue a report containing findings of fact, conclusions of law, and an order regarding sanctions, if any are levied. The hearing panel may order dismissal of the charges, diversion, restitution, assessment of costs, admonition, probation, reprimand, suspension, or disbarment. The panel's order is final subject to the parties' right to appeal. Appeal is to the Supreme Court of Arizona, of course. I am the presiding disciplinary judge. The lawyer member, seated to my right, is Mona Gonzales of Prescott, Arizona. The public member is Henry Davos. Henry, for the record, is seated to my left. All right. The burden of proof rests with the State Bar of Arizona so, counsel, you may call your first witness."

Demosthenes wasted no time. "The State Bar of Arizona calls Jonathan Logan, the complainant. Mr. Logan, please come forward and take a seat in the middle below the presiding judge."

Jon Logan walked brightly to the witness chair, smiling and nodding to the hearing officers as he came forward. He appeared confident and controlled, as if he had no ax to grind and he were out to hurt no one. Thaddeus, from his vantage point at counsel table, knew better. Logan was there to rip his license off the wall and set it on fire if possible. The poisonous diatribe was just about ready to begin.

The witness was sworn and took his seat. Then Demosthenes started in.

"Your name, sir?"

"Jonathan Logan."

"Your job?"

"Assistant District Attorney, Coconino County DA's office."

"How long have you been an assistant DA?"

"Going on fourteen years in March."

"How long have you held a license to practice law in Arizona?"

"Fourteen years in March. I was a winter bar exam taker."

"Are you acquainted with Thaddeus Murfee?"

"I am."

"How long have you known Mr. Murfee?"

"Oh, it must be about three or four years now. Probably closer to four."

"In what capacity do you know him?"

"Professional. He defends the criminals I prosecute."

"Objection," said Shep. "He means Thaddeus defends the people he prosecutes. They aren't criminals until the jury says they are."

The presiding judge was having none of that. He waved a hand dismissively. "Please proceed, counsel."

"You were the prosecuting attorney on a case involving a defendant named Sheila Lowenstein, were you not?"

"I was."

"And, later, you prosecuted Sheila's daughter, Patricia Jean Walston?"

"That is correct."

"Who defended those cases?"

"Thaddeus Murfee."

"For the record, Mr. Murfee is in attendance today?"

"Seated right next to his attorney, Shep Aberdeen, yes."

"Please describe for the panel your experience with Mr. Murfee in the first case of *State of Arizona v. Sheila Lowenstein*."

"Mr. Murfee misled me, and he misled the police investigators, from day one. The mother confessed. The daughter, PJ, was questioned by the police on the scene when she told them she didn't shoot her stepfather. After that, everything came unglued. Suddenly, the daughter steps up and says she did it, the L.A. video people said they measured people in a video, of all things, the daughter's dentist said she was bit by her father, and the mother presented a video that she had forgotten to tell anyone about. The chairs were moved around in this one, nothing was as it seemed, it took a mastermind, a very ingenious lawyer, to pull this off, and that's Thaddeus Murfee's calling card, sleight-of-hand, a magician, a card shark. It was, after all was said and done, a deceit on the court."

The diatribe continued in this manner for another ten minutes, then it was Shep's turn.

Shep bored right on in. "Did anything happen, though, in these cases, that doesn't happen in all criminal cases?"

Logan's eyes opened wide. "Didn't you hear what I just said? Everything was a deceit and a fraud, sir, everything!"

"Please answer my question. I'm asking whether anything happened in either case that doesn't always happen in criminal cases? Things are taken out of order. Witnesses say surprising things that no one expects, confessions are recanted, exhibits are denied as having been at the scene, all of the ups and downs and sideways of a rollicking criminal trial. Isn't that really all that happened here?"

"Let me back up. A mother confessed to murder at the scene of her husband's shooting. She goes to trial. Out of the blue, her daughter then confesses to the murder. The case evaporates because the daughter had clearly been manipulated by Thaddeus Murfee. The mother walks off scot-free. So I prosecute the daughter. Now Mr. Murfee begins producing evidence that the daughter didn't do the crime. He brings in video evidence that's been produced out of thin air. He brings in the mother who produces a secret video that she says portrays her arm and hand in the process of shooting her husband. First time anyone's been made aware of the video. He calls it impeachment evidence. The judge agrees—wrongly, I might add—and the case against the daughter evaporates. So there's the crux of why he violated all of a lawyer's ethics—two people walked when a man was shot dead. All because of Mr. Murfee's manipulation of a minor witness, manipulation of phony video facts, and hiding away video of the actual shooting. He deserves to be sanctioned at a minimum and deserves to be disbarred as a warning to other defense lawyers that there are limits in our courtrooms."

"You sound really angry," Shep states.

"I am really angry. Someone literally got away with murder here. Thanks to Mr. Murfee."

"That is all, Your Honors."

44

The State Bar, through counsel Demosthenes, then called the police, the detectives, and the medical examiner as witnesses. Shep felt like none of them hurt Thaddeus enough to spend much time with them. The Bar then called Judge Watertown. He testified in a reserved manner, correct in appearance and diction, and wouldn't come right out and say Thaddeus had done anything untoward in his courtroom. Then Shep got him on cross-examination.

Shep posed the first question to Judge Watertown. "Judge, during the time Thaddeus was defending Sheila Lowenstein in your court, did he ever make any representations to you that weren't in fact true?"

Judge Watertown looked around the city council chambers as if searching for his answer in the faces of the politicos whose official photographs lined the walls. He pursed his lips, then said, "In the mother's case, I was under the impression the only person on trial was the mother. Mr. Murfee's entire defense seemed to be directed at proving the mother acted with the intention of protecting her daughter. I'm referring specifically to the defense witness, Dr. Mangrum, who said the mother's psychosis becomes apparent when she could not see any other course of action than shooting her husband. I fail to see how Mr. Murfee intentionally misled anyone with this testimony. It seems to me it was garden variety psychiatric testimony, not especially compelling, but enough to raise reasonable doubt. Which was Mr. Murfee's job, to raise a reasonable doubt."

"Was it troubling to you, what he did?"

"What is troubling to me is that I consider the State Bar investigation and this hearing to be nothing more than witch hunts. Defense lawyers need to be able to raise any and all defenses, even if totally bizzarro, without fear of having their licenses yanked by the State Bar all because some prosecutor got his feelings hurt."

"That's what you think we have here?" Shep asked.

"That's exactly what we have here. I admire Jon Logan, but he was way off-base in filing this Bar Complaint. I personally see no wrongdoing, and I personally never felt misled by Mr. Murfee. Not one iota."

The city council chambers fell quiet. Only the blowing air of the forced air furnace could be heard. Shep cleared his throat and said he had no further questions for Judge Watertown. Demosthenes definitely had no further questions and seemed anxious for his own witness to leave the place.

The State Bar then called Judge Stormont, who was a little more friendly to the Bar, saying that he felt the case was "extraordinary" in both aspects, mother and daughter, and said he "felt lost" at times during the daughter's trial, as if he had no idea what to expect because the evidence "was lurching all around like a bucking bronco." At the very end, he made a damning comment, saying he felt Thaddeus Murfee had been less than forthcoming with the truth and that he played "fast and loose" with the rules of court and rules of evidence. Demosthenes asked these same questions three different ways in an effort to pound the judge's answers into the judicial panel's ears. Shep feared he was having some success. Thaddeus merely sat at the table, arms folded, staring ahead at the floor while Judge Stormont had his say. He didn't shake his head in disagreement or roll his eyes in disgust. He was stolid and unmoving and didn't indicate in any way that he was affected by what Judge Stormont had to say.

On cross-examination, the judge was unflappable. He did say that he didn't think Thaddeus intentionally lied to the court, but he maintained his position by saying it was his opinion that Thaddeus's conduct fell below the degree of honesty a lawyer owes to a court.

In the end, Demosthenes had made a *prima facie* case of attorney misconduct. He now couldn't be dismissed at the close of his case. He announced he was finished adducing testimony and sat down as if he'd just won an Academy Award.

Shep was unimpressed, but Thaddeus's demeanor hadn't changed. Shep felt in his bones that Thaddeus was closer than ever to just hanging it up and walking away from law. He hoped he was wrong, but actually, deep down, he wouldn't blame him if the young lawyer did spend his days doing other things with his life. Shep was saddened by the whole spectacle. He couldn't imagine how sad Thaddeus must be.

But it was his time to present evidence so, like all erstwhile lawyers, Shep ignored his feelings and trudged ahead, calling Thaddeus as his first witness.

45

He definitely didn't want to be there. He wanted to be out on the high desert on Hearsay, galloping until the horse was slick with lather and breathing through its mouth, or trailing at a slow walk along Forest Service roads in the dense Ponderosa and aspen forest behind his home. He wanted to be anyplace but in that city council chamber defending a license he no longer believed in. A license he no longer even wanted. For Thaddeus had come to that point that all lawyers reach eventually when they begin to realize they aren't enjoying life, that the practice of law is sucking the joy out of every single day in a long, slow march to self-defeat that actually began the first day they sat their butts down in a law school student chair and surrendered to the air around them, air thick with precedent and procedure, air thick with tradition, air that never forgave human frailty and the short-comings of all human beings. He was, in a word, done with it.

He heavily raised his right hand and swore to tell the truth. The truth he told was a truth no one expected, least of all Thaddeus himself.

"Yes," he said on cross-examination by Demosthenes, "I did manipulate the facts. All lawyers manipulate the facts, in case you've forgotten, Demo. We manipulate the facts, we manipulate people, we manipulate institutions and judges from the time we get up in the morning until the time we go down to sleep at night. Hell, we even manipulate our own children so that they might become better citizens with rules and proclamations about how they should behave if they're going to achieve success in this life. So yes, I did all the things you've complained about in your bar complaint, everything except one."

Demosthenes was beside himself with glee. So much so, that he asked the next obvious question: "What thing didn't you do?"

"I didn't manipulate the young girl, Patricia Jean Walston, PJ. I never even talked to her before she took the stand to testify in her mother's trial. I hadn't spoken to her beforehand, though my investigator, Turquoise Murfee, had spoken to her. But Turquoise's notes only indicate what the girl said. Turquoise, I am quite sure, wasn't a person who might've planted in the child's mind the notion that she should lie in order to save her mother. That isn't something Turquoise would do, but hell, why ask me? Ask Turquoise yourself. You have the power of subpoena. Get her up here and let her tell you what actually was said. I'm not worried."

"But you will say whatever you need to say in order to protect your license, Mr. Murfee. We're comfortable you're human enough to do that like all men will."

Thaddeus looked at him askew. He looked at him as a querulous old lion might look at a young zebra before pouncing and devouring. "You're sure I'll say anything? Well hear this, Mr. Demosthenes. Early today, I removed my law license from my wall and inserted it into a twelve by fifteen FedEx mailing envelope. I mailed that license to the State Bar of Arizona along with my letter of resignation. The very idea that the State Bar would countenance a complaint such as yours, a complaint of pure bullshit, is just too much for me to endure. I surrender my license and I take back my life from the practice of law. I am finished here, and I am leaving now. Enjoy the rest of your hearing, all of you."

Nobody was more surprised than Shep, at first, who stood and watched Thaddeus march out of the courtroom without one glance back. Then, as the outer doors were swinging shut, Shep began clapping. Clapping and nodding at the astonished hearing judges and the floored Bar counsel, Demosthenes. Suddenly, they were without a lawyer to kick around and bully. They had outdone themselves and removed one of the finest among them from the practice of law. The judges and prosecutor sorely began packing their bags and briefcases, unable even to speak.

Again, the only sound was the hiss of the forced air furnace of the city council chambers in Flagstaff, Arizona. Air that was dead, air that no longer contained the contention, argument, and disagreement about right and wrong.

Right and wrong had left the room with Thaddeus, leaving behind only empty formulas and rules that he no longer gave a damn about.

It was finished.

46

They sold out and moved to Durango. Colorado was a state of mind. It was a place to move and lick old wounds, heal old injuries, and recover from a lifetime of law. Both Thaddeus and Christine were in love with their new ranch house and their new five-hundred-acre spread. They were in love with the small town, a main street still vibrant and active after all these years. The San Juan Mountains showed clearly in the near distance while the Animas River scooped around the side of the town. The Animas River's official name was *El Rio de las Animas Perdidas*, roughly translated meant, "The River of Lost Souls."

Plus, Durango offered over 300 days of sunshine a year. A person couldn't help but be happy with all that Vitamin D shining down on them.

Their children were all thriving, happy, and full of their own dreams and schemes. The school system and town was small enough to feel intimate, yet large enough to offer all types of sports, events, arts, and activities. Living outside Durango, the

Murfee parents felt like a taxi service, T-ball, piano recitals, ballet, football, and the competition for adult time was tremendous. Finally, the kids had their parents' attention they had always wanted. Every day there were more smiles and less fighting. Every day Thaddeus woke up to the adventure of parenting, not an easy task by any means, almost as challenging as law. But the idea made him smile. If nothing else, he loved it as much, so it had been an easy trade. No more nannies for the kids. Christine and Thaddeus were doing it all.

Turquoise had found a nearby condo, and she was out to the ranch every day or so and could be counted on to haul kids in her pickup every so often. She wasn't sure what work she was going to pursue. Local law enforcement perhaps? Even local private investigation. She wasn't sure but wasn't rushing her decision.

Mostly all the driving fell to Thaddeus, who seemed to be always coming from or going to town, and it was all right; he had never felt happier to be a parent.

For the first month, Thaddeus rode Hearsay as he scouted the ranch and met with cattle experts to discuss grazing possibilities. "Do you want to sell cattle at a year old?" asked one. Thaddeus told him no, he didn't think he wanted to sell them at all. He just wanted cows to look at. It didn't take long for that kind of talk to make the rounds. He was definitely a new kind of neighbor to the working ranches around Durango.

He went with new friends to try his hand at fly fishing. He caught rainbows and browns and released them back into the streams.

Then he got into light planes, bought a Cirrus, and soloed after fifteen hours of training time. It was fast becoming a favorite pastime. At one point, he did a cross-country to Flagstaff, landed and refueled, but spoke to no one there. He had planned on calling Shep for dinner but decided against it.

Three months after the Arizona bar hearing, he still hadn't received any notice regarding any disciplinary action. He did notice, however, that his name had been erased from the roll of attorneys as per his request. He could no longer practice law there, and that was fine. Thaddeus had obtained reciprocal admission to the bar in Colorado years before. If he ever changed his mind about law, there was always Colorado where he could try his hand, but so far, the thought hadn't even crossed his mind. He was enjoying being a civilian again without ties to any court. It felt wonderful to be free.

Christine had taken to driving the ten miles into Durango alone, which was a huge achievement for her. She still spent much of her time around the house with the children and her own hobbies but was coming back from her injury and was stepping out again and living life on life's terms. She told Thaddeus she had climbed out of the bottom of a well. She was taking golf and bridge lessons— two pastimes that had seemed out of reach until now. Out of reach because her Flagstaff legal workload had become overwhelming.

One day, as Thaddeus sat on Hearsay and watched his horse drink from a fast-running stream, it occurred to him that his life was perfect. Christine was all but recovered, the kids were happy and excited with their new house and making friends, and Thaddeus had no battles to fight, no worries of any kind, only the kind of peace that comes after a great battle.

Then his cell phone chimed. Karl, Christine's father, a lawyer in St. Louis.

He two-fingered the phone out of his snap-button shirt pocket and jammed it to his ear.

"Go ahead, Karl."

"I've talked to Reuben. They won't budge. I'm a dead man."
Reuben was the brother of Matin, the man Karl had defended and
lost to the penitentiary.

Thaddeus grimaced. Hearsay began edging backward, slowly
cropping new spring grass.

"You talked to the people in Juarez?"

"Reuben himself," said Karl. "This is a cold man."

"He's not a man, Karl. He's a drug kingpin."

"I'm sorry to drag you into this."

"You're my father-in-law. If you're Christine's family, you're my
family. I'm in."

Long pause. Then Karl asked, "What should we do?"

Thaddeus said, "No choice but for me to go to Juarez."

"Jesus."

"Hold on," said Thaddeus. He placed his hands behind him on
his horse's rear end and looked out across the Colorado prairie.
In the far distance were the ridges of the Rocky Mountains.
There was a long phone silence while Thaddeus watched
Hearsay crop grass. He considered Karl. Thaddeus barely knew
the man. Karl lived in St. Louis. He was a lawyer there, a man
with financial troubles who'd done the unthinkable: defended
the Juarez drug cartel on an unwinnable case. For a $25,000 fee, a
drug lord's brother had gone to prison, and now it was all Karl's
fault—according to Juarez. The cartel was blaming Karl so much
so that a contract had been placed on him. His last-ditch effort to
buy his way out of the contract with Christine's money had

failed. He had called Thaddeus before he went under for the third time.

"When will you go?" Karl said, his voice hollow and shaky.

"This afternoon. You're lying low where I put you?"

Thaddeus had flown Karl out of St. Louis in the dead of night. His Gulfstream jet had deposited the man in Amsterdam. He would be safe for another forty-eight hours—maybe less—depending on who ratted him out first.

"Still here. I don't sleep, I can't eat. I don't understand what anyone's saying in Dutch. I'm constantly looking over my shoulder."

"It's like fighting snakes to keep Christine from swooping in and carting you off," said Thaddeus about Christine. She was prepared to die to protect the father she loved with all her heart, but her emotional health wasn't 100% yet. Thaddeus had managed to convince her she was too close to the situation, that she should let him handle it. For now, it was holding her off. He just didn't want her to act impulsively, which he'd never known Christine to do, but this was about her dad. Who could say what might happen?

"She does love her dad," said Karl.

"We all do," Thaddeus reminded him. "We all have skin in the game."

"Will you phone me as soon as you talk to them?"

"You're on your sat phone?"

"Yes. You?"

Thaddeus smiled. "Only ever. Yes, I'll call. And I may have to move you again. But I'll tell you. I'm fresh out of ideas if talking to Juarez fails."

"What about handling Matin's appeal?"

"I've thought of that. Drug appeals are never successful, Karl. I shouldn't have to tell you that."

"But I thought you might try. It would at least buy me more time while the appeal's working its way through the court."

"Maybe, maybe not."

"I could have more time to hide."

"Your options are running out, Karl. We tried buying your way out. Our money's no good with Juarez. That makes them very dangerous people."

"Oh, my God. Why, oh, why? How could I have been so stupid?"

"Don't beat yourself up. Money twists everyone."

"Except you and Christine. You two are pretty damn straight despite your success."

"That's nice of you to say, but we've got our skeletons, believe me. Okay, I'm going to head back home. The next time we talk, I'll be in Mexico."

"Goodbye, Thaddeus."

"So long, Karl."

Thaddeus reined in Hearsay and stopped. He tore open the rear case of his sat phone and dug out its innards with his fingers. Then he flung the batteries and card as far as he could, like a relief pitcher winding up in the bottom of the ninth with two out. He rode a half mile and suddenly wound up again and flung the phone itself down a rocky arroyo. He couldn't be too careful with these people. They were everywhere.

He rode into Hearsay's corral and climbed down. Wiley was waiting with a bucket and brush.

"Take him in the barn and wash him down good, Wiley. He ran hard."

"Worked him out, Mr. Thaddeus?"

"I did that, yes."

Thaddeus stroked his horse's shoulder as Wiley took up the reins and began leading the quarter horse into the barn. Thaddeus followed alongside, talking softly to his mount. Then they parted ways at the barn and Thaddeus went west toward the house and the mud room. Inside, he pulled another sat phone from its charger. He dialed a Durango prefix.

"Monty, it's Thaddeus. Thirteen hundred hours, we're off. Juarez."

The pilot, Monty, understood exactly. They would lift off in the Gulfstream aircraft at one p.m. Monty made no reply into the phone; it wasn't necessary. He would be fully fueled and waiting when Thaddeus arrived.

Christine found him in the mud room as he sat with a pick, digging horse manure out of his boot seams and dropping it into a running sink. He heard her come up behind. She encircled him with her arms.

"What?"

"Have you spoken with him?"

"I have," he said. "He's very frightened, but he's safe for now."

"What was said?"

"I'm heading down to Juarez. One last plea."

"Will you offer them money?"

Thaddeus turned to her and rested the boot pick on the side of the tub. "You know better. Reuben is Matin's brother. I either spring him out of prison, or Karl is no more. That's what it's going to come down to."

"So why go to Mexico at all?"

"I want an understanding. They let me do my thing, and in return they leave Karl alone while it's pending."

"Will they buy it?"

He went back to picking bits of manure from the soles of his boots. "Doubtful. But I've got to try, don't I?"

"Thank you, Thaddeus. Would it be too much to ask to tag along?"

"Yes, it would be too much. Your health. And the kids. We can't desert them so soon. Not when we just got them settled and happy for us to be around."

He meant at least one parent had to stay safe. Two of their children had lost both parents before. It couldn't happen ever again. Nor to the rest of the kids.

"I know. Are you hungry?"

Thaddeus spun the faucets, and the flow of water stopped. He set his boots on the mud room counter on top of a rubber mat. He shook his head. "I'll grab a sandwich on the plane. I want to get out to the airport and start going over Matin's trial transcripts."

"Who's the bad guy?"

"Probably the narcs. They tapped his phone without a warrant. They swear they didn't, but I know better. Your dad knew better, too. He just couldn't prove it."

"Is that enough to get the case reopened and a new trial?"

"It better be. If it isn't, Karl's days are numbered, and I don't want you to think otherwise, Christine. You're a big girl. Karl's a big boy. He had no business defending Matin in the first place. It's a death sentence if you lose."

"He knew that, you're right. He should've come to me about his money problems."

"Coulda, shoulda, woulda, oughta. He didn't. I'm off to Mexico. Keep the bed warm."

"Always, Señor Murfee. Thaddeus, *lo siento por mi padre*."

"*No hay necesidad*. No need to apologize for him."

"*Adios, mi amor*."

"Goodbye, Chris."

He still had one active law license—Colorado. It was enough to practice in another state. There were rules about such things.

Rules.

He felt the old curse closing down around him, but he also felt Karl was about to die. He knew Christine would never forgive him if he didn't try to do something.

At 1:03 p.m., the Gulfstream was in the air and climbing. Thaddeus looked at the spreading prairie below the wing just as they danced beneath the clouds. It had been a wonderful freedom.

But it wasn't to be. There would be one more trial, that much was sure.

Then there would come another. And another.

He'd never felt so alive as he did just then, just knowing it was coming, one more fight.

Then they were in the clouds and gone.

THE END

UP NEXT: LA JOLLA LAW

"Loved the excellent diverse characters. Fast paced plot development and good bad guys and great good guys!"

"John Ellsworth's newest addition to the Thaddeus Murfee collection of legal thrillers doesn't disappoint."

"I hope my review will encourage someone who has not read his books a try. You will be so pleased you did and can look forward to enjoying a wonderful legal novel. Each of the 5 stars were earned!"

"This book was the best Thaddeus Murfee yet. It was constant edge of your seat excitement and surprising twists and turns with a bone-chilling ending."

Read La Jolla Law: CLICK HERE

FREE BOOK FOR EMAIL SIGNUP

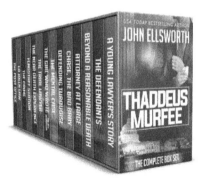

Can't get enough John Ellsworth?

Sign up for our weekly newsletter to stay in touch!

You will have exclusive access to new releases, special deals, and insider news!
Join today!

ABOUT THE AUTHOR

I'm an independent author. I'm independent because I enjoy marketing, selecting covers, reader communications, and all the rest. But I do need you to tell others about my books if you like them. Also, if you liked *The Defendants*, would you please leave an Amazon or Goodreads review? It would mean a lot to me.

Presently, I'm working on my 31st novel. I published my first book, *The Defendants*, in January 2014. It's been a wild ride and I was self-supporting four months after my first book came out.

Reception to my books has been phenomenal; more than 2,000,000 have been downloaded in 60 months. All are Amazon best-sellers. I am an Amazon All-Star every month and a *USA Today* bestseller.

I live in San Diego, California, where I can be found near the beaches on my yellow Vespa scooter. Deb and I help rescue dogs and cats in association with a Baja animal shelter. We also work with the homeless.

Thank you for reading my books. Thank you for any review you're able to leave on Amazon.

Website and email:

ellsworthbooks.com
John@ellsworthbooks.com

CPSIA information can be obtained
at www.ICGtesting.com
Printed in the USA
FSHW011300130921
84736FS